THE
Gift

Tor Books by Patrick O'Leary

Door Number Three
The Gift

THE Gift

Patrick O'Leary

TOR®

A Tom Doherty Associates Book   New York

*Patrick
O'Leary*

(fantasy)

This is a work of fiction. All the characters and events portrayed in this novel
are either fictitious or are used fictitiously.

THE GIFT

Copyright © 1997 by Patrick O'Leary

All rights reserved, including the right to reproduce this book, or portions
thereof, in any form.

This book is printed on acid-free paper.

Edited by David G. Hartwell

A Tor Book
Published by Tom Doherty Associates, Inc.
175 Fifth Avenue
New York, NY 10010

Tor Books on the World Wide Web:
http://www.tor.com

Patrick O'Leary's Homepage: http://users.aol.com/patri10629

Tor® is a registered trademark of Tom Doherty Associates, Inc.

Design by Bonni Leon

Library of Congress Cataloging-in-Publication Data

O'Leary, Patrick
    The gift / Patrick O'Leary.—1st ed.
        p.   cm.
    "A Tom Doherty Associates book."
    ISBN 0-312-86402-7 (acid free)
    I. Title.
    PS3565.L4G54   1997
    813' .54—dc21   97-13323
                                        CIP

First Edition: November 1997

Printed in the United States of America

0 9 8 7 6 5 4 3 2 1

For Fred Banzhaf

Acknowledgments

THE TALE GREW WITH THE TELLING. My warmest thanks go to those who listened and inspired. Ken Ethridge, who never stopped believing. Claire, who was always there. Anthony Ambrogio, Anca Vlasopolos, Jane Schaberg, Robin Watson, Claire Crabtree, Carol Campbell, Peggy Stack, who patiently bore its disjointed genesis, and will now know the rest of the story. The many cousins of Corvus Frugilegus who've haunted me over the years—the fat one in the tree in Royal Oak in 1975 who started it all, the pesky ones who kept bombarding my window last winter, and the greedy ones at the Hearst Castle in San Simeon—all right already, it's done—leave me alone! Kathryn Cramer, whose keen eye and faith meant more than she could know. Gene Wolfe (who never read it, but), who set impossible standards and showed me a way. And, especially, David G. Hartwell, my most faithful reader. Words fail me, but gratitude never will.

P.O.

THE
Gift

Prologue

THIS IS A STORY ABOUT MONSTERS.

The real ones. Not the ones we tell children about.

The Captain at the helm and the little Teller in the bow watched the sailors one by one leave their hammocks below, and admitting the impossibility of sleep, make their groggy way up to the deck where they stood restlessly together in groups of two or three, looking warily out over the sheer water as smooth as any mirror and as black as the pitch that sealed their hull. The full moon cast the only light in that windless night, a comfortless light that made the shadows darker and all their faces white as the body they had pulled up in their nets that afternoon.

No one spoke of it then or now. She was beautiful, or had been. Beautiful and blond and not a stitch on her. No blood either. No marks or cuts or clues. That would have been enough—more than enough, even if her sagging belly hadn't born the purple stripes of a recent child.

Once they had untangled her from their nets, everyone stood around the body waiting for someone to suggest what to do. Strangely, none of the sailors asked where she had come from. In fact, they acted as if none of them had ever seen a woman before. Some would not look at her. Some could not look away. Some thought of their wives. Some thought of their daughters. Some, of their mothers.

Finally, the Captain, a tall, hard man with a white beard and one hand, instructed them to tie something to its feet and toss it back. There was a prolonged search for something expendable and weighty enough to do the deed. Theirs was a modest vessel, sparsely supplied and fit only for small trips to stock the fishmarkets on the rocky coast; a three-day journey out and back, barring storms, was the usual. In truth, there wasn't really much debris, or comfort for that matter, to be found onboard. But eventually one mate discovered in a forward hold an old anchor net of rocks that had rotted out of use. Reluctantly they lashed it to her ankles and dragged her to the edge. Her hair left a wet mop smear on the scale-laden boards of the deck and it was still there, twelve hours later, splitting their boat in two with a black stream that reflected the stars. The men stepped over it.

There was no more fishing that day. No one felt like talking or eating. And they had all retired early, leaving only the Captain on watch and the Teller in the bow of the boat to continue their silent feud. Anyone who spent any time on deck knew there was something of a grudge between the little man in the bow and the old man at the helm. They never showed each other their backs. They regarded the opposite across the wooden planks and double holds as if at any time the other might produce a knife and throw it. None could say what this unspoken spite was about, unless of course they were family—which, frankly, did not seem likely. They might have been playing the childhood game of shadow, daring each other to be the first to move, to blink, to buckle. What were they on about anyway?

As far as they could tell, the Teller had been decent enough company. Though, it was true, judging by his silence over the last two days you'd be hard-pressed to find any evidence of his calling. He'd staked out his place there up front when they'd taken him on in Sotton's Bay and he rarely strayed from it. A little bald man with a scarred mouth who wrapped his body in a thick gray cloak that piled about him as he squatted in the bow, so that it seemed to those who glanced his way that he consisted entirely of a head resting on a small mountain of cloth, like a white cherry on a pudding. Yet, occasionally a pale hand crept out of the folds of the gray mountain to pull it tauter; then, on his pinky finger they'd see the silver ring the King had gifted him, which granted him free lodging anywhere and free passage on any boat he chose. And perhaps explained the Captain's begrudging. He was not, in their experience, a generous man. So who could blame him if he felt he was being freeloaded? After all, the custom was that every night the Teller would tell a story. Though not strictly required, it was considered a courtesy that most Tellers were obliged to perform. Two nights and not a peep out of him. Some thought: A Teller who doesn't tell is hiding something—a guilty secret perhaps?

But no one had asked for a story that night, not after her.

Then as they settled in their hammocks and blew out their oil wicks, the songs began. Oh, such songs. Most sailors have been told the tale, but few have actually heard the music of the Mer: the ladies who lived beneath the waves, who sang keening wordless melodies that echoed off the hull. Only a dead man could have slept through that sound. And the only silence and refuge was above decks, above the water, above that hideous wail. So they stood on the main deck looking out at the flat salt sea (they did not know it was an ocean then), waiting for it to stop.

Their silent vigil was broken by a ruckus on the stairs. Nib, the Go-Boy, burst through the hatch, tripped, and landed on his face. "What is it? What is it?" he cried.

The Captain's laughter gave the crew a much needed excuse to jest.

One cracked, "It's your momma calling you home, lad!"

Another shouted, "It's a she-demon calling us all!"

Then it became a sport.

"It's a dead whore's song!"

"It's a dragon giving birth!"

"It's the hungry beast of dark water and she likes boys best!"

They all chuckled as the boy's head swiveled to and fro, fearing and believing each revelation more than the last.

Such teasing was not an infrequent occurrence. The sailors all were Mouthers: They couldn't read anything without pictures. Little wonder then that they resented the Go-Boy. "The Captain's Right Hand," they called him (out of his earshot, of course). The man was almost superstitious about his signature: He never put his name on paper, never signed for anything—inventory logs, port tallies, slip taxes, even their payroll—once he learned the boy could scribble he had delegated all such tasks to Nib.

Perhaps they thought he was paid extra for these services. He was not.

The sailors' laughter snagged when a voice from the bow cut through the night, a small whisper of a voice with nothing like a joke in it, but with the power of a nightmare, a voice that'd make you sit bolt up in bed.

"It is the Song of Mother Death," the Teller said, only his white face visible in the shadow of the bow, like the face of the moon on the water. "Has no one told you the story?"

Sometimes, as the sailors looked at the Teller, they got the uneasy feeling that somehow he was inside of them, looking out through their eyes. The Teller stood then, and all the sailors watched as he motioned the Go-Boy, Nib, to his side.

"It is a fearful tale," he said solemnly. His eyes glided across the men until they rested on the Captain, who stood above them at the helm. "But I see you have a taste for such. It is a coward's appetite: to take pleasure in someone else's fear." His body indicated the Go-Boy without any gesture. "It's one of those dark gifts we learn as children. Many never outgrow it."

A snort came down from the Captain, and he stroked the yellow jewel lodged in his ear. "I have a *crew* of children," he said in that voice that made all the sailors still until he had finished. "They've never seen Leviathan."

After a moment the Teller retook his audience by saying, "Your captain knows a secret. But that does not mean he knows a truth. That's what Tellers are for."

Then he looked up at the moon and let his grey cloak fall to a black pool at his feet. It was the Telling Stance, which marked the Telling Time, and no one but a King dare interrupt. He was a slight man, no taller than a boy, whose body was marked by a tangle of white scars that clung to his

14

hands, arms, legs, and face, as if once he had been wrapped in the web of a giant spider.

The wizard Tatoan was the last of the great race who fell out of the sky, he began. *When Tatoan knew his time was dwindling and soon he would die, he flew to the White Moon Mountains, to the tunnels that twisted through them like a brood of sleeping serpents, to the home of the Watermen.*

There he lay down for the last time: a thin white man floating in a shallow pool of green, surrounded by the creatures whom his brother wizards had spelled from simple frogs into something that could master chants and tongues and magic.

"My dear friends" *he whispered hoarsely.* "Do you recall what I have taught you? That every fire can light or burn? And any pool may quench or drown?"

The Watermen were silent. It was one of their first lessons.

"Everything must have a gift and a price. We wizards once were spirit. But we longed to be human. What was the price we paid?"

"Death," *the Watermen replied.*

"And the gift we gave?"

"Magic."

"Yes. You know it well. Now, listen. I have stepped Between and I have seen a dark time yet to be. A someday when a man may try to take death from this world. And he may succeed. If he does, everything will spoil. The water, the wind, the earth—everything.*

"Should all this come to pass, a strange one will be born: a Guardian. The only one who can stop this spoiling. The only one who can bring back the gift of dying. The one you will call Mother Death.*

"I have spelled it so. And it has taken all my power."

He closed his eyes, and the tiny creatures watched his eyeballs roaming under pale lids and heard his breath like a cloth being ripped inside his chest.

"Do you see, my friends, that there is no other way? Death is the price. Magic is the gift."

Silence in the caves of the Watermen.

"I have one last thing to teach you all. It is a song. You must sing it over and over until *it has found a place in you. You must sing it every day. And you must teach it to every creature of the water, for it is their song, too. Will you do that for me?"*

All the Watermen consented.

And as the wizard sang, a great wind filled their home. And in its arms it carried both the last breath of Tatoan and his last song. It echoed off the twisting cavern walls: a simple four-note melody that rose and fell, rose and fell, like breakers at the base of cliffs, waves looking for a rest they'd never find on any shore. A grieving song. The song of creatures who once had the gift of magic but have lost it forever. The Song of Mother Death.

For a time no one on the deck said anything. Then the Go-Boy, Nib, thinking there was something wrong, laid a hand upon the small man's arm and met him eye to eye. "Is that all, Teller?"

The man came out of his daze, looked at the boy and smiling sadly, said, "No. That's just a beginning."

And then, on that sleepless night under the moon, he told them the rest.

Chapter one

THE ALCHEMIST HELD HIS HAND over the candle, speaking the old words quickly, determined to finish the spell before the pain grew unbearable and his hand would wrench away of its own accord.

He stood over the body of a huge black rook. It had not been easy to catch. Its beak had gouged his hand repeatedly as he drowned it: the hand he was now burning.

He could smell his smoking flesh, but he could not stop. He had come too far to stop. To gain this one glorious spell he had taken many chances, ransacked many book houses, and stolen more magic books than he could remember. Until one day, he smothered the ailing old witch and found The Book—tucked away in a cupboard under a sack of flour— found the chapter, found the page, found the words, and he embraced the dusty volume as if it were a lost child. After years of searching, years of humiliating failure and countless spells gone bad, years of botched experiments and twisted useless abominations (their names like bitter seeds upon his tongue: Bodoneenon, Cronic, Agulie, Griff), creatures doomed by unforeseen flaws in their concoction or conception—after fruitless years of blunder he had succeeded. He would never forget the months spent sleeping in the woods, begging for bread, spurned by women, teased by children, and tossed out of inns with scornful laughter—but none of it mattered now. He had found it.

Not the spell for gold, but something more precious and astounding, something that promised him a powerful ally and an end to his misery: the spell to raise the dead.

He stood beside the Great River at twilight, fiercely holding his shaking hand to the candle. He finished the spell, the words rushing out of his mouth as if they fled an enemy: "Elbane. Erotser. Sisats d'nepsus. Wake up now! Now and forever!"

Then the earth cracked.

He fell to the sandy bank, dropping the candle and folding his mutilated hand under his arm. As the ground tore open, molten fire spewed forth from the bowels of the earth; it spilled into the river with a roar and a hiss, and a cloud of steam slipped up into the air as the liquid flame dropped about him like fireworks. He moaned in triumph.

In the instant before the cleft had cooled and sealed itself, a creature squirmed out. It had waited centuries to emerge. It had simmered and fumed with rage, clinging to the knowledge that no cell was completely secure: One day its unleashing would come, and it would do what it had longed to do for ages. It would eat.

The alchemist did not see the creature crawling toward him—for outside its natural element it was invisible. What he did see was the body of the dead rook twitching, and he marveled as the smoke curled out of its beak. He could have wept at the beauty.

He saw the bird rise on awkward legs, but he did not see it smile at him as if he were a meal.

"Master!" it said, the words scraping out of its throat. "You have burned yourself!"

So unaccustomed was he to success that for a long minute he stood dumbfounded, staring down at the black rook, half expecting the air about him to break into applause. For the first time he felt tall and proud and a little giddy. He longed to turn to his old Tender and say something that would hurt.

The memory still scalded. Orphaned at birth and deposited on the steps of the King's Book House, he had been taken on and raised under the strict hand of an old Book Tender: a woman who dawdled over the two lean brown hounds with whom she shared a bed, who let them lick her hands clean after every meal, a toothless woman with a hard mind who taught him elaborate courtesy, the alphabet, and fear of the switch.

"I can see why (Swat) your mother had no use for you (Swat)," she'd say whenever he had broken anything (Swat), missed a lesson (Swat), or had an accident (Swat). "But what she abandoned (Swat) . . . I will perfect (Swat). I will make of you the perfect little man."

In his bed he'd watch the moon outside the window slit and feel each stripe upon his back. And think, I will grow up. Someday I will grow up.

When he was five, the old woman had climbed the tall ladder which leaned against the shelves that filled one whole wall of her tower room in the Book House. Her hounds watched attentively as if she were fetching them a treat. From the highest corner she snatched down a book. She crossed the five-pointed star on the marble floor, paused briefly before the huge empty fireplace, and stood before the boy, her thin body glowing in the shaft of golden light that fell from the ball of flame set in the high stained glass window behind him. She held the thick volume before the boy and loftily said, "This is the knowledge that all men hoard, the wisdom they feel no woman worthy of. This will be the reward of your education. When you have worked your way through all the books on the wall, when you have mastered them all down to the last one in the lower corner—this will be your gift."

The embossed words on the faded leather binding read, *The Secrets of Nemot*.

"Thank you, Dear Mistress," said the boy, repeating the required phrase he had learned by rote, though in truth, he would have preferred a picture book or a bag of sweets.

"It is not yours yet. You must earn it." And she replaced the book, taking out the next volume in the row. "Sit," she said, and the boy sat on the stool. "Stay," she commanded, as she settled into her high-backed chair and began to read, the words filling the dusty room like smoke.

It seemed to the boy that he spent the rest of his life sitting on that stool, his legs dangling and sore, the old woman's voice piping away, demanding attention. He soon learned that attention and memory were the only ways to get off the stool. He was taught not to dabble but excel—to subdue knowledge like an enemy.

In the long monotony of lecture, the book slowly became an obsession. It grew easy to believe that all those hours of boredom could not be in vain—only something splendid could redeem the endless tedium. At night the book crept into his dreams, transformed into something luminous and magical. It came to symbolize not only his reward, but the end of his trial and just reprieve.

At least it was something to hope for.

In time it became impossible to learn from the Book Tender. She often lost her place or fell asleep in her chair. Until one day she asked the adolescent to read to her. And so he read. But when the old woman dozed off, he would switch volumes, or move onto the next chapter without finishing the last. Until over the years he read and skipped his way to the last book at the very bottom of the shelves: an obscure work on Alchemy. He browsed the final pages and snapped shut the binding with a sharp clap that woke the Tender and her precious hounds.

They watched befuddled as the young man stood tiptoe on the ladder and reached up for the promised book. His hand found an empty corner of darkness, a gap in the top shelf where once a heavy volume had rested.

"Dear Mistress," he said over his shoulder, "where's my book?"

"Your book? What book?"

"The one you promised. My reward."

"I don't recall . . . promising a book," said the old woman.

It was all too much, her forgetfulness. He sighed, asking wearily: "What did you do with the book in the corner?"

"Oh. That book . . . I sold it."

It cost him a great deal to stand still. Slowly, he stepped down from the ladder. He would not believe it until he saw her face. He turned.

He believed.

"I needed a quilt!" the Tender whimpered.

"You promised," whispered the student, his voice cracking, his mind clinging to some wounded sense of fairness. "My reward . . ."

The Tender replied solemnly, as if pronouncing the issue dead. "Knowledge—as all men know—is its own reward." She pointed a quivering finger at her pupil. "I am an old woman with little left me. I don't expect a stripling like you to understand the needs of an arthritic body or the chill of a solitary bed. I merely hope you understand that certain sacrifices are essential in the pursuit of science . . ."

How convenient, thought the student as the old crone droned on, that the message of this missing book should coincide exactly to the Tender's needs. How wonderful a woman's mind. He no longer listened. It was simply one more tangent in a life devoted to digression. The words floated over him and dissipated in the air. From that moment on he hated words; he would scorn anything not as useful as a knife, simple as a cup, practical as fire.

And that night, before he left her forever, while she was sleeping, he strangled the hounds with a rope and left them cold at the foot of her bed so they would be the first thing she would see when she awoke.

He searched for the book for years. Yet after he had found it and the great spell, after he had said the words that cracked the earth, after he had seen his power bring life to the creature before him, he realized he had not been searching for mere words bound in worn leather, not the book, not knowledge, not even—as he had once thought—revenge. But this: this beautiful black bird. This word made flesh. This pet who called him master. This was his reward.

"What is your name?" he demanded.

The black bird walked slowly toward him, flexing its wings.

"You may call me Tomen." Its black eyes shone. "And I will call you The Usher of the Night."

For a moment he thought he feared the bird. But it passed, and he swallowed the title like an overdue compliment. It never occurred to him that he had just surrendered his name.

Chapter two

"IS THERE SOMETHING WRONG, CAPTAIN? You look as though you just saw a ghost. Nothing? Then I'll continue."

The Water Sickness spread like a shudder through the kingdom. First the fishing went bad on the Great River that ran from the northernmost ranges like the spine of a great dragon: Albino fish floated on the surface like leaves in a bowl of broth. Then came an outbreak of stomach cramps in the far villages under the shadow of the White Moon Mountains that stood over the Long Tall Forest. Soon after, a rash of pox struck the families in the forest; young mothers had stillborn babies and died: A relentless fever wore them down like a plane shaving wood into kindling. The sickness rolled on, gathering victims as a legging gathers burrs, from Northland to Southland, from the steep face of the Shear to the fishing port of Derry, and back again. The sickness followed the route of gossip: All the towns scattered along the road leading to old King John's castle were stricken. No one was spared its touch. Whatever the disease, there was no rallying from it. A broken leg, even properly set, could prove fatal from putridity. A cut finger, even properly loached, took weeks to heal. People began to walk warily, as if the ground were ice. The smoky taverns squatting below the looming castle walls were unusually quiet. There was much whispering and few smiles. Many heads were shaken and many said the land had lost all luck.

But the worst blows were yet to come.

One day King John locked himself in his chambers in the castle's tallest tower. He shaved off his beard, took off his crown, and drank a bottle of his finest wine. He took time to write an unintelligible note to his son, the Prince. Then, as the sun dipped below the horizon, he stepped up to the window ledge. A few peasants saw him in his white bedrobes. They waved. He waved back and shouted out, "Long live the King!"

Then he leapt.

The peasants who watched said they would never forget the sound of his landing. "Melon," said one. "Like a ripe melon."

At the coronation young Simon, the new King, kept insisting the trumpeters blow harder. His bodyguard and tutor, the massive Jason, had to reassure him that they played quite loud indeed. The golden crown, which did not quite fit him yet, rested on his ears and he swore the metal was affecting his hearing. To him the songsters were barely a hum as they sang out their final chorus. The old Physician was called: a doddering, secretive man who had more reputation than reliability. Yet his prognosis was correct: King Simon was going deaf.

Immediately, a remedy was called for and a reward proposed. Jason summoned all the healers, herbalists, and tricksters in the Kingdom to court. Whosoever could cure the King would be given a sack of gold and the Lordship of an old Summer Book House far to the south. An enviable dwelling—three times as large and as well appointed as any main house in the land. But the great house had stood empty for years, abandoned after the Queen had died.

Remedy. Reward. Healing. The words spread through the land like a secret bit of good news, to be spoken softly lest it spoil. But privately people scoffed at the plan. They had little doubt it would end poorly. They had long ago surrendered.

So it happened that one night, down the long torchlit corridor leading to the great oak doors of the throne room, came a small man, darkly dressed. He was in no hurry. He walked quietly, boldly passing the long line of healers who had waited patiently for their audience with the King. Strangely, no one called out in protest. Even those who had waited all day turned away from this imposing figure. When questioned later they were unable to describe him. To some he was tall and black, and his long cape lapped behind him as if from a personal wind. To others he was nobly dressed and smiled warmly. Some took note of his many rings. Others said it was obvious the stranger wore gloves. In fact, the only detail recalled and confirmed was the way the dogs who swarmed about the castle cowered as he passed.

An old woman who had come a long way to bring a specially prepared charm necklace walked out immediately after his arrival—muttering, "People oughtn't look at people like that!" A black-headed green-breasted magpie tethered to the wrist of a dark man from the northern isles, squawked, "Bad Bird! No Cage!" and tried vainly to escape her master. A small boy who had been napping against his father, a healer from the mountains, awoke and whispered: "Why, he's got a bird on his shoulder!" But no one else saw it. And as the stranger passed, the shadows in the hall-way seemed to stretch and thicken, while the light from the torches appeared to shrink. Guards stationed at intervals along the corridor grew respectfully alert, though they puzzled why the young King was receiving so royal a guest at such a late hour.

The guard at the oak doors was said to be the largest and most loyal of the King's army. He had frightened many foes by his stature alone, and he was accustomed to being addressed with a nervous politeness. One moment he was thinking of his warm supper and his warm wife and the next he was looking down at a small dark man who appeared neither young nor old. "Small and dark," he would say later, "that's all"—emphasizing his estimate with a level palm held at his stomach.

"His Majesty will see me now," commanded the stranger.

"Of course," said the guard, opening the doors which gave their usual solemn whine.

"Your wife and supper are waiting," said the stranger as he stepped inside. "Tell the others to go home." The huge guard obediently turned to the corridor, cleared his throat loudly, and waited for the attention his announcement deserved.

In the several moments before his presence was noted, the stranger scanned the room with abrupt birdlike glances. There were six tapestries on either side, woven of red and golden thread, hanging heavily from ceiling to floor. Under each, a guard stood in polished armor holding a spear. Everywhere he saw the gestures of fatigue: Eyes glazed, nostrils flared, bodies were discreetly scratched. It was a room drained of anticipation, a room where failure was expected. He could see there had been too many apologies after too much enthusiasm. He heard the silence of a room without hope.

Across a long floor of checkerboard tiles he saw Jason—a huge, ugly, bearded man—resting his hand on the King. The young man wrapped in a purple cloak sitting on the throne was quite handsome, though he looked like he wanted sleep. His skin hung pale on his thin body, and he tugged his rings with distraction. The stranger whispered over his shoulder, "Are you awake, Tomen?"

"Awake, Master."

"Good. I may need you."

Chapter three

THE FIRST THING THE KING'S bodyguard—Jason—noticed about the stranger was his hands. He did not look at his face—it was hidden in the shadow of his hood. And he had fought sword to sword often enough to know that you never look into your opponent's eyes. To anticipate a blow you watched his hands. The stranger's right hand was crippled, frozen like the claw of a dead bird. The other hand was taut with control, the forefinger and thumb pinched together as if bracing themselves for a performance. The hands betrayed him: He was straining to be casual.

Despite his suspicions, the sight of the crippled hand made him pause. He vividly recalled the night his own finger was severed at the knuckle. He had been the youngest armsman ever recruited into the King's escort—a privileged troop of a dozen men picked from the army's finest. On the King's yearly stag hunt they were ambushed by a band of wood thieves. Only Jason and King John survived the attack. Their horses had fled. So they were forced to walk the twenty miles back to the castle, both wounded and weak, following the dim trail by moonlight.

He would never forget the moment. First, the fraction of time before the pain when he knew he had lost it and he knew it would be bad and he knew it would botch his aim, then, hearing the blade clink against the hilt of his sword—and cursing himself because he had made the amateur's mistake of looking into the glint of gloat in the moon-reflecting eyes of his enemy just before the blow. To his luck, however, the triumph had lingered in the thief as he wound up for the final stroke. It was the hesitation that killed him. Even as the pain seared through his hand he thrust

his blade through the man's neck. It was a useful memory. It kept him careful. He would not forget the mortal pride of a man who had rejoiced a
blow too soon, or the bright agony of his wounded hand: the price of the
lesson. He had looked into his eyes.

Jason glanced from the approaching stranger to the young King on his
throne. To lose a finger was one thing. But to lose a sense, and a father?
He understood his dark mood, though he had little patience with grief.
To his way of thinking, young Simon had drawn an imaginary line; he had
made the mistake of giving life an ultimatum: Do not cross this line or I
will be crushed; do not take this from me because I cannot bear it. But life
ignored him; it crossed the line and he had taken it as his cue to despair.
You can't decide beforehand what you can or cannot bear. Nobody knows.
When Jason's father died after coughing blood for days, when his mother
had not woken up one morning, both times he felt he could not bear it.
But he did, and what seemed at the time to be the end of all things was
just one of the many endings life continually discharges. You didn't tempt
life with ultimatums; you didn't draw lines if you wanted to survive. You
turned and went on.

Simon beckoned him to his side. "Is there something wrong, Jason?"

He had to be careful. The young King was uncanny in his ability to
read moods. He must never show his true distaste—it would hurt him.
He shook his head, then mouthed the words the King would read on his
lips: "Perhaps this one . . ."

"Yes," said Simon dryly. "And perhaps not."

How like his father he was, so quick to despair. King John never recovered from his wife's death. In the years that he clung to his grief, Jason
was often embarrassed by him. But he had never lost his love and respect
for John. The old King had won them quickly, convincingly, on that night
of the ambush, the night he lost his finger. They had no business surviving that night.

There was something about being alone in the woods—at night, with no fire—that made you want to talk. On their long trek back to the castle they discovered they shared a taste for poetry. As they walked slowly, sometimes limping, they recited to each other—the music of their voices the only sound of the night. Jason had never spoken to a King before, so it never occurred to him that such talk was uncommonly intimate given the gulf between their ranks. Once the King fainted—he had suffered an ugly chest wound—and Jason carried him on his back for five miles. The King awoke and realized he was being carried.

"What's your name, armsman?"

"Jason."

Then he fainted again. The next time the King awoke he insisted on being set down. As Jason caught his breath the King fixed his bandages and asked where he had learned to fight. Jason took this as a compliment. He had seen the King drive his opponents stumbling backward with furious blows.

"My father taught me. A blacksmith. When I was five he made me a sword and told me never to use it unless I used it well. He'd stand me next to a small pine and I'd have to cut off all the branches before he'd count to fifty. Not just cut them off, but clip them so they left no nubs."

"Quite a challenge."

"It was. I didn't get it right till I was eight." Jason smiled, and when the King had looked away, he winced. The shock was wearing off.

"Perhaps you could teach my son someday."

Then they walked silently a while, side by side. Once they were startled by a dark shape that darted across the trail. A stag, its rack silhouetted against the night sky. In that brief moment of fear their eyes met; trust passed between them and they were friends. When dawn broke Jason crested a hill and saw the castle in the distance, then shifted the burden on his shoulders and carried the King the long last mile. He set the King down gently, knocked on the gates, and collapsed in a heap.

During the three days that Jason lay unconscious, King John seldom left his side. He hovered over his physician as he tended to the wounds and slept in a chair beside the bed of down that sunk under the great weight of the man. On the second day he interviewed the Lieutenant who had recruited Jason. A tall nervous man who stood uncomfortably at the foot of the bed, sometimes casting a wary eye on the quiet hulk that sprawled under the quilt.

"I need to know," the King began, "the kind of man he was."

"*Was?* I pray the wounds aren't fatal!"

"He has a chance. As you know, he is a strong one."

"Stout of heart and quick of sword," agreed the man, "and . . ."

"And what, Lieutenant?"

"If I may be frank, your Majesty . . . a gift for trouble."

"Be specific," the King ordered.

"He rose through the ranks quickly. Quietly. Some say 'like a weed.' He soon made sergeant."

"Unusual for a young man."

"Indeed, Sire, it seemed hasty. He was not a typical armsman, not given to gambling or carousing with the other troops. A man of few words. No one knew where he'd come from, and he couldn't be cajoled into speaking of his past. This made him . . . suspect. Then there were the books."

"Books?"

"He was caught reading in the barracks. Poetry. Naturally, this struck some of the men as uppity."

"Naturally," the King conceded.

"Three of the veterans took it upon themselves to break him in. They teased him about the books and laughed in his face. Had he only laughed with them . . . but he ignored their taunts and this struck them as intolerable. So Kuma slapped him."

"The big one? The one who lifted the dead horse over his head?"

"The same, your Majesty. Jason's a quick man, but as the saying goes, 'Nobody's quick enough for three.' They beat him senseless. Again the next night they caught him reading and beat him and threw his book in the fire. The next night he joined the other men at the bonfire. Bruised but cordial. They were satisfied. He was one of us. I mean, he was one of them."

"I know what you mean," said the King, the suggestion of a smile on his lips.

The Lieutenant paused. "The rest is rumor."

"Go on."

"A week later we fought the Battle of Tartoon. It was a bad night for the enemy, and for us. You could barely step without tripping on a limb." He spared the King the worst of the memory: the cries of dying men in the aftermath, men becoming boys again, wailing for their mothers. "In the morning the scouts went out to collect survivors. They found none. But they did find three peculiar casualties."

"Peculiar?"

A hint of bitterness crept into the man's voice. "They were three of your fiercest armsmen, your Majesty."

"I've lost many brave men." The King sighed. "But you said 'peculiar.'"

"The three who broke in Jason just a week before. They were beheaded." The man swallowed. "Their heads were found together on a stump, facing outward."

The Lieutenant glanced at the bed as if he might have been overheard. The King worked hard to keep a solemn face.

"And the upstart Jason?" he asked.

"Started reading his books again." Inadvertently, the man began to address the figure on the bed. "From that night on he struck us all as a really very decent fellow—slow to anger, soft-spoken, not one to sit upon a laugh. Given half a chance he proved to be a very respectable armsman indeed."

"And the troops found no occasion to tease him again?" said the King dryly.

Tight-lipped, the Lieutenant nodded.

"You've been most helpful," he said, dismissing him.

Jason remembered his bewildered awakening: emerging from a dream of endless rolling clouds against a purple sky—a soothing journey, a vast serenity. He was in a strange bed with a strange man sitting beside him.

"You damn horse!" said the man. "How dare you scare me like that?"

He wished he could get back to the peace of the dream. His body felt as if it had been trampled and his hand pulsed with pain. Who was this man beside him? Why did he like him? Could you like someone and not know their name? What was wrong with his hand?

"You nearly died you know. You lost a bucket of blood. My physician didn't expect you to live, but I commanded him to change your prognosis."

Commanded. That was a strange word. Commanded. Suddenly his memory tumbled back into place and he spoke his first words in days. "You're the King!"

"John." The King smiled, touching his arm. "Call me John."

A week later he was well enough to attend the ceremony appointing him personal bodyguard to the King. This abrupt promotion scandalized the Court. Whispers filled the castle: He was a common armsman. He was crude. Worse, he would contradict the King to his face. But what irked them most, as the King and Jason became inseparable, was their smug camaraderie, their secret smiles—as if they shared a private joke. The Court could not understand the attachment to one who has saved your life. Such danger and loyalty was beyond them. They speculated that the King had been blackmailed.

As this remembrance faded and Jason gazed down upon the small dark stranger who stood at the foot of the steps leading to the throne, he found himself taken by the sudden hope that perhaps this one wasn't a fraud. Perhaps this stranger would have the remedy for King Simon's deafness. The word clotted in his mind: remedy. He sighed deeply and looked into the shadow where the stranger's eyes should be.

Chapter four

WOULDN'T ANYONE OFFERED A MIRACLE be curious? Grateful? Amused? No. King Simon had sat through too many magic shows as a child. Jason would explain each trick and they would lose their charm. A hidden pea under three walnut shells, an egg into a dove, a coin behind the ear; all miracles were scrutable. The real trick was locating the moment of deception: when the deck was stacked, when the dove was nudged out of the secret pocket, when the innocent hand—the one you shouldn't have been watching—slipped neatly behind the back. Jason had taught him to be a hard audience. How ironic, then, that this endless procession of healers was Jason's idea. Could he really believe they would find a remedy—a remedy in the crafts of repulsive little men like this one? He stared covertly over the rim of his goblet as he drank the sweet cider—stared down and saw the silent approach of the small dark stranger: the shadowed face, the wretched dangling hand. He scratched at the beginnings of his first beard and felt Jason's hand settle on his shoulder. Could he really be so deluded after three days? It was like watching a troop of minstrels flub their juggling—then starting over, insisting they would get it right this time. This time. This time! How long was he expected to endure it?

On top of it all there was the pity. The mouths exaggerating around him as if he were an infant. The insult of depending on a Scribbler to transcribe all conversation. Pity followed him everywhere, like an ugly mutt lapping at his ankles. He'd had his fill of it as a child—a sickly boy, prone to many ills, he quickly learned the leverage of the bedridden. Everything was his for the asking, tantrums were tolerated, griping acceptable, and when he was bored he could always boss the servants. But for all their devotion he never quite got well, and he concluded that their sympathy was useless.

One day he hid deep in a closet. He waited a long time for the shrieks, the frantic search, and the tears of relief. He waited especially for one nurse who had a way of touching his head. She didn't come. Then he must have fallen asleep because he awoke with the cool stone floor against his cheek. He was hungry. And when he tracked down his nurse, she said, "Not now, Simon, I have to finish this mending." He understood then for the first time that it was their job. They were paid to serve him. From that day on he became the terror of the castle. He set his bed aflame with a candle. He had his nurse fired. He began to lord his office over grown-ups. He learned how to snub. You may be healthy, he thought, but I am the Prince. I will never pout to be pampered. I will brook no pity. But now it was back again. Everyone was so understanding, so impossible to patronize, so inexhaustibly kind. There now, they seemed to say: Now you are one of us. The pity was so thick it felt like revenge.

When he was very young—perhaps in one of his many fevers—he had gotten the idea he was being punished. One of his earliest memories was a rare meal with the King, sitting opposite him across a long table, his chin just above the edge. They ate in silence until he suddenly realized most children had dinner with their mothers, and most fathers had wives to eat with, and wasn't she ever hungry? "Where's my mama?" he asked, and the King left the table. He asked his nurse and she burst out of the room holding her apron to her eyes. Then the Physician told him sternly: "You'd better not ask such questions, little Prince. They upset the King." All this confirmed the peculiar notion that he had done something terrible, so terrible that no one would ever tell him what it was.

Yet he got everything he asked for: The King gave him a pony, a boat, a bow, a leather fencing vest, sweets, a toy castle of wooden blocks, a sword—everything. But the thing he wanted most, he could not put into words. The Prince used to wish: "Someday, someday . . ." But eventually, even if that someday had miraculously appeared, it would have been too late. He stopped asking for gifts. Then he stopped thanking him for them. Then he began to hate them. Each new present seemed to say: This didn't cost me anything, it doesn't mean anything, you don't deserve anything, but let's pretend. He learned to hate pretending. And any game of make-believe was joyless to him.

This did not help him make friends. The castle children were either stupid or frightened of the Prince, and his father wouldn't let him play with the peasant boys and girls: It would be unseemly. Eventually he found companionship in the most unlikely prospect: the only person he could not intimidate. The Prince had a passion for a new game of logic that the spice traders had brought back from the East. It was called chess. He considered himself a master of the game, for in three years he had never lost once. One day, when there was no one else to play, he challenged the King's bodyguard to a match. It was his first encounter with a man who had always struck him as rather gruff and dull. The game was new to Jason so Simon patiently instructed him in the moves, the power value of the pieces, and some rudimentary strategy: "Watch the mages, they move at angles; horses are graceless and crude leapers who do not know their place . . ."

Jason beat him in twenty moves. He was furious and demanded a re-match. They played again and again. Simon always had Jason cornered; he was always two moves away from checkmate—but Jason would grunt and nudge an innocent pawn that crippled his defense and sabotaged his game. They played six more games before the Prince conceded it was no fluke. Jason was his clear superior. He brooded about it all the next day until he realized the wonderful truth of the matter. Jason was very simply the only man in the castle who had never let him win. Elated, he went to his father and demanded that Jason be made his tutor. He had finally found some-one to trust.

He had also found something he had not bargained for: a tough taskmaster. Jason taught him to be a crack swordsman and almost as good with a bow. He taught him galloping, jousting, and hawking and made him ashamed of his sloppy mind. He taught him to think harder than ever before: how to memorize a long poem, how to put himself in the mind of his enemy and outguess him. It was a refreshing education, for Jason made no allowances for his office or frail body. "Pick up the damn sword and do it right this time!" he'd scoff. His tutor was immune to tantrums. He quizzed him ruthlessly on his digits. And he never once lost at chess.

Jason also taught him about women. They had gone fishing on the Great River and after lunch went into the woods to relieve themselves. They were standing side by side, the Prince doing his best to make his puddle as big as Jason's, when they saw a flattened patch of weeds with intersecting tracks. They followed the tracks for a while then Jason said they should sit down and no matter what happened be absolutely still.

Four deer stepped into the clearing a stone's throw away: a doe, a fawn, and two yearlings. When they saw Jason and Simon they froze but were too young and weak-eyed to be alarmed. They must have smelled the salt of their sweat because the doe ambled over, leaving the others tense behind. She ignored Jason, went right up to Simon, and sniffed him with her black nose. It was hard not to move. She smelled wild. She then took two licks on his cheek and flopped her tail once, signaling the others. They retreated lazily and she followed them without hurry, glancing back once before she was lost in the camouflage of the forest.

They sat silently for a while until Jason spoke. "It's time you were told about ladies and such." And he talked about children and bleeding days, and where to put it and how to touch and that it was good if it was gentle but better if you loved the girl (for then there was something to talk about afterward), and how certain women liked certain things and on and on. Finally, the young Prince burst out laughing because he thought Jason was telling him the damnedest joke he'd ever heard. But the tutor was serious.

"Such things actually happen?" asked the Prince.

"How d'you think you got here?" Jason replied.

Simon made him repeat the whole story—the hows, the wheres, especially the whats. Later, as they lay under the stars, he found he could not sleep: His imagination buckled under a whole new vocabulary.

In the morning he demanded more details, and when they were supplied he was still not satisfied. As they trotted home he blurted out his misgivings: He could accept something complex, but he could not swallow a mystery.

"But why?" he demanded. "Why would anyone *want* to?"

Jason stared at the Prince, then began to laugh. He could not stop laughing and had to dismount and lean against his horse. After Jason wiped the tears out of his coarse red beard, they rode quietly for a while— the silence occasionally punctuated by his chuckle. Finally Jason said: "I suppose I've saddled the pony a mite early."

There came a time when Jason's words about women began to make sense. He had lately begun to avoid them. They gave him strange feelings, they smelled odd, and he found it difficult to keep them out of his dreams. He had seen what a woman had done to his father, and he didn't think they were worth the trouble. Yet there was this hunger to know. He had only one question for Jason. It had burned inside him so long that he approached it quite indirectly, as if it were too tender to lance.

They sat in his bedchamber before a roaring hearth and he asked if she was beautiful. The question seemed to hurt Jason, and he turned away saying, "You've seen the pictures."

"But paintings can flatter."

"And so can words," said Jason.

"Then tell me the truth," said the Prince.

The tutor stared off into the flames. When he spoke, the Prince did not recognize his voice—it was steeped in memory and loss. It never occurred to him (until much later) that like most of the men who had met his mother, Jason had fallen in love.

"She was beautiful. But I don't think it mattered to her."

To see that she had moved a man as solid as Jason confirmed his worst suspicions. They were dangerous creatures.

Then he asked the real question. The one that mattered. The one that hurt to ask. "Did I kill her?"

Jason turned and saw the look on Simon's face. "Of course not!" he said, shaking his head, dumbfounded. "Whatever made you think that?"

"Are you sure?"

"Oh, Simon! Of course I'm sure. It wasn't your fault, lad. Has no one ever told you about it?"

"I asked, but I wasn't answered," he replied bitterly.

There was a long silence, then Jason asked, "Do you believe in magic, Simon?"

"Not since I was a child."

"I thought not. I want to tell you a story. Some time ago, I was on my way back to the castle. I had stopped for the night at Donaldson's Inn, and I saw this ring of travelers gathered round the Tale Teller—Donaldson himself, an old bald man with no eyebrows. Most of what he said wasn't worth pissing on, but he knew how to tell a story. He was like a liar who couldn't help slipping in a little truth in spite of himself.

"It was very late. And when he was telling that tale, there was the fire snapping in the hearth, there was his voice piping and chiming like an old woman, and that was it. I'll bet you a golden not a man in that tavern slept decently that night. I know I didn't."

The Prince smiled. "Are you trying to scare me, Jason?"

"Maybe I am. You could use a little fear."

"It takes more than a story to frighten me."

"Really?" said Jason. "I would think that would depend on the story."

He continued. "The strange thing was, the old man told it two ways. Finished one, downed his mug and started the other. The first goes something like this:

One day the Maker was very angry at the wickedness of his people and he decided to punish them. On that day he sent down his wrath to men in the form of a huge black bird. The bird flew across the skies like a great thundercloud, spitting magic rain upon the land. And the spittle flooded into the rivers and moved like a cloud of ink, backward against the current, until it had spoiled all the waters. The people called this spoiling Mother Death, because though it poisoned many men and children, it took its greatest toll on mothers. This was so the wicked could bear no sons, and their names would die with them.

What a strange name, thought Simon. In all the legends told of the Water Sickness since it had begun, he had never heard that one.

"That's the first one. The second one goes like this:

There was once an evil spring hidden deep in the crevices of the White Moon Mountains. And wicked little emerald creatures lived there. They were ugly and froglike and only came out at night to steal fish and piss magic poison into the streams. They were called Watermen. They hated people, and they spoiled the waters, poisoning many men and children, but they took their greatest toll on mothers. Now, the Maker was fond of his people, so he fashioned a creature to rescue them—a creature made of magic, spoiled water, and the spirits of all the dead mothers. He called this creature Mother Death because she destroyed the evil Watermen and purified the waters and became the guardian of all those children who had lost their mothers.

Simon smirked in spite of himself. He felt sure Jason was trying to frighten him, and he was proud that it hadn't worked. Checkmate, he thought. Just another peasant legend about the Water Sickness. He had heard them before. Such simple people, he thought: They must explain their suffering. "It's a riddle isn't it? In the first legend Mother Death is a curse. In the second Mother Death is a remedy. Right?"

"Does it matter? I daresay you could find something riddling about this fire. It works both ways: It can burn or warm, light or blind, depending on how you use it. It's a riddle, but that doesn't make it any less real."

He won't admit he's lost this one, thought Simon. He began to tease him. "But surely you're not saying those legends are *true?*"

Jason looked deeply into the fire.

"I'll tell you what's true then. I knew I wouldn't sleep that night so I rode straight to the castle. When I arrived I found the King had locked himself in his chambers. I heard a baby crying. The Physician met me in the hall and said the Queen had been dead for hours. He told me her last words were 'Call him Simon.'"

The Prince felt a sudden chill. "But that's impossible! That was nineteen years ago! The Water Sickness—"

"Didn't start until four years ago," said Jason. "Your mother died almost exactly when the old man was telling those stories."

Jason had won after all, and though he obviously didn't relish it, it felt like a terribly cruel trick.

"You didn't have to tell me like that."

"You wanted to know what she died of," Jason replied. "I'm trying to tell you. She died of magic."

"But that's nonsense!"

"Is it?" Jason asked. "There's too much snicker in you, Simon. You're too young to snicker at a world you don't understand."

He replied bitterly to the memory in his mind. He understood all right. He understood that his mother had died without his ever having known her, and no creepy legends were going to change that. His father had lost his mind and he had lost his father. They'd put the King's body in a stock chamber off the throne room where shields, pillows, and candles were kept. Stacks of candles everywhere like perfect kindling pyramids of unblemished birch. The white body was laid out on a table—hastily, for there were pale candles strewn all across the floor. It was covered with his favorite cloak—a fuliginous wrap so dark it seemed you could plunge your hand right into it, as if it were a window looking out into the night. His father's dead face (practically the only part of his body that was not

41

broken, that did not resemble meat). His father's dead nose and mouth and brow. He fingertipped the mound of skin below his dead eye. It felt pliable, used, like cooling wax. And he recalled thinking, My father is a candle.

That's the kind of world it was. It was a world that would always be missing something. It was seeing a teacup spill and shatter on the floor and having to remember the sound—or imagine it. It was never hearing a bird call, a child laugh, a book shut, a waterfall, a fire crackle, and never hearing the voice of the only man you loved. He understood all too well. The only thing he didn't understand was why Jason had told him those riddles and found it necessary to frighten him.

He felt his tutor's hand on his shoulder and resisted an urge to shrug it off. He looked down at the stranger at the foot of the steps. Apparently, he was speaking. His mouth curled into contempt as the ugly little man melodramatically lifted one fist above his head, then floated slowly upward until there was a gap of air between his feet and the floor. And as he hovered in place, an impish smile was visible under the shadow of his hood, and the snicker in the King's throat died quickly.

Chapter five

SOME TWENTY MILES SOUTH OF the castle at the foot of the White Moon Mountains, the Long Tall Forest stretched out deep and green and full of cool shade for many miles. Near the center of the forest was a small clearing and a well of stones. A worn path extended from the well to a log cabin at the edge of the clearing. There lived a couple and their only child, a boy named Tim.

Tim was proud to be a woodcutter's son. He loved to stand beside his father in the cluttered workshop that smelled of sawdust and resin. Above the bench and worktable was a wall covered with different tools hanging on pegs—some wooden, some metal, each uniquely shaped for its special task. As a child Tim had imagined this to be a collection of musical instruments, for his father would select one with deliberation, pause before he pressed it to the wood, and then, as he began to stroke, a song and rhythm would emerge. To Tim, it was magic.

Indeed, it took such magic to keep him planted in one place for more than a moment—he was a restless boy, given to frolic. And it was not uncommon for his mother to hear him sprawling on the shingles of the cabin's roof, having leapt from a nearby tree. Yet year by year, for hours at a time, he'd watch his father working at his craft, carving toys, rocking horses, signs to be hung above inns, oxen yokes and wagon beds, stools, tables, and occasionally a door which bore the family crest upon its knocker.

Each of his father's pieces was a glimpse of another world. A world outside his own, a world not circumscribed by the clearing, the well, and the comforting silence or whisper of the trees that surrounded their cabin.

As it was for his father until he'd made his first journey out of the woods.

The path became a trail and then a rutted road. I saw a horse: a fine stallion, black as night with flashing blue eyes. The woods is mostly shadow, you know. When it opened onto grassy lands I thought that all the trees had picked up their roots, like a woman lifting her skirts to cross a stream, and retreated to join their brethren in the woods. Then: golden farmland, the wheat ripe and chewable and waving in the wind.

There was the occasional farmhouse. And I slept under a cherry tree and woke when a ripe one fell on my head.

My first town was just a few houses and a well. Cattle stood so still in the knell I thought they were sleeping. Then their tails would whip at flies.

There's a ferry at the Great River, and I rode across with a troop of cavalry. There was a big man with a horse face accompanied by a young boy on a white mare. He asked what I had in my pack and I was showing it to him before I realized he'd been suspicious. It was a sign I was delivering to an inn—my uncle had won me the commission, out of pity I suppose. He was always saying I'd never amount to anything. The big man held it and examined it like a woman checking herself in a mirror. Then he held it up for the boy to see with a grunt. The boy (he was pale and wore a shimmering purple cloak) smiled. The horseman grunted again and called it "fine work." I blushed and said I could do better.

"Better?" he asked.

Then I told him of the chair I had made in a dream. A mad maze of antlers and horns carved from oak, sanded and burnished till it shone like gold.

The horseman said it sounded splendid. "How many goldens?"

I don't think I understood immediately that he was serious. Then I said it would take me months.

He turned, deferring to the boy, and said, "Your father could have it in spring. For his birthday."

The boy shrugged.

The horseman reached into the leather pouch at his belt, and I saw, as he pulled out the coins, that he was missing a finger.

He put three goldens in my hand and said, "Three now, three when you deliver it after the last snows."

I felt like a man to whom the Maker had revealed his life's purpose.

Stammering, I asked where I should deliver it.

The horseman laughed. And the ferryman who tugged the rope snickered, saying, "Do you not know who yer addressing?"

I was silent and ashamed until the boy spoke—sympathetically, I recall—"It'll make a splendid throne for my father."

After the word throne, *I, who had never seen a King, knelt, imagining the horseman was him. He stubbed a laugh and laid a gentle hand under my arm to help me up.*

"On your feet, man. Save your bowing till spring."

Then he introduced the Prince on the white horse (he seemed a humble sort and not altogether unkind). And I bowed and the boy bowed back and the horseman bowed to both of us as if it were a great joke.

And by the time we made shore and the ferryman lashed us aground, Jason—that was the horseman's name—had told me a story of the Battle of Tartoon that I swore I'd remember all my life.

King John's throne turned out to be his finest work—a maze of elkhorns that meshed to form a chair both stately and mysterious. The design had so pleased the King that he commissioned the woodcutter to carve a relief of figures that told the story of the great Battle of Tartoon. This was the piece that absorbed Tim's father now. And the boy watched intently as he labored over the wheels of a coach, turning the spokes into winding serpents that licked the axle with their tongues. "What's that, Father?" Tim asked, pointing to a peculiar detail.

"What's it look like?"

"Three pumpkins on a stump."

His father chuckled deeply and said, "That's right."

To Tim this was true magic; it was as if these figures had always been in the wood, waiting and yearning for his father's touch to be made real. Perhaps they slept and dreamed of someday waking from the wood. Or perhaps these figures: hawks and horses, dragons and armsmen, castles aflame, arrows launched and soaring in an arc—some shot so high they pierced the clouds above the battlefield—perhaps these were the dreams of the trees his father had felled for carving. Of course! It made sense that something so locked in one place would fill its dreams with so much freedom. Who wouldn't long to ride and run and fly after being forced to stand still for so long? Perhaps his father had found a way of freeing the dreams from the trees. Or maybe he could tell when a tree was dreaming, the way it bent and creaked like a snore. Was there a signal only woodcutters knew to tell when trees were ripe with dreams?

Soon he would learn such things, for this was the day he had waited for and dreamed of: the day he would become his father's apprentice, his twelfth birthday. His mother had made his favorite stew, his father had given him his own set of carving tools. That night after supper, as they sat before a blazing hearth—his mother in her rocker, his father in his chair sipping hot spiced cider, and he at his father's feet sucking a maple and wrapped in a quilt—he was so happy he wouldn't have believed the day could get any better. But then the woodcutter asked if he wanted a story and his face lit up, for his father was a craftsman of words as well as wood. He wondered if the story would be remembered or created. It didn't really matter—either way it could make him cry and laugh at the same time.

"Mother says you were doing some 'flying' today."

Tim cringed inwardly. She'd caught him treebending that afternoon—a sport that panicked her but delighted him. The trick was to scale a young tree whose trunk was not yet stout, grasp the narrow tip, and fling yourself backward into the air. The tree would bend down quickly, as if it meant to dash you to the ground, but at the last moment (this was the best part) its trunk would recoil, spring up and down, up and down, dragging you with it. Finally, it would settle you gently. You'd let go and the tree would whip back into place. To Tim this sport was sheer joy, to his mother it was suicide. She could not understand that trees were his only playmates.

She was a careful woman, a woman who searched out things to fret about. A born worrier, she felt compeled to supplement the woodcutter's meager income by doing odd chores for travelers: washing, seaming, loaching, and she had acquired something of a reputation as a palmist. It was a task she took reluctantly though it paid better than all her other chores combined. She told Tim once: "It is a useless skill: to glimpse the future. Believe me, no one wants to know their future. They want to know if someday they'll be happy."

"Well?" his father said. "Were you flying, then?"

"I know what I'm doing," he said. "I'm twelve." He hoped this wouldn't be one of those stories that taught you a lesson and made you feel awful. He had gotten more than his share of those.

"But did you know there once were men who really could fly? Men who could ride a cloud like a horse."

"Really?"

"You'll frighten the boy, John," his mother warned. "The old tales are best forgotten."

But Tim truly enjoyed being frightened and he quickly asked: "Is this a remembered story?"

"Yes. A little friend told it to me."

Long ago, the woodcutter began, *before things were set down in books, the wizards came out of the sky like falling stars. They lived among the creatures of this world for ages unseen, for outside their natural element they were invisible. They were spirits of great power, but as they observed the ways of men they grew lonely. For though they could see and hear, they envied us our other senses—especially the gift of touch, the gift we mortals take for granted. They begged the Maker to relieve them of the burden of their immortality,* to grant them the privileges of our form, especially the gift of touch. The Maker promised to grant their wish on one condition: that they share the ways of power.

At this the wizard Nemot faltered. "Could they be ready for such power?"

"As ready as you are for death, Nemot. For that is the price of this gift."

So the wizards agreed. And from that day forward they were human. They could taste, smell, touch, and die.

Now, they were true to their promise. To their favorite creatures, the frogs, they gave the gift of speech; they taught the chants of Water Magic. In time, they became the Watermen. To the human apprentices they gave all the spells and formulas of Earth Sorcery: the ability to command matter and light, the power to read the thoughts of the mind at will. But for themselves alone, they reserved the most potent magic: the Way of the Wind, whose currents were said to carry the Maker's spirit, whose true form is invisible outside its natural element.

The wizards lived the lifetimes of a hundred men. They flew across the skies of the world bringing their tales and power and wisdom to all. And in their time they were held with such awe and love that it was said that good fortune rested upon the house that a flying wizard's shadow had crossed.

But eventually they began to die. Most were saddened to leave their adopted home. Some were weary of their mortal flesh and its pains. But one wizard went so far as to deny his death. He had grown accustomed to his power and he was loath to relinquish his stature. In the waning years of his life, he grew so desperate for his lost gift of immortality that he spelled an evil spell. Unheeding of the Maker's decrees, he cast his spirit down into the depths of the world—into the lowlands where there is fire—and with this spell he forged the deeper elements into a new creature that could survive though it died a thousand deaths. A creature made of spirit untouched by time. Worse still, he wrote an evil spell into a book, leaving it for someone to find.

It was the spell to raise the dead.

This was the wizard Nemot, and the Maker knew of his evil. For punishment the Maker took away his heart, the heart with which he had been gifted when he chose to be mortal: for hearts are what make people human. And the Maker banished him into the center of the world, closing a huge spinning ball of stone about him to keep him from the upper lands.

The wizards died, and without their guidance and wisdom, the powers they had gifted the world soon became forgotten and passed into legend. The winds they had awakened and ridden soon fell into a deep fathomless slumber and drifted aimlessly over the land. Sorcery grew dim, recalled only by a few who wrote the spells in fine books bound in leather. These they passed onto their descendants. But the language of magic was old and it grew strange to the ear. And over many years much of it was lost. Only the Watermen clung to their beautiful chants—and thus their magic was preserved.

Tim's father sighed deeply. He took a sip of his cider, which had gone cold, and looking down, he saw his son asleep and leaning against his knees. He chuckled and turned to his smiling wife.

"Just look how much I've frightened him."

"He was tired. He had his usual reckless day. Besides," she added, "I don't think he understood."

The man frowned slightly. "I wanted him to."

"He's still a boy," she said. "Darts about all day like a bird. I don't see how you expect him to have the patience for woodcutting."

"I wasn't talking about woodcutting."

"I know." His wife sighed and looked at the floor. "He frets me." She gently stroked the open palm that lay upon her lap, as if it held something she wanted to wipe away. "I look at him and I see . . . a great shadow."

A helpless hurt rose in the woodcutter's eyes. "Your palming days are over, love."

She looked darkly at the sleeping child. "I fear him sometimes."

"The drowned mutts? But that was an accident!"

"Was it?"

"Hush, now."

"I fear for him." She shuddered. "What he could become—"

"Is anybody's guess. My love, trust a little bit, eh? He has a guardian."

"Much good may it do him," she said darkly.

The woodcutter gave her a wistful look, then stood and stretched. "I'll tuck him in."

Turning to the sleeping boy, he extended his arms in a peculiar gesture that his little friend had taught him, and said an ancient phrase.

Tim's limp body lifted silently off the ground like a tuft of white dandelion and floated gently into the outstretched arms of his father, who carried him up the ladder into the loft, to bed.

For the longest time, the Teller kneaded his eyes between his finger and thumb.

Then, he continued.

Chapter six

AS THE STRANGER ROSE INTO the air, the dull silence broke; the throne room echoed with the sound of shock: the unanimous gasp of dozens of mouths sucking air. Jaws dropped as if on cue. Jason drew his dagger. The old jester wet himself.

Simon stood and tried to conceal the shaking of his voice. "What are you?" he cried.

"A Wizard of the Wind," was the reply.

To anyone who'd ever seen a true wizard fly, the counterfeit would have been obvious. The posture was wrong, the attitude and words incorrect. Clearly, this was a different sort of magic. An impersonation. Anyone with a wise eye would have said the stranger was hanging not floating. But wizardry had long since passed into legend.

Tatoan had been dead seven hundred years. It had been ages since anyone had spoken with a wizard, or felt the learning in their hands, or glimpsed through the portals of their fallen star the work of silver gears and jewels within.

No one was alive to remember all this when the Prince had lost his hearing. Memories had become songs. Songs had become tales. Tales had become legends.

You see, the wizards gave us many, many things; but the most precious thing they left us is something no one ever recalls coming from them.

Can you guess what it is?

Here's a clue. Until the wizards, our ancients were very much like children: They believed they disappeared when they closed their eyes. They believed anything. Memory was such a feeble young thing back then; it had not been exercised to the point where it could retain more than two or three things at once. There was no difference between lies and truth, gossip and witness, fancy and fact, for the world was full of deep mystery and constant wonder. There was very little past to compare things to. And Time had not yet been discovered. All was devoted to that moment, that hour, that day. And people didn't expect much more than a warm fire, a successful hunt, and simple shelter.

Until stories.

Stories were the only thing that made us different than animals—nothing else.

Perhaps the First Story Teller was a blind girl who knew the worth of words, who sat all day in the cool cave, listening to her family come and go, imagining their faces to match their voices, weaving words to capture a life she could only listen to. Or perhaps it was a hunter lost for years, who passed his time remembering his clan, and retold in his mind the long lonely life he'd led in the dark woods, rehearsing for the day he'd return from his wanderings to be welcomed back, to be fussed over and fed, wrapped in a warm skin and begged to tell of his adventures in the wild and frightening world. Or perhaps the first Teller was an old woman with a long stick who drew words from the air, dazzling her tribe with strange tales of The Boy Who Lost His Wings, The Joker Who Forgot How to Make People Laugh, The Dancing Fruit, The Chronicler Who Stepped Between Worlds and Cheated Time.

Only much later did it become a craft, a trade. Story Tellers roamed with troops of players from place to place, earning their lodging with tales told before hearths at inns, bonfires on beaches, or, perhaps, under a full moon on the deck of some creaking boat . . . like this one, eh?

52

THE Gift

Do you see?

There were no stories before the wizards came. That was their gift. The gift that made us human.

But there was a price to pay for these stories. Stories gave us pleasures we had never imagined, and hungers we had never known. And once we became listeners and Tellers, stories became our strongest appetite. But we kept it at a cost. What do you suppose it was?

Endings. They left us endings.

You see, you've always feared death. It wasn't always so. Your ancestors only feared pain. They did not fear death until they learned about endings. Stories taught them that.

Some say magic was the wizards' greatest gift, others say flight. Though we have lost both. Yet, I believe—though no doubt my calling colors my judgement on the matter, I think if I were a woodcutter and not a Teller I might feel the same—stories are their greatest gift.

Do you recall where I left off, or have I strayed too far from the telling?

The stranger rose above their heads and claimed to be a Wizard of the Wind.

The King read the transcript that the Scribbler handed him. "How can I believe you? The songs say the last wizard died seven hundred years ago. The wind, they say, has long been sleeping."

"It wakes!" said the stranger triumphantly, and the King needed no transcript for that phrase.

"Who are you?" cried Jason, stepping forward.

"You may call me the Usher." It was a proud cultivated voice that took pleasure in its own sound.

"No man alive has the wisdom to wield such power," objected Jason. "That's why the wizards let their secrets die."

"Not quite," replied the stranger. "They were only sleeping, like the wind."

Jason strode toward the small floating man. He reached up, grabbed his collar with one hand, and dragged him down so that they faced each other. His dagger shone under the Usher's throat. The smile disappeared from the Usher's face.

"Jason!" yelled the King.

"I can smell a fraud. And this one stinks like a pig! If you're a Wizard, little man, you'll prove it. But not by any birdy trick!"

"Jason, what are you doing?"

"A fire without a flint! That's the way to tell a Wizard! You conjure up a fire with your bare hands, and we'll know you're what you say you are!"

The Scribbler hastily transcribed this for the King.

"Is it true, Jason?"

Jason nodded.

"Then let it be done."

The Usher's face was red when he snapped, "Call off this horse and I'll make you a fire you won't forget!"

Jason let the Usher down and backed off. The Usher dusted himself with his good hand, then turned a fierce look to Jason. "If you ever touch me again, you'll lose more than a finger."

Jason snickered at the little man and sheathed his dagger.

"Come to the window," instructed the Usher. Jason and the King followed him to the thin gap in the wall. As they leaned out, a warm summer draft lifted the fringes of their hair. It was a bright moonlit night. In the distance, beyond the castle walls and the roofs of the town, they could clearly see the Long Tall Forest stretched out like a huge dark rippling lake to the foot of White Moon Mountains.

The Usher rolled his hands around an invisible ball. "Watch," he commanded. "Watch and believe."

Soon they saw a great black serpent creep slowly out of the middle of the forest and mount the air in a coiling spiral: a pillar of rising smoke.

"Watch," whispered the Usher.

A crown of silent orange flame appeared, lapping the treetops like a wave. Simon wept. He turned to the Usher and held out his hand. The Usher tucked his bad hand under his belly and bowed to the King. He looked sidelong at Jason. "Well, big man?"

"You're a wizard, all right. But can you heal the King?"

The Usher laughed through his nose and directed the King back to his throne. Simon sat, then looked with wonder into the eyes of the stranger. Slowly, the Usher placed both hands on Simon's ears, holding his head like a piece of fruit.

One might ask at this juncture: What happened next? The truth is, only two men know. And, frankly, they will not say. Did the Usher place a device inside King Simon's ear? A glowing jewel perhaps? What do you think, Captain? Did he incise the lobe, or prick the nodule at the base of the skull? Was his cure chemical or magical? What did the Usher do?

We do not know.

What we do know is this: Jason flinched when blood came out of Simon's nose. The room became still and hushed.

"May you hear all," said the Usher.

Then quickly, he crooked a finger at Jason and led him to the oaken doors on the other side of the throne room.

"Call to your King," he whispered.

For a moment Jason stared at the dazed Simon slumped in his finely carved antler throne. He felt not elation but dread. And he wondered what to say. Reluctantly, he spoke in a voice only the healed could hear.

"Simon? Rook takes mage." It was something of a private joke he used whenever Simon got too cocky: the first checkmate he had ever sprung upon the young boy.

All eyes in the room were fixed upon the King when his brow wrinkled as if he had sustained an inner pang. He blinked rapidly, several times in succession. His eyes were wide and tearful as he lifted them from the floor to find his tutor's face.

"Jason?" he cried. "Jason! I can hear! I can!"

The young King raced across the room and flung himself into the huge man's arms. A cheer rose up from the chamber guards.

After a long embrace, Jason cradled Simon's face in his trembling hands. "Wine!" he shouted. "We must have wine!"

The Usher interrupted with a solemn command. "No! The King must immediately be isolated for one week in the most remote and quiet room of your castle."

"I do not understand," Jason said. "Is he not healed?"

"Most definitely," replied the Usher. "But a period of recuperation is necessary. If this is not done, the cure may not keep."

No doubt it seemed a small price to pay, to delay their celebration.

It was agreed. Simon was led to the highest tower. The Usher rode the next day with their gratitude and gold to his Book House in the south. A great feast was planned for the last day of the King's isolation, and in the bustle and excitement and joy, it never occurred to anyone that the Usher had not put out his fire.

Chapter seven

ON THE LAST MORNING OF his childhood Tim watched his father sling an axe over his shoulder and walk whistling past the well of stones until he disappeared into the woods. In the dark blue sky that hung above the cabin small clouds rolled over themselves, and Tim recalled part of his father's story from the night before: something about ancient men who had fallen from the sky, who knew how to ride a cloud like a horse. The memory made him catch his breath. He longed deeply to ride the clouds, to be like a bird, able to see where the woods ended, where his father said there were villages and towns, farms and the occasional armsman on horse-back. He knew someday he would. His father had promised that next spring he would take him on a tinker trip to sell his carvings. He couldn't wait.

As he stood by the window he noticed a smudge on the cloudy glass. He was polishing it clean with his cuff when he heard a noise. An odd noise. It sounded like the noise his parents made when they twinkled in the bed below him. There was something funny and comforting about their love sounds. It always pleased him to know they were getting happy. But this sound was different somehow. It had some of the tongue against the teeth sound of twinkling, but it wasn't as slow and rhythmic. It was fast and frantic and—goodness, what could it possibly be?

He looked up and saw a flock of birds fly by in close formation. Then, to his surprise, another flock flew by, and still another. Soon the sky was full of birds: a dark speckled cloud rippling over the clearing. It suddenly grew very dark where only moments before there had been bright sunlight.

"Mother?" he said over his shoulder. "What are the birds doing?"

His mother, who had been cleaning the chimney, stooped back into the room, her face smeared with soot. Immediately she noticed something wrong with the light. Puzzled, she walked to the window and looked out. She made an odd noise like a hiccup and covered her mouth, then taking Tim's hand, she led him outside.

In the middle of a sunny day it was darker than dusk. The great shadow that flickered over the clearing had taken all the color out of the morning; everything was grey. The sound the birds made passing overhead was now like nothing he had ever heard: a distant, unbroken scream that went on and on. The boy gazed with open-eyed delight at the stream of birds. He saw then that his mother had fallen to her knees. She covered her eyes and wept. And feeling very grown up, he went to her and held her close, saying: "It's all right, Mother. It's only the birds." He did not become alarmed until his father came running breathlessly from the woods without his axe.

He'd never seen his father's face like that.

The woodcutter took them in his arms and held them tightly, whispering, "I thought I'd never see you again."

"Can't you . . . ?" cried his mother.

"I've tried, but nothing works!"

In the distance Tim thought he heard the sound of trees crashing to the ground. Then he smelled smoke. His father looked frantically about the clearing. Without a word he grabbed Tim's hand, ran to the well, bent his head into the shaft, and whistled.

Following them, his mother cried, "What are you doing?"

"He'll be safe in the well." His father touched his shoulder. "You're not afraid?"

"No," said Tim. "Is it a fire?"

"Yes."

"But what about you?"

In the pause before he answered, Tim saw his father's face pass through a lifetime of expressions. There were tears and the ending of tears, hope and the fear of its loss, tenderness and hurried joy, helpless rage and stony courage, grief and victory over it, sadness and the place beyond sadness—and finally, the almost interchangeable looks of agony and love. Tim would never forget his father's face as the fire closed in and its light played along the tangles of his full red beard.

He recalled it often.

"Don't fret." His father smiled. "We'll be back soon. Stay in the well till someone comes for you."

His father gave him a long hug and he kissed his mother. Then, standing on the wall of stones, Tim grabbed hold of the rope and put his feet in the bucket.

"Careful!" his mother cried.

"I know what I'm doing," Tim said.

His father held the spindle crank and slowly let him down. He hadn't expected the water to be so cold, and he caught his breath as it soaked him to the skin. He held tight to the rope and found a foothold under the water. His parents heads leaned over the ledge above him, blocking out the meager light at the mouth of the well.

For a moment no one knew what to say.

"Remember," his father warned, "wait till someone comes."

"It's cold."

"We won't be long," his mother said. Then his parents looked at each other.

"Good-bye, Tim," said his father.

"Take care, my son," his mother said gently. "Don't be frightened."

Then they were gone.

Tim stayed in the well for hours, shivering, listening to the crackle, spit, and roar of the fire as it devoured the forest. Waiting. Eventually night fell, and looking up the dark cylinder to the orange glow at the mouth of the well, it seemed as though the moon had burst into flames. Finally, the sound of the fire receded. He waited and waited, bored and fidgeting, till he could hardly stand it any longer.

Time is a slow and difficult thing for children; they haven't yet learned how to fill it.

There, alone in the dark well, Tim found himself recalling the last thing in the world he wanted to: the only story that had ever given him nightmares. A tale told by a stranger, a passing tinker with green teeth who had stopped to get a drink from the well. Tim remembered his grimy face and his sharp clever eyes that fed on his fright, as the words of his story hooked themselves into his mind and would not leave go.

One day long ago, before people had sense to get out of the weather, before they learned to place stone on stone, or branch on branch, when shelter was still ages away from entering their minds, there was a clan who lived under trees. They ate the fruit and played in the great plain that surrounded them and watched the many beasts go by in bands that dawdled on the way.

This was before beasts and people had learned to eat each other.

One day they saw a great light in the sky, as if a star had fallen from the lake of night above. It smashed into the plains on the horizon and they saw great streaks of light rise from the spot and dash up to the clouds. They were frightened, but they were curious, too. And their elders went off to find the fallen star.

When they returned, their bodies were burnt red as if they'd fallen asleep under the noonday sun. And their eyes were full of terror. They said the People of the Star were voices that sang in the air like hidden birds. And the voices came from a giant fish that smoked at the bottom of a huge pit.

And asked what the People of the Star wanted, their elders said simply, "A child. A child they would teach how to fly like a bird."

THE Gift

At this, all the children danced and cooed and each was more eager than the other to learn to fly. And finally an Elder proclaimed his son would be the first child to learn. And the next day he walked off with the boy.

And when he returned alone they asked, "Where is the flying boy?"

But, for a long while, the man would not answer them. Finally, he said that the People of the Star wanted more children. A new child every day. And the children were delighted. And the fathers were proud for they too would have a flying child. But the mothers began to speak amongst themselves, and they hissed at the fathers, saying, how stupid could they be? It was obvious to them that the Elder was not telling the whole truth.

And the Elder grew angry and threatened to strike them with his arms if they spoke like that again. But finally it was agreed that each morning a new child would be sent to learn to fly. From the eldest father's down.

And so it was.

But after many mornings when none of the children had returned, the men grew as suspicious as the women. And they questioned the Elder, and they argued with the Elder, and eventually they hit the Elder with their arms and then he said it was a lie.

The People of the Star had made him tell the lie about the flying children. He told them that when he first brought his son to the fish in the great pit, the fish had grasped him with a blue tongue and swallowed his son and the People of the Star said if he wanted to see his son again he must send other children to them. And if he didn't, then the silver fish would eat their clan. All of them.

Then the clan banished their Elder for his lie and he lived under a tree a long throw from their own and no one would give him words. And when the next morning came and none of the mothers would let their children go to the fish, they saw, walking toward them across the plain, a boy.

It was the first child the fish had swallowed. The Elder's child.

And he went to his mother, who clung to him and washed his face with her tears. But when she saw the faces of her clan, she said, "Why do you look at him like that? Can't you see my son is returned?" And the mother wailed, and slapped her hands on the dirt, and wept.

He looked like the child they had sent away to learn to fly, but something was not right, something was different. His skin was red, as if he had fallen from a high branch. And he spoke strangely, saying many words they could not understand. And he smelled like rotten fruit. The child watched them with wary, dark eyes—eyes that none of them could meet.

And finally the new Elder stood and addressed the child. "Who are you that rides in the body of my nephew like a worm in an apple?"

The child replied, "I want my brothers."

But the people would not listen. They set upon the child and hit him with their arms until he breathed no more. And they left his body under the tree where his mother cradled it on her lap and wept and tried to nourish it with her milkless breast.

And the next day the other children returned from the fish. They, too, were red as the sky at dusk, and this time, they did not talk. They grabbed the new Elder and broke his body into pieces. And they stood over the pieces and spoke to the clan.

"This is what will happen unless you send us all the children now."

Weeping mothers grabbed their children and tried to run away. But they were found and pulled to pieces before their children's eyes. Fathers attacked the red children and they were dealt with quickly. And finally, all the children of the clan were gathered into a circle. And the red children marched them sobbing and terrified out from under the trees in a line, over the horizon, to the silver fish.

And they were never seen again.

Soon after, Tim's mother had come out to the well and chased the man off. "He's a pest," she'd said. "You keep clear of him."

Tim had always wondered why the tinker with green teeth had told him that story. Had someone told it to him when he was very young? Did he enjoy retelling it and scaring children? There was no one to explain this to Tim. All he knew was that the story had frightened him. Frightened him so much that he could not spend another minute in the well.

Forgetting his father's warning, Tim pulled himself hand over hand up the rope and over the top. The first thing he noticed was how warm the stones were at the mouth of the well.

THE Gift

A full moon illuminated the smoldering ruin of the deep woods. A carpet of smoke hovered over the ground, randomly twisting into whirlpools, coiling around the trunks of charred black trees. Sparks still drifted down from the treetops. He saw the body of a squirrel curled up and roasted. There were no sounds, no bird calls. Nothing remained of his home except the chimney and the hearth. Everything—the furniture, his father's carvings, his workshop—was gone. Among the ashes of the cabin he found his set of carving tools: tarnished blades with scorched handles.

Tim stood in the middle of the decimated forest, surrounded by the dark ruin of his life and he had a very understandable reaction: He did not believe it. He could not. Nothing had ever ended for him before.

Suddenly, he sneezed. Tim tucked his arms about him and tried to rub some warmth into his muscles. It did no good: His clothes were soaking.

In the distance he heard a noise that sounded like a whistle.

The silhouettes of the dead trees about him began to resemble giants with enormous outstretched hands, crouching animals ready to pounce. A cool wind brushed against him and raised the flesh on his arms. He sneezed again. Then, from somewhere high in the treetops, he heard a voice.

"Bless you!"

Tim felt his stomach drop to his knees, and his teeth began to chatter. No strange voice in a desolate forest in the middle of the night had any right to be so casual.

"Bless you!"

Tim began to cry. He wanted the voice to stop. He wanted to wake up in his bed in the loft of hay with his mother making soup and his father outside chopping wood.

Something flickered above him, and looking up he saw an animal hanging upside down from a scorched branch like a sleeping bat.

It was a huge black bird with glistening black feathers and golden claws. It seemed both graceful and obese. In each black eye a bright orange ring glowed. Tim smelled something sickening and the enormous bird caught his eye and laughed.

"A child! I was expecting something more satisfying. Ah, but times are hard and company's scarce."

The bird's voice sounded as though it had passed through thorns— the words seared and cracked and wrenched themselves free. But its manner was shrugging nonchalance. It snorted and flexed its wings.

"It is my custom to acquaint myself with all my guests. I am Tomen."

Tim found himself remembering something his father had told him while carving the battle relief, something about a warrior's tradition: enemies exchanging names before battle.

"You've not heard of me?" It seemed surprised. "Then allow me to introduce myself. . . ."

Snapping its head to and fro as if it were being slapped, the black bird began a type of song the likes of which Tim had never heard. For it flirted on the borders of melody and rhyme, though it never quite entered, and it was a music that, once heard, no one would ever want to hear again. The branch gripped by its talons shuddered as it sang. And, for the length of the song there was nothing but the bird and the night.

I Am Bird. I Am Not Bird.
I Am Fire. I Am Not Fire.
Death Knows Me. Death Fears Me.
I Fear Nothing. I Eat Fear.
No Body Can Flee Me. No Mind Can Know Me.
No Rock Can Keep Me. No Wind Can Move Me.
No Water Can Swallow Me. No Fire Can Touch Me.
No Night Can Fill Me. No Light Can Find Me.
No Time Can Count Me. No Mirror Can Hold Me.

THE Gift

I Am Victory. I Am Power.
I Am Hunger. I Am Perfect.
I Am Tomen.

The song seemed to echo in Tim's bones. And as much as any child can, he felt the hand of death upon him.

The bird peered at him for the longest time. "You mustn't be frightened of me. I like boys. And so does my master, the Night Usher. He's a fine teacher. He's starting a school where you can play the most splendid games and learn the cleverest tricks. Do you like games? Do you like tricks? Would you like to learn how to make fire?"

The bird burped and liquid fire dropped out of its mouth to the ground, where it lapped and rolled like kindling doused with grease.

"You started the fire." Tim gasped.

The bird took pause from its upside-down swagger.

"Yes. But how did you survive it, peculiar child?"

Tim didn't know he was feeling hate; he'd never felt it before. "You started the fire!"

"Child, it is bad manners to repeat yourself. I do hope you make better nourishment than company. Now, step over to my fire, won't you?"

If birds could grin, Tim would have sworn that Tomen wore a grin wide enough to swallow the moon. He found himself walking toward the small fire. Part of his mind wailed resistance, but his body gave no protest. Indeed, after his initial hesitation, it felt a very natural, pleasant thing to do: step up to the fire, get a little warmer. But strangely, the fire gave no heat.

"Now," said Tomen, "lie down in the fire."

And Tim would have done it too—had not a deafening crack broken through the spell. A bolt of lightning flashed and lit up the forest. Immediately, a thunderstorm was drenching everything in sight, including the black bird's fire.

Tomen cursed in supreme annoyance and lifted up into the night. Its great wings flashed, and guttural squawks came from its golden beak. It swooped up higher, pausing for a moment at the treetops to scream down a threat.

"I warn you, boy! I never leave my guests hungry!"

Then it was gone. Tim breathed huge desperate breaths, fell to his knees, and yielded to the refreshing rain.

Chapter eight

"YES, OF COURSE, YOU'RE RIGHT, my son," said the Teller to the Go-Boy. "They did not exchange names. The boy never gave his . . ."

The Teller smiled. "Nib? Fetch me a skin, won't you? I'm parched."

When the boy had gone below, he twisted the silver ring about his pinky and continued. "It is, frankly, a tradition I do not care for: speechi-fying before the clash. Still, a Teller has his obligations. And inevitably, there are some stories which he'd prefer not to relate. I fear I must tell you one now. Not that this story is unimportant. But it sometimes happens that a tale must be woven out of fancy. Perhaps, because there were no witnesses. Or no surviving witnesses. Perhaps the minds of those who could recall are enfeebled by age or disabled by disease. Perhaps only a blind man was present at the murder, only a deaf man saw the argument, only a lonely man witnessed the wedding and never understood the grief that came of what he took to be the happiest young couple in the land. You understand what I am saying? Some Tellers should not be asked for directions."

The Captain laughed through his nose and leaned against the tiller, resting his jeweled ear against his only palm, lightly drumming his head with his fingers. He seemed much amused by the proceedings. For a moment the Teller paused and shook his head. Then opened and closed his eyes several times. If the men hadn't known better, they might have believed he was drunk.

"I'll be candid," he continued. "I hate castles. And I am reluctant to return to a place so fraught with evil memories.

"In all my years in a castle I never liked it. In fact, I would go so far as to say that it is a wretched place to live: drafty and never warm enough. And the smells! Has no one ever told you what a castle mostly smells like? It smells of dog. Mutts in every corner. A filthy, filthy place. Cold in winter. Rancid in summer when the walls sweat and the corridors are full of flies. And it is at all times swarming like a hive with the intrigue of small minds and empty hearts who dress up to resemble humans. It is appalling how empty a place so imposing can be.

"Where was I?

"Yes, I was saying that in regards to this tale the witnesses are either mad or dead. And I am loath to presume an authority I have no claim to: I wasn't there; I wasn't told; I can only imagine.

"So I will say it happened like this . . .

"All week the royal kitchen cheerfully prepared an elaborate feast of pheasant and pork; the trumpeter rehearsed a new fanfare of rejoicing (he would never play it—which was a blessing no one reckoned at the time); the vain, gluttonous guards polished their armor and washed their best uniforms. Old banners were brought out of storage to be washed impeccably, repaired of any rent, and hung high on the castle walls, where all the loyal citizens could pretend to admire them. The throne room was scrubbed and sheened until one could see the beamed ceiling beneath one's feet, the horses were groomed to a shimmering gloss for the royal parade, and all the dogs were roped together and taken to the river to be drowned.

"I'm sorry.

"There's nothing humorous in what I am about to say.

"I have a joke lodged in my mind and it will not be shut out."

The Teller frowned and shook his head. "Captain?"

He looked up at the one-handed man. "Captain, are you enjoying yourself?"

"Immensely." The Captain smiled, as if someone had just told a stitchingly funny joke.

The Teller's eyes suddenly seemed clear. And when he spoke it was in a startling low voice that sent shivers up the sailors' spines. "Enjoy it while you can," he croaked.

The Captain's face went pale.

And the Teller continued.

All was ready. And an air of joyful anticipation pervaded the Kingdom as news spread that a remedy had been found and the King was healed.

It was the eve of Celebration Day.

That night, the last of Simon's isolation, from the highest window of the highest tower, horrible screams broke out. They echoed down the winding steps that led to the King's room. Dogs barked and guards were startled at their stations on the walls. Jason burst out of his room at the base of the tower and dashed naked up the steps. He grabbed a torch from its stand in midflight and quickly unlocked the door. He kicked it open and poised himself to leap upon whatever enemy he might find. The sight that met his eyes made him drop the torch and step back stunned. Simon knelt alone in the middle of the room, his hands clenching his ears, his body swaying back and forth, gripped by violent spasms; he shook his head wildly and wailed. Jason stared. This was no nightmare. The King was spellbound.

Years ago he had seen the crude work of a mad magician. A crowd had formed to watch his tricks and the madman had saved his best for last. To the delight of the watchers and to Jason's disgust, he had cruelly spelled a cat into dizziness. He remembered the bewildered, anguished look in the animal's eyes as it chased its tail. He saw it in the King.

"Make them stop!" Simon cried. "I can hear them! Tell them to go to sleep!"

Jason took him into his arms and felt his body taut with fear. "Who does this to you, boy?"

"Please! Make them stop talking! I can hear. I can hear . . . their dreams. I hear their whispers. I hear their cries. The baby will not stop crying!"

The old Physician appeared in the doorway, out of breath.

"Help him!" demanded Jason through clenched teeth. "He is afflicted!"

Holding one finger to his lips, the old man looked a long moment at the sobbing King. Finally, he pulled from one of his many pockets a vial of blue syrup. Warning that the taste was bitter, he emptied the potion down Simon's throat. After an initial grimace, the King drank quickly, eager for relief. Gradually he relaxed and his cries were reduced to low moans.

"He will sleep now," said the old man.

Under the potent narcotic the King slept for two days, occasionally calling out in pain. The celebration which had been so lavishly prepared was postponed. The physician and Jason met in counsel.

"You are certain," inquired the old man, "he said 'I hear their dreams'?"

"He screamed it," Jason replied solemnly.

The Physician spoke as if he hesitated to divulge a trade secret. "In my practice I have known only one such case: a woman who could read palms and eavesdrop on dreams. She was a simple thing with no heart for evil. She made a modest living by telling futures and recalling the dreams of passing travelers—sweetening the darker passages, of course.

"Now, I heard of her gifts, and curious, I sought to judge if they were authentic. They were. She recalled a dream of mine that had repeated itself for years. She told me she'd been given the art by a small man who lived a hermit's life on the outskirts of her village in a filthy hut swarming with wild dogs. An alchemist, she said, who spent every waking hour pursuing that foolish craft. She scoffed, but I could tell he had terrified her: Her eyes shivered when she spoke of him.

"One day he told her that the magic formula for gold was locked in his mind and he needed her help to recall it. He said he was a Dream-

Reader but that he could not read his own dreams. He asked if he could lend her the gift so she could read for him. With a touch he gave her the gift and she read his dreams—apparently not to his satisfaction. The answer was not there. He left her with a curse and a gift. For, later she realized he did not take back his loan. She never saw him again."

"DreamReader?" asked Jason.

"A rare and wonderful gift," said the Physician. "It shouldn't afflict the King as it does. I suspect there's more magic here than we know."

"Why?"

"His Majesty said he heard a baby cry. That was no dream; I heard it also. But I was on the other side of the castle, far out of his range, tending to the birth of a willful little boy. Jason, I'm afraid the King is either deeply spelled or mad. A man who hears a baby cry at such a distance, who reads dreams, who claims to have heard voices . . ." The Physician shook his head. "It requires thought."

"I think we waste our time. Let's rage on the villain's Book House in full armor!"

"Challenge a Wind Wizard with an army? You have more boldness than good sense! He would call up a twister and demolish you!"

"Then ambush the cur in his sleep," spat Jason.

"Better we wait till tomorrow," the old man advised, adding darkly, "Perhaps it's just a fever and will yet fade."

Early the next morning Jason peered into the cell through a hatch in the door. The King stood very still, gazing out the lone barred window, his back towards his tutor.

"No, Jason," he began, "it's not a fever."

"Simon!" Jason cried, unlocking the door and rushing into the room. "You are recovered?"

"And it's not the gift for recalling dreams as you supposed last night."

There was a tone of menace in the lad's voice that disturbed Jason. How could he possibly have known about that conversation?

"I heard it," replied Simon with a smooth hysteria. "Don't you understand yet? I can hear you, you big fool. I can *hear* you!"

He turned and something in his pale face made Jason bite his lip.

"I know you're horrified," said Simon, stepping toward the tutor, who backed away. "This moment you're thinking: What have they done to him? You want to run! You're crying out to your mother in your mind now, saying, Help me, help me, I need your calm, your insight—"

"Stop it!" cried Jason, aghast and retreating from the grotesque creature who was violating his mind—repeating his thoughts even as they formed.

"A monster?" the King laughed. "Your pupil a monster? Why, how can you think such a thing, Jason? I have two hands . . . two eyes . . . I have no tail—"

"*Stop it!*"

"No, I will not! And I will not be fed another drop of that sickening sleep syrup as you are planning. Yes! It *is* hideous! Yes! I hear every thought! Yes! Every fear that creeps into your mind!"

"Please, Simon. There's bad magic here!"

"Why don't you say what you think, Jason? That I'm raving like my father. That I should be locked away. After all, that's what they do to people like me: freaks. They hide them—like you've hidden me these past few days."

"I never meant you harm!"

The King spat out the words. "You let that man touch me! Yes! It *is* your fault—stop thinking that it isn't!"

"I wanted you healed."

"I *am* healed! I hear more than any man deserves to hear. An abomination? All right, that's what I am—and someone is going to pay!"

"Simon, I swear I will find a cure. The Physician—"

"The Physician! The Physician?" the King mocked.

"I am sorry," Jason whispered.

"You are a frightened old man who is calling on the spirit of his dead mother for aid! I never knew how weak you were—how many cowardly thoughts you've courted. Right now you want to run and hide! You were always so strong, so wise. But now I know the truth! I can't *help* but know the truth! The guard outside—I know the names of his children; he recites them to keep himself awake. I know the fantasies of every guard on the night watch. And the women! The women think so much nothing it's painful! I know the inmost thoughts of children: They are deafening! I hear everything, Jason! *Everything.*"

The frenzied King fell to the ground sobbing.

"Everything!"

When Jason knelt to hold him, Simon did not resist. The man rocked him in his arms whispering soothing thoughts of care.

The next day they found the guard posted at Simon's door tied up and gagged. A pouch of gold was missing from the King's private chest and his special horse was gone. The gate guard said, "Yes, indeed. His Majesty took a night ride. Said he was feeling much better. Said he'd be back presently. He's running a bit late, eh?"

A note was found in his vacant quarters and brought to Jason.

Old Horse,
Expect my return when justice is done.
Simon

The news of the King's madness and escape spread through the castle and a great sadness overtook the people. They had lost their King. And, perhaps more important, there would be no celebration. The Physician sadly noted that given the proper time and study he could have found a cure. "What are thoughts but a type of music?" he had wondered. "Music unplayed in the air. Perhaps his Majesty has become an instrument. Perhaps someday we all will have such instruments that will retrieve such invisible music." But Jason was in no mood for philosophy. He sent off a search party, then stormed out of the castle alone on horseback, heading south.

He never returned.

Chapter nine

"THANK YOU, MY SON," HE said as the Go-Boy handed him the brown skin. He drank long, letting the water trickle down his cheeks and neck.

"Before I continue, I have a question to ask you. . . ." For a long moment the Teller gazed out over the rail. Eventually, the sailors followed his gaze, only to find there was little to see. The flat slate water. The night sky pocked with stars. The full moon, pale. It was a night of nothing: a silence that made them feel lost and small, an emptiness that seemed to slant their minds toward their worst imaginings. After a time they found themselves wanting the Teller's voice again, eager for it—anything but this dreadful silence that surrounded them.

"Have you ever seen a sea monster?" the Teller asked suddenly.

"Captain, you smirk?

"Anyone? Let's see a hand. None of you? They say that sailors see all sorts of things. Yet not one of you has seen a monster?

"Now, I must tell you: That is what I expected.

"Is that because there are no monsters anymore? Or because they never existed? Or because they are shy? Or because they only come when your back is turned? All these are possible given the lack of witnesses and evidence.

"But now it is enough to know that before any man on this boat was born, creatures that can only be called monsters lived well below the calm sea we ride upon and no human eye has ever seen them. Nor ever will. They, too, have passed into legend.

"Such is the case of the Watermen.

"Who knows their substance or origin? Who knows their purpose? Were they just one of the many creatures the wizards tampered with? Beluga. Leviathan. Dauphin. Were they the discarded earlier drafts of the creature they were perfecting? Who knows? The only thing that we can say for sure is that they are no more."

For hours Tim hid behind the well, listening for the flap of huge black wings in the treetops. He felt surrounded: The night was too quiet, the forest too vast, and the full moon cast a pale unnatural green light. If only he could stop his hands and lips from trembling! It felt as though something had been shaken loose inside him. He had only one thought: They should have been back by now. They shouldn't keep me waiting. And his mind kept repeating it, clinging to it, afraid to stray too far. He understood for the first time in his carefree life what it was to be alone. His parents had never been more than a shout away. He never knew how safe he'd really been, and he recalled how much he resented the interruption whenever his mother called him back to the cabin.

How he longed to hear her voice now.

A sudden creaking startled him to his feet. Behind him the rope on the spindle of the well quivered as if, as if . . . Slowly he started to back away. The spindle began to turn round and round, lazily winding up the rope until the wooden bucket appeared. It swayed a bit and was still. Tim backed into a tree and stared.

For a moment: silence.

Then a tiny emerald hand crept out of the bucket and three long fingers gripped the rim with indented tips like the shallow bowls of acorn caps. Two sad black eyes rose up like mushrooms resting on a squashed head, and between them on the snout, two seedlike holes. A thin smile wrapped around the face. It had no chin or neck, but a milky sack bobbed under its curved jaw.

It was the biggest frog he'd ever seen, and as it climbed out of the bucket he saw its underside was white, but blue-green skin the texture of tongue stretched taut over its knobby back and rump. Its arms were thin and bony but its legs were muscular, and it sprang to the ground with ease.

"Don't be frightened," it croaked, like a tiny old man or a hoarse puppy. Yet it walked toward him like a toddler—awkwardly, legs akimbo, arms out for balance—and its thinly webbed feet made a squish with every step.

"What are you?" Tim asked.

"They call us Watermen."

Bright red membranes, just below and behind the eyes, trembled like the skins of twin drums.

"You're bleeding!" Tim cried.

The creature reassured him with a smile. "No. I'm listening. These are my ears."

Tim stared for a long minute. He couldn't decide if it was ugly or beautiful.

"Can you come with me? I must show you something."

Tim followed the frog, whose head barely reached his waist, until they came to a huge black tree with an odd branch much lower on the trunk than all the others. If Tim reached up he could almost graze it with his fingertips. Then he saw a glint of charred metal imbedded in the bark and he knew what it was: his father's axe.

The frog touched his hand, saying, "I'm sorry."

Tim looked at the scorched black handle and asked, "Are you sure?"

It nodded. Tim reached up and touched the axe handle. His fingertips came back black. He looked at the wide black eyes of the Waterman. The creature looked at the ash on Tim's fingertips.

"I knew the woodcutter. I taught him magic. He would have taught you too one day. When you turned twelve."

"Twelve? I was twelve yesterday." Tim sighed. "I don't believe in magic."

The creature looked at him hard. "Then there's no time to waste. Are you hungry?"

Tim nodded and the frog did something very odd: It spit on the ground, then croaked three times a phrase that sounded like "Healium Beluga." Turning to Tim, it said, "I'll take you where there's food and magic to spare. Stand back or you'll fall in."

The spittle at his feet had grown into a little pond, wide as the mouth of the well. He bent over and was shocked to see no reflection: The surface was aglow with a light that didn't come from the moon. The creature began to dance awkwardly around the pond, slapping its feet on the ground and clicking its tongue in a way that reminded Tim of water dripping into a puddle.

"We'll take the Bubble Sleep now. It is safe passage, so don't be frightened. Take my hand and we'll jump in together."

Tim took the creature's hand warily, shuddering as the cool, damp fingers (strangely lacking knuckles) wrapped twice around his hand. He felt suction where the tips touched his wrist.

"Close your eyes," instructed the creature solemnly.

"Wait!" cried Tim. "What's your name?"

The creature smiled. "They call me Marty. Now jump!"

They jumped together and disappeared into the pond. The next thing Tim knew, he was floating upward.

Out of the forest.

In a bubble.

He could feel it about him: round and soft and slippery; he tried to stand but could get no footing. Marty lay beside him curled up and sleeping, and together they shot past the tips of the tallest trees. Far below he glimpsed the glimmering pond as it receded into the burned forest that spread out for miles like the briared back of a giant porcupine.

Tim thought: It's a dream. It was a nightmare before, but now it's just a dream.

How else could he explain the most surprising property of bubbles? They cannot be seen from the inside. His view was unobstructed; the bubble was as clear as the clearest stream. In fact the only way Tim knew he was in a bubble was the sensations of roundness, coasting and dipping with the wind. Otherwise, he would have said he was merely floating. Or being carried. Or being rocked in the arms—but he didn't want to think about that.

A strange silence surrounded him. He had always taken certain sounds for granted: crickets, wind through the trees, leaves crackling underfoot, his breathing. But in the bubble he might as well have been deaf. Even his movements were noiseless.

But if this is Bubble Sleep, thought Tim, why am I not sleeping?

Their journey was swift; the bubble rocked slowly in the night breeze, floating them surely toward the mountains that glowed white under the moon. They had barely gotten underway when a sudden descent stole Tim's breath and plummeted them toward a wildly churning river. He felt sure he was falling to his death when they splashed down and the bubble burst. Gasping for air, he surfaced at the bottom of another well: a round canyon with steep grey walls that rose so high he could not see the top. There was a starry dawning sky above him and a loud silence around him. The water was cool and full of dark green shadows. Surrounding him, in the flat rock that encircled the pool, were a number of tiny caves just above the water, like many small mouths yawning.

It was then he realized he could not swim.

Chapter ten

IN A SMALL VILLAGE A long ride south of the castle, in a quiet tavern, there lived a man of some renown: Donaldson. He was a permanent fixture at the inn, where nightly he occupied the small table closest to the hearth. Every evening he would snuggle up with a mug of beer, and between luxurious swallows, tell stories. He was a weathered old man—totally bald and without any eyebrows. Brown loaches rode the top knuckles of his right hand—to soothe his joints. He was given to long discourses of questionable substance. The regulars preferred the hunting stories, but the war tales were also favored for—if Donaldson was to be believed—the old man had played a decisive role in every battle of the last two centuries. When the stories ran out he would tell fables, jokes, sing songs, and offer assorted wisdom to anyone with the ears and patience to hear him out.

One night the bald man talked of dragons.

A word about dragons. Everyone has heard about their lust for gold, but no one seems to know its source. "Greedy" they are called. But this is merely a human dodging fault by pinning his shadow upon another creature's feet, however unlikely or blameless. It takes but a moment to consider that no one has ever seen a dragon at market, or changed coins with a dragon, or gone so far as to wonder if coins had yet been conceived as a currency of exchange when dragons (though there were never many) still flocked to make their yearly passage to the south. No. The simple truth is they hoarded gold because it was the remnant of their ancestors. Or so they thought.

THE Gift

Ages unimaginable ago the dragon were the only flying creatures. They ruled the sky. But once there came a shower of molten rain upon the deep south where they flocked once a year to mate. The land became so hot it was impossible to roost. The air became an oven that would bake away the film between their wing bones and thus rob them of flight. And so as the sky rained fire, their flock died cowering in agony on the boiling land, or they died slowly in flight, their wings aflame, the snouts expelling wails and smoke as they spiraled to their deaths. Few escaped the rain of fire. But those who did returned the next season to find the roasted bones of their family scattered over a vast obsidian plain, glazed and blistered like the skin of a charred goat. And coursing through the shining black rock were frozen rivers of bubbling gold, rivers that caught the sun and wound between the bones, so that the dragon thought the rain of fire had turned the blood of their ancestors to this glowing precious rock. And from that day on they hoarded every gold remnant they could find as a memorial to their great flock that had been devastated by the fire. They did not know that gold was the residue of the molten rock expelled from the ball of fire at the heart of the earth. They took it for their blood. So, as you see, a legend may arise from spurious reasoning grounded in grief.

As I was saying, one night Donaldson was talking about dragons.

Apparently he had become acquainted with the very last one. Several guests at the inn gathered about him, half listening, half watching the fire. One young gentleman with a thin beard sat away from the others in the corner furthest from the hearth. He was partially hidden in shadows, so no one could see how intently he listened.

A vicious grey brute he was! All smoke and ash and scale. Any fool could see he was waiting to die. He had eyes that could look right through you, enormous red coals that steamed when he was angry! And he was angry! Why, one of his claws could rip out the side of a mountain, and—and—one of his nails was as big as a King's guard. He spoke to me in an evil voice that bubbled out of his molten heart:

"Fool! I know what you're here for! I know you want me treasure! And I may be the last dragon, but I'll die before you set your stinking human hands on it!"

The old man burped and continued. *But I was a sneaky lad, I was. Dusted me jacket and strode up smartly to him, I did, and says: "Look here, dragon! Keep your filthy treasure—all I want is souvenirs!"*

The audience broke into riotous laughter, and bald man took this opportunity to drain his mug and call for a fresh one. With perfect timing he continued just as the laughter crescendoed and had begun to fade.

"Souvenirs!" he says. "Souvenirs?" And if you've never heard a dragon laugh, it's a good thing for you! It's a foul and fearful sound! The whole cave took the echo and all his gold and jewels were quaking. And, I tell you true—I plugged me ears good and hard lest the racket do me damages! But he sizzled and he laughed and the whole damn place got hot enough to roast a rabbit! So he looks at me with those deep red eyes and says, "Fool! Why should I let you even touch the least of me treasure?"

And—O, Day—I could see him licking his bloody chops, just waiting to have me for his dinner. But what that mighty dragon didn't know was he was talking to Donaldson. And my great-great-uncle being a direct descendent of the top Wind Wizard and all—I had him where I wanted him. I smiles and says all quiet like, " 'Cause I know your name, you filthy beast!"

And you should have seen him pull back! It was like I was poison, see? 'Cause it's common knowledge that dragons can't kill you if you know their name. You didn't know that, did you? Well, now you do! So, he was right miffed. Worked up a mean appetite he had, and I done spoilt it. What's more, he didn't know what I was then! I could have been a wizard for all he knew—and dragons don't fool with no wizards!

So I shouts out his name all bold and kinglylike—and damned if he didn't cringe like a poacher from a hangman!

Someone said "What was his name?"

"Oh no. Not *that!* See, that was part of the bargain we struck. I rummaged up what I could carry—some rings, a crown or two, and other niceties—that was his part. My part was never to speak his name to a living soul. Otherwise—well, you know what happens to a man who breaks a dragon promise!"

The captured audience uniformly shook their heads and the old man continued with relish.

"They burn up on the spot! Like they walked into a flaming pit."

A gasp went through the crowd.

"Saw it happen to a third cousin of mine. Stupid man! See, dragons don't touch you if you know their names. But they cast a spell so strong on you that you wear it all your living days. If I were to tell you his name, this room would get a little too hot for my liking."

Chuckles swept through the inn. Someone loudly asked, "What'd you do with all the treasure, Donaldson?"

"Ah, that's a good one! You don't suppose that I lived every day since without a trade and all the beer a man could reasonably tip without bidding a bit of that treasure good-bye, do you? No sir. I sold it all to merchants. I bought land; I own this inn and my son runs it. And, I might add, my good wife, bless her, dressed the remainder of her days in a wardrobe as fine as any court lady's. I'll tell you! It's all gone. Invested. There's none left to that story!"

The listeners soon trickled away or turned back to their tables, and the bald man was left to his corner by the fire. It was then the thinly bearded young man stepped out of the shadows and made his way to the old man's table. "Those are finely woven tales, sir."

"Oh, tales they may be—nothing but beer-talk to a good many of these fools who haven't traveled farther than their noses. But there's a lot of living in those stories, no matter how you take them. Young man, hope that someday you may live as long and as fully as yours truly! Ha!" He winked, then, peeling the loach off his index knuckle, he inspected the raw slime patch where it had feasted.

"Respectfully, sir," said the young man, "there's only one thing that bothers me about your tale."

"What's that, lad?"

"You left out the part about the book."

The bald man set down his mug and yawned.

"This beer is getting too close to the bottom for me." In one deft grab he scooped the loaches off his hand and dropped them clinking into his empty mug. "You'll have to excuse me; I should be heading for me bed."

As he made an effort to rise, the young man put a strong hand on his shoulder and forced him firmly back into his seat. The old man sputtered a weak curse and turned his eyes away.

"Look," he warned, "I don't know what you want from me, but I'll call my son—"

"You'll do nothing of the sort. You'll be very quiet."

The old man looked warily into the stranger's eyes. "You're a hard one, lad. You've no pity for a poor old man who only wants his sleep."

"You can sleep after you tell me about the book you stole from the dragon's cave. You didn't bid that good-bye, did you?"

"How . . . ?" whispered the bald man in amazement.

"Never mind that. Just tell me what you know."

"It's a special book to me, lad. Promise you won't take it."

The stranger shook his head and the old man whimpered quietly. Finally he spoke: "All right. It's a book of magic spells."

"That's better. But you can't read, can you? Why do you keep it?"

"It's beautiful!" cried the old man. He glanced furtively at the stranger. "Well, not *that* beautiful. Actually, it's a rather plain old book. Dusty, damp. You know, I don't think you'd even like it."

The stranger's face was expressionless. "Drop the dung and tell me why you keep it."

"The pictures. It has the tales of the true wizards. I can tell that by the pictures."

"It was your great-great-uncle's book."

"Yes!" said the bald man, flabbergasted that he knew.

"On his deathbed he asked you to retrieve it from his hiding place—a place no one would ever dare to look for it. He told you the dragon's name."

"Yes!" the old man replied, now frightened of the stranger's knowledge. "He was the wisest, kindest man who ever walked or flew. He was everything I ever wanted to be."

An heirloom, thought the stranger—a useless heirloom in the hands of an old fool. But in the proper hands it could prove a most powerful tool.

"I'll buy it from you," the young man offered.

"Please. It's not for sale. This inn, my land, mean nothing to me, just the book."

"Come on, old man. I'll give you twelve goldens for it! That's enough to buy a hundred better books!"

"I don't want your gold—I just want the book. I'm keeping it in memory of my great-great-uncle."

The stranger grabbed the bald man's arm as he signaled for another mug. He lowered it to the table and leveled his eyes at him, enunciating the words precisely and coldly. "Your great-great-uncle wanted the book so he could destroy it. He made you promise to burn it. You broke that promise."

The bald man covered his face with his hands. "The pictures," he whispered. "The pictures."

A tall man was standing next to the table saying, "Look here—what's going on?"

"A friendly chat," replied the stranger with a crisp smile.

The tall man scowled.

"Billy boy," said the old man weakly, "I'm so glad you've come! This man here is—"

"I'll bet you're glad," his son replied. "Look, Dad, there's a fresh bunch that just come in, or didn't you notice?"

"Billy boy, please . . ."

"It's story time, Dad. If you ain't talkin', they ain't drinkin'."

"He's threatening me!" the old man pleaded.

"What?" cried the tall man regarding the stranger, who had begun to doodle casually on the dusty tabletop.

"He said he would—he said if I didn't—"

"What are you babbling about, you old cinder?"

"I swear, I'm telling the truth—he's, he's—" but something made him pause. Perhaps it was the amiable smile on the face of the stranger. Out of the corner of his eye he saw something bright in the firelight: the stranger's hand moving calmly, deliberately, repeating the same motion over and over on the dusty tabletop. What at first appeared to be an idle scratching, upon closer inspection became a legible symbol. The bald man shook uncontrollably as he recognized the familiar rune his great-great-uncle had sketched below the figure of the dragon on the book's opening page.

It was the name of the dragon spelled out. The name, in fact, that every dragon wore as his own, for their creators used it as a rein. It is the word, though Donaldson didn't know it, that means dragon. He only knew it as a name that, if spoken by the stranger, would burn him to oblivion.

"I'm going to be sick," said the bald man, standing up.

"I'll see to him," said the gracious stranger.

"Just you be sure he's back here lickity-split with a story!"

"Don't worry," the stranger replied as he escorted the stunned old man out of the room, back to his quarters where an ancient book lay hidden under a thick feather bedding.

As the King mounted his horse, the old man begged him to return the precious book someday. Simon rode off, saying curtly over his shoulder that the book was of no real use here; it had a higher purpose.

He left the old man sobbing outside the tavern under a full moon.

86

Chapter eleven

FOR A LONG WHILE THE sailors listened to the creaking of the masts. An abrupt sound which frightened them after so much silence. One of them imagined that a great sea beast was passing underneath the boat, lifting them slightly as it scratched its back upon their hull. But the older sailors were familiar with the sudden currents that coursed throughout *Fishrun,* and paid it no mind.

The silence returned.

"Where was I?" said the Teller, finally.

"Ah, yes. The King now has the book—much good may it do him. But I ought to go back to the boy, Tim. He was drowning when we left him, no? That was a crude Teller's trick, but it never fails.

"He did not drown, I'll tell you that. The strange frog saved him."

Marty croaked and scolded, "Why didn't you tell me you couldn't swim?"

"Why didn't you tell me I *had* to?" replied Tim with a cough. He sat naked and shivering in a narrow tunnel of rock before a hissing fire, his clothes laid out to dry beside him, while this smelly child-sized frog roasted a row of fish on a stick. The fire gave meager heat, though it made the damp air smoky and cast fluttering shadows of gold on the mossy walls about them.

"Where are we?" asked Tim.

With one hand Marty stripped the cooked fish off the stick into a pile. They were barely mouthfuls but Tim ate eagerly, burning his tongue and fingers, grateful for any food and warmth.

"They say long ago a great worm chewed his way through this rock and made these caves and tunnels. It is our home now."

It sounded like a legend his father might tell. In fact everything around him had the look of something imagined. He kept wanting to compare it all to something real. The cold floor was pocked with many little craters, like rings with empty sockets; in each a tiny pool reflected the golden pulse of smoke that rolled across the ceiling. The tunnel was slim—Tim would have to stoop to walk—and it began and ended in darkness.

"Is this a dream?" asked Tim. "It feels like a dream." He was suddenly angry. "If this is a dream I want to wake up!"

Marty laid a cool hand on Tim's arm, but the boy pulled away.

"I'd forgotten your people dream," said the creature.

"Doesn't everybody?"

Marty chuckled. "Child, but for the bubble, we don't even sleep!"

Tim didn't like being called a child, especially by such a little creature, and he didn't like being laughed at either, so he said: *"You* slept in the bubble, but *I* didn't."

This amazed Marty, and the frog insisted that Tim recount every detail of his journey through the air. So, grudgingly, Tim told him how the streams looked like fallen trees with many smaller branches that couldn't decide which way to go. How a line of hills rose single file like the knobs on a man's spine. How the land was sprinkled with dark stones that might have been dropped like seeds from the fist of a giant. How a bird had circled the bubble once in curiosity.

Marty sighed. "You have the Telling gift, like your father."

Tim wondered: Could Marty have known that all the time he was describing his journey, he had been thinking of his father? "You said you knew him," Tim said, though he wasn't sure he believed the frog.

The creature rubbed its hands over the fire; it sounded like his father sanding in his workshop. "He saved my life. When I was very young I slipped into the pool one night and chased a school of minnow down the river. I got tangled in the waterweeds and couldn't get out."

"Your magic?" said Tim sarcastically.

"I knew no magic then. And I still believed what I'd been taught: that I would die if I saw the sun. The family calls it Day Fire. But the sun rose and it was glorious, like a bright moon. Then I saw this huge monster with a beard full of sawdust and I thought I was dead for sure."

"He freed you?" It was something his father would have done.

"Very gently. He showed me how to make a fire as well. He told me many stories and made me promise to visit him. I'm sorry, I see I've made you sad."

Tim said nothing. He was thinking of his father's bright red beard: how it smelled when it was speckled with sawdust, how his mother used to comb it out.

Marty continued: "When I returned, the family couldn't believe I survived the daylight. They treated me like a ghost."

"Do they all look like you?" asked Tim, making little effort to hide his distaste.

"Exactly like me. But I'm afraid you'll have to take my word for it. They're very superstitious. Won't go out in the day. Won't go near my fire. Won't talk to people. Even *I* make them uncomfortable. They smell the woodcutter on me."

"You said he could do magic. Why couldn't he stop the fire?"

For a moment Marty looked puzzled and sad. "I don't know. He surprised me when he called for help. We had a signal: When he whistled into the well I could hear him in these caverns. The wizards laid a linkage in between. I am told they did not believe in distance." Seeing that the child did not understand, he added, "I came as quickly as I could, but I had to take the long way to avoid the fire: through the underground streams that fed the well."

Tim broke a stick in half and tossed it into the fire. "You had to take the long way," he repeated bitterly.

"I wish I could have saved them, Tim."

"Not as much as I do," Tim spat. "And if *I'm* ever caught in a fire you can be sure I'll not call for the help of a frog!"

The creature clamped tight its lips, and after a moment, croaked, "John-John said you had a temper. I wasn't going to tell you this, but . . . I sent the rain—too late to help them, I'm afraid. The clouds had to come a long ways."

"*You* did that?" said Tim, amazed. "But you're just—" He stopped.

"Just a frog?" said Marty with an odd smile. "Once my family were frogs. But that was long ago, before the wizards gave us words and taught us chants and magic. We were many then; now we are few."

"Why?"

"Mother Death," said Marty quietly. "Our mother is barren. I was the last child she bore."

Again, Tim saw a sadness descend into the creature's eyes and thought, What a strange name for a mother's barrenness.

When Tim's clothes had dried, Marty led him deep into the caverns to a chamber where the very walls perspired and a strange echo repeated the end of their sentences. High in the corners yellow globes pulsed and glowed: nets of something sticky coated with fireflies. In the pale light Tim noticed damp tapestries on the walls: woven patterns of fluid lines in shades of green. His father had taught him to admire such craft. Marty noticed his curiosity and explained: "Weed quilts."

"They're lovely," Tim cried.

Lovely, lovely, lovely, went the echo.

Pointing to a small pool hidden in shadow, Marty said: "I want you to meet the Listener. He heard the woodcutter's whistle." Something drifted slowly out of the shadows into the soft light, something floating on its back in the black water. Tim wanted to leave. The body was stiff and twisted like the frozen carcass of a dog found in a snowdrift; and as if it had been drained of blood, everything was white: the skin, the fingers, even the eyes, dull white orbs that hung in the wretchedly cocked head, looking into Tim's shocked face with the bewildered, pleading expression of a dying animal. It was a tiny crippled Waterman.

"He's blind," said Marty.

The figure spun slowly, one of its pale hands flicked the water with weak random strokes. Tim could not stop looking at it. Marty squatted by the pool and began spooning water over its head.

"The Water Sickness?" asked Tim, biting his lip.

"Yes."

"Does it hurt?"

Hurt, hurt, hurt, went the echo.

"Yes," replied Marty. "But his sickness has given him a great gift. He hears thoughts from very far away. He is our Listener."

Wonderful, thought Tim. He must feel very lucky.

Then Marty whispered something Tim didn't understand. "Little One, the Wind Tamer doesn't believe in magic!"

The white frog gave a little giggle that became a cough. Marty stroked its belly until the fit had passed. Tim stared transfixed at the floating pulp of white, wondering how the same power that could call up a thunderstorm, douse a fire, and make a bubble could not protect this innocent thing. It didn't seem a very reliable magic. He recalled the day his father had found a wounded deer in the woods: an arrow through its neck. Some lazy hunter had not trailed it. The deer was in great pain, so his father had slit its throat and given it a merciful death.

"Is there nothing you can do?" asked Tim.

Do, do, do, went the echo.

Marty looked hard at the boy. "He is not a pet to be pitied! He is family—my blood." The creature continued spooning water over the white frog's eyes. When it spoke again, the harshness in its voice had disappeared, replaced by the hint of a smile. "There is a ghost window deeper in the caves. It shows stories like moving tapestries. But it has bled itself of any color, so that everything is told in pictures black and white. Though, I must say, it is still beautiful."

Tim did not understand, but the frog continued. "When I was young, much like this child, I watched a story once about some jewel thieves."

They stole a pearl as big as an egg. But in order to sell it they had to remove its one special feature—a flaw, a black speck which clung to the pearl like a birthmark. They gave it to a master gem cutter and he trimmed and chipped and polished—a little here, a little there—ever so careful not to shatter the pearl. Finally the speck was but a tiny freckle on the smooth pink skin. They took it back to the scoundrel auctioneer who had originally appraised it as priceless. He looked at it a long time. Then he smirked and offered them a price. A price that wouldn't even cover the cutter's fee. They were dumbfounded. "But the flaw is so much smaller than before!" "Indeed," replied the auctioneer. "And so is the pearl."

Pearl, pearl, pearl, went the echo.

Chapter twelve

FURTHER SOUTH—SET OFF FROM the road and hidden in a thick wood—Simon found a row of shallow caves in a thin cleft of earth. Thieves had long sought refuge there, but they had rampaged and bullied the people beyond patience and a troop of marshals was sent to scourge them. Now all that was left of their abandoned retreat was soot, ashes, filthy piles of straw, and several broken, dried-up barrels of wine. All their booty had been collected and portioned to those who could prove offense. So it was as empty as any place could be when the King, seeking shelter and isolation, came upon it. He was hungry for a place to study undisturbed.

By firelight he devoured the intricate runes of the journal set down by a Wind Wizard who had succumbed to vanity in his old age. Boasting of his adventures, he had unwittingly preserved a record of magic—powers that in the hands of the uninitiate could have the most devastating effects. Which was why such a book was forbidden.

Though Simon floundered at first, he pressed on, skipping the more cryptic spells till eventually he found he could easily absorb secrets that unlocked the most profound magic. He soon learned it was always easier to destroy than to create. The crudest spells were transformative in nature: simple mixtures of combustibility and decay. The trick was in the essences—the embedded forms in all nature: Once their superstructures were memorized, they could be manipulated. He marveled at nature's repetition of form: the way the leaf echoed the tree, the snowflake echoed the cloud. He learned to see the great dance of tiny stars at the heart of all matter, how adjustments in their orbits and momentum released pure fire.

The spell for making matter still was simple. He spoke the words into the fire and it oozed into a lovely, wild paralysis. He was so pleased with himself that he leaped into the air, tripped, and let his hand fall into the flames. Although the fire was frozen it was nonetheless hot and he howled in pain, and soon after howled in terror, for the burning would not leave his hand: It, too, was still. After several long minutes of anguish he realized that he had failed to learn the counterspell which would restore the fire to its natural motion—releasing his hand from its relentless agony. Cursing and frantic, he finally found the page that brought relief. It was a lesson in wizard sense that even the greenest apprentice knew: Never do a spell you can't undo.

As magic became a more intimate companion, he sensed a strong seductive pull that drew him deeper into the realm of power. At times it felt as though the magic had a life of its own, and it beckoned him to follow. Perhaps because it all came so easily to him, he began to suspect he was not fully in control. Sometimes the magic spoke to his pride, applauding him like a crowd of peasants after a harvest blessing. It called him to surrender to his great gift. Other times it spoke to his fear in the voice of his stern and distant father, demanding his complete obedience. All this made him cautious. He studied his spells fervently, yet he held back a part of himself that was critical of all he did. He reminded himself that after all, this power was merely a tool for revenge. Nothing more, nothing less.

For two weeks he studied the journal. He learned many useful and just as many useless things. He could work many minor spells: to give sleep, to purify water, to curb appetite—and several major spells: to change form, to heal (strangely unworkable on himself), to enter dreams, to divert weapons, to tell when a man lied. But most curious of all were the passages about the wind; they puzzled him deeply. The wizard claimed he could fly. He gave a long list of wind names and illustrated different postures which would make him a conduit of the power of the wind. Yet throughout these long and obscure passages there ran a thread of meaning, an implied secret which totally escaped the King. Somehow something was missing for, try as he might, long and loud, he could call up no wind. He vigorously practiced all the magic he dared and soon became quite fluent. But when it came to the wind, it was as if the spells were elaborate hoaxes designed to frustrate him. After many failures he gave up. Obviously, the silly wizard had left out something vital. He resolved, henceforth, to perfect the skills that came more readily. And many did.

The first tangible benefit of his study was the control he was able to gain over his Listening Curse. He had nearly gone mad in those first days after he fled the castle. Whenever he came to a town his mind would be drenched in moods, memories, voices—everything from the stupid drone of infants to the repetitive whine of hatred. The thoughts mobbed his brain with noise. It was like being forced to concentrate on every conversation at a feast—all at the same time. But now that he had learned to narrow his new sense and "focus" it where he wanted, it would not be so difficult anymore to go among people.

One night by the fire he realized he had been lingering for days, repeating spells he knew inside out. He had absorbed all the magic the wizard's book would yield. He was ready. So why did he hesitate? The image of a small dark man scraped across his mind, and despite his new power, he trembled. Disgusted with himself, he threw the wizard's book into the fire and resolved to leave the caves in the morning and head south.

He woke after a fitful sleep with the nagging memory of a dream: a dream which prompted action but offered no direction. He'd been reading the wizard's book when, suddenly, the list of formulas and spells had turned into a story, "The Story of the Last Armsman." And it stood out from the rest of the magic book because it wasn't written in the wizard's scrawl. Indeed, its borders and lines were so uncannily even, it was difficult for the King to even imagine a Scribbler capable of so impeccable a manuscript. The pages seemed the product of an impossible device which had perfected the alphabet: Each letter was equal in proportion and impression.

Yet as flawless as the writing was, the tale itself was hazy.

There once was an armsman coming home from years of battle. He carried a heavy sword and a great darkness, which over the miles of his return, had eaten away at his insides until he felt that he himself was nothing but a great hollow space within his armor.

There were no more wars to fight. No more enemies to kill. No more victories to win. So on his way home he decided to kill himself.

He rode his horse deep into the night, deep into the woods, to the darkest place he could find.

It was there he came upon a light in the forest, like the last ember of a dying fire. It was a cabin in the dark. And inside by a hearth, he found a dark old woman stirring a black pot with a long spoon.

"What took you?" she asked.

He sat down and found himself telling her a long story about the war. And when he had finished she said, "Little child, you don't know what you've been suffering. Come. Give me your sword."

So he did. And she dipped it in the pot, the big black kettle over her fire. And she cleaned the years of blood off it, the years of killing, the years of being right. And she said, "Now you have a clean sword. But you must do something for me. You must show your sword to your sister."

"My sister?" said the armsman.

She said, "Yes. You know: the one who wears the red dress."

He hadn't thought of her in years. But he remembered. A childhood playmate who shared secrets with him, who always wore red. They did everything together. She had probably been the last person he had ever trusted.

"I don't understand," said the armsman. "Why should I show my sword to my sister?"

The old lady replied, "If you don't show your sword to your sister, you will show it to your enemy."

She smiled and slapped him soundly on the face.

The armsman woke up.

His horse was looking at him. And he thought, It was a dream. It must have been a dream.

But he got on his horse and he rode like the wind. It was as if he had lost some weight in the night, as if his horse had grown wings. He made it to the castle just as the sun was rising, cladding the towers in pink. And he asked the gatekeeper where his sister was.

"Where she always is," he replied, as if the armsman were having a joke at his expense. "In the tower."

The armsman dismounted, dashed up the steps, and knocked on her heavy door.

"Come in," she called. He found her standing at the window in her blazing red dress. He remembered now: She was dark and beautiful. "Why, Brother! I hardly recognize you! You've been gone so long. Did you kill all your enemies?"

"I must show you something," he interrupted. And he pulled it out and he laid it on his open palms and knelt before her.

She looked at it a long time, then gave a small familiar smile. "That's funny. I've got one, too." She laid a warm palm against his ghostly cheek. "But I keep it better hid than you."

Late that day he came to a small village in a valley: several stone houses, a flock of goats milling about a pond, and a comforting curl of smoke rising from one chimney. The people were guileless and kind: They offered him a sleeping place and food and he stayed for two nights. He answered many shy questions with many polite lies and for the first time in what felt like years he was made to feel at home.

On the morning he left, he woke refreshed and calm. He found his steed thoroughly groomed and munching on a bag of oats. He noticed strange pouches strapped to his saddle and was amazed to find them filled with smoked meat, dried fruit, and nuts. There was even a clean red blanket spread neatly under his saddle. He heard the gentle reassuring hum of simple minds busy with their chores, content. He wished that his formal gratitude of the previous nights could have been warmer, could have expressed how much their casual kindness meant to a lonely man made welcome. Riding off, he sent back a spell of good fortune on the village, wondering whether such spells really took effect, or if they had been mere courtesy in the days of wizardry. Indeed, he wondered whether, under his curse, good fortune could ever be his to give.

He practiced spells that day. Walking deep into the woods he picked out a spot by a huge tree whose peak he could not see and sat among the dappled red wildflowers at its base. After toying with some elementary charms he toiled through the more difficult ones. Finally, to top off a very satisfying day he decided to split the tree in half. It was no easy task: In the end he had to combine several motion spells and repeat them twice. The split began at the top with a faint cracking sound, then it came soaring down the tree dead center, sending wood chips flying. There was a huge groan which echoed throughout the forest and the tree came crashing down—perfectly halved. The roots sprang up and rich black dirt rained over the King. Smaller trees bent and flattened under the enormous halves. Then there was only dust and the angry cackling of fleeing birds. It had all taken about fifteen breaths. I'm getting very good at this, he thought, and sat down trembling and exhausted.

He slept off the road that night under another fallen tree, snugly and soundly in his new blanket. But his dreams were vaguely troubled: full of evil portents and the sound of wind and fire. Once he woke and glimpsed a big bird poking about the ground nearby. He threw a pebble at it and it flew away. He woke late and longed deeply to return to the castle. His thoughts were full of Jason.

For hours he had been following an old, unused trail deeper into the south woods when he came upon a small cabin in a clearing. It had been a long time since he had crossed water. He decided to ask for hospitality. His horse protested as he edged into the clearing but he ignored it.

Dismounting he saw a smiling old fat woman approach him from the doorway.

"Welcome," she said.

"Your pardon, ma'am. I would be grateful if you could spare some water. My skins are low."

"Plenty for the asking!" she responded cheerfully and led him inside. As she filled his skins in a barrel, Simon took a seat by the window and looked about. The place was perfectly neat: The air was fresh; the smallest corners were free of dust. Strangely, small mirrors of every shape and size adorned the walls of the room; they made it thick with light—odd beams of gold shot out from every angle and in one corner the King saw the old lady reflected many times over; he did not see himself. Above the mantel was a crouching figure bound in chains, coarsely sculpted out of stone. A grotesque thing about the size of a small barrel, it had webbed feet, the wide eyes of a child, and no mouth. The more he looked the stranger the room became. Little things felt out of place: a broken dish here, a stubby broom there (with burnt bristles); the wooden floor was so smooth and polished it looked wet.

Simon felt an overwhelming urge to bolt from the room, mount his horse, and flee—as quickly as possible. But he was also thirsty, and he swallowed the dread and sat still. He was, after all, a man of power.

"You've come a long way, my handsome one," said the old lady as she handed him his dripping skins. "We get meager company in the woods. I was hoping you might stay and rest a while."

Not really hoping, thought the King, reading her mind—positively desperate.

He nodded graciously. "You are most generous."

The lady made a great effort to conceal her delight. "Splendid! I'll make us some tea."

Obviously, she wants something from me. But what? Is she a witch? In disguise? Perhaps. Is she so confident in her art that she's oblivious to threat? Or am I? He ran his finger over the wooden chair and felt a tingle dance up his arm. Be very careful.

As the woman was rustling over the fire, a shadow passed in the corner of his eye. He turned and for a moment he could barely control his feelings. There in the doorway stood a young lady of stunning beauty, simply dressed yet radiating elegance. A golden clam pinched her maroon robe at her pale neck. She smiled at him. "Mother, you should have warned me a stranger had come."

The voice was sweet and gentle. It kindly rebuked the old woman.

She began to stammer nervously. "I didn't expect you home this early."

"Still you might have called." She turned to Simon with a shy, embarrassed smile. "I'm a mess. I was picking berries." With a giggle she showed him the red stains on her lovely hands and apron. As she stepped closer to the table he saw the clam brooch at her neck was actually a small golden claw. Tentatively, he reached out to her mind and found, to his utter amazement, nothing. She was void of feeling and thought—a complete cipher. In his brief time as a mind reader he had never met such a soul. To be sure he had read the minds of idiots whose thoughts were like the meaningless murmur of sleepers. But this was different. He found he could not take his eyes off this hollow creature. Something stirred inside him, but her deep gaze met his and he dearly hoped she would never look away. Wait! So lovely. Wait! So sweet. Too late. He could look into her eyes forever.

When the young King had subtly sought her mind, he was vulnerable. Not only had her beauty disarmed him, but his defenses were dropped in order to attune himself to her. That moment was all she needed. As the girl walked to his side, the King sat spellbound: frozen, dumbly believing that he was still locked in her gaze. She reached down, picked up his hand, and bit his nail to the quick. She released his hand and it dangled in the air above his head. The girl smiled and chewed. "Oh, that was simple. He went for the eyes."

The old woman approached her crossly with the steaming kettle in her hand. "You promised! You said the next one was mine!"

"He is rather smart-looking, isn't he?" said the girl, stroking his hair with her long nails. "He'll do nicely."

"But it's my turn!" whined the old woman. "You promised!"

"Goodness, Mito, how you do nag!"

"But, but, but——"

"Stop it!" she said harshly, then continued in a gentle sing-song voice. "You're forgetting your place, dear. You lure them in and I take my pleasure. Occasionally, you get the crumbs. The important thing to remember is that it's only through my charity that you're even allowed to meet strangers."

"But I get hungry, too!" she whimpered.

"You're human. You can still eat your soups and such."

"But I *like* people!" she wailed.

"I know, dear. But my appetite is ravenous compared to yours. Dragons must have flesh or they will wither. How many times must I tell you?"

"Greedy!" snapped Mito. "You just had those boys who marched by yesterday!"

A word about witches. They were notoriously untrustworthy. Partly because their magic was of a decidedly lower rank. Earth Sorcery grudgingly passed on by men of power who treated women as chattel. No wonder their magic was steeped in illusion and bogus ritual. Like most magic, it promised more than it gave and gave things unwelcome. The unforeseen side effects were often as powerful as the initial spell—something King Simon, for all his accomplishment as a novice, had yet to learn. In fact, most witches were either half-mad or age-simple. Magic has a way of warping the levelest minds, so strange are its ceremonies and so twisted the powers it conjures. Though most had a few charms (minor spells, usually temporary in effect), any witch worth her thunder harbored at least one major spell that could secure her a regular income (it was a business, after all). Yet even these were hazardous. The wizards' original gift was spoiled over time by bad workers and false Tellers who twisted it to their own dark ends, until it became like a tale told poorly or a rumor distorted by repetition, a thing so marred and tepid it could not be remembered, or so outlandish it would not be believed. It also bears repeating—most witches were half-mad.

The beautiful woman continued to ignore the witch. She watched the King intently. "Would you believe that even now it takes every bit of my strength just to keep up this ridiculous body and hold this silly pilgrim in check? You know, I do believe he has some power. He didn't go under immediately; I had to give him extra—"

She screamed as the scalding water came upon her. "Ohhhh! You dare touch me! I'll smash you! I'll gosi-suck your blood! Ahhh! What have you done to me?"

The old woman dashed for the door, but the steaming girl leapt and caught her ankle and set her teeth deeply into flesh. Mito howled and Simon emerged from the dream where the beautiful one was speaking so eloquently about dragons. Dazed, he saw her maroon robe puddled on the floor beside the fighting women. As he watched, the golden claw emerged slowly from under their wrestling bodies, like a sand crab inching its way toward shore, its knuckled fist opened and closed, opened and closed, creeping away.

The young girl's form began to change before his eyes: Her black hair became grey scales which shimmered like glazed stones, a sharpening tail sprouted from under her dress, her thin hands curled into claws, and as her lips sucked the woman's leg, the faintest suggestion of wings emerged from her shoulder blades and strained against the delicate fabric of her blouse.

THE Gift

The King stood quietly, assumed the pose of magic, and said one word: the only dragon name he knew, the only one he needed. The dragon, who was now fully formed but strangely miniature, recoiled as if its spine had been pricked. It spat out the woman's leg and left an awful wound, then rolled into a ball and—still steaming from the kettle—looked up at the King and shuddered. A raw hissing sound began to form in its throat. Simon spoke the words of a fire spell that could destroy a house in minutes and the dragon began to writhe and spit smoke—choking to death on the flames that swelled up inside its belly.

"Don't do this!" it pleaded desperately. "I have many treasures hidden nearby. I will show you!"

"Die, dragon," commanded Simon.

"I know the Prime Spells! Changing Spells! Wind Spells!"

"Die, dragon."

"I can make you the greatest wizard that ever flew! I'll tell you everything!"

The King nearly faltered at that: Dragons were notorious for their knowledge; they were said to be the oldest creatures alive. Then Simon realized that this was a sick dragon who depended on the help of an old witch to survive: a weak shrunken creature that had lost its power to fly. It most likely had no magic to give him, much less treasure. He doubled the spell and watched as the foul creature was consumed by its own fire, till finally there was nothing but a wisp of smoke and ash that swirled and settled softly in the golden beams of light.

He turned to the dragon's helper then: The wounds were deep and fatal and she was half-mad. He gently touched her forehead and let her ruined spirit pass away into sleep.

Simon felt a tapping on his boot, and looking down, he saw the golden claw knock at his heel as if it were a door. He did not know how, but he felt sure he understood the brooch was asking for something. He had never listened to jewelry before.

103

Then he knew what it wanted. It was asking to die.

What sort of magic made this? he wondered dizzily. Magic did not spring up fresh like a stream. It needed precedence and forethought. The wizard's book had said clearly that all magic created variations on given things. But there was nothing given about this shell. It seemed a new thing, the embodiment of an idea so original that he could not imagine the mind that had conceived it: talking gold? Working metal? It was as if two contradictory notions had been harnessed together to create a bizarre third. And for a moment he found himself caught between wonder and revulsion.

No man made this, Simon thought. It is impossible.

Then he caught himself standing very still, staring at the golden crab that tapped insistently on his heel as if it were a serpent that had crawled into his boot while he slept. He was a man of power; he had just destroyed a dragon. Yet this shiny little trinket at his feet terrified him in a way he had not thought possible.

Simon crushed it thoroughly.

As he left he saw that every mirror in the room was cracked. His horse was terrified and would not be mounted until he cast a spell of calming. He rode off quickly and did not look back.

Chapter thirteen

"Do you know what a legend is, Tim?"

"Sure. It's a story that somebody made up that nobody believes."

Marty chuckled. "John-John didn't know when he was being funny either."

Tim bristled whenever the frog mentioned his father. He did not need to be reminded he was dead. And he hated to think his father a liar, a man who lived two lives, one of them a secret he had never even told his own son. Why hadn't he? And how dare this stranger presume to share his grief?

"I want to tell you a legend unlike any other. Because this is one you should believe."

"Why?"

"Because it will be true."

"Will be? You mean it hasn't happened yet?"

Marty nodded.

"That's not a legend. That's something else. A legend is something that happened long ago, only it didn't."

"And nobody believes it now?"

"Right."

Marty laughed again. "I wish you weren't such a serious boy. You'd enjoy yourself more."

Don't laugh at me, thought Tim, wanting to smack the creature across its ugly mouth. He wondered why he put up with the frog. He wondered why he stayed. He didn't belong here. He could feel he wasn't welcome.

How often had he turned a corner in the caves to hear the squashy scamper of tiny feet fleeing down a passage? Sometimes he even heard the distant echo of their chants. But whenever he came close to the source the music would abruptly cease. He roamed restlessly through the labyrinth of caverns, but he never once saw another Waterman. Often he'd come upon rooms that looked hastily abandoned, weed quilts half-made, bowls of fisheye soup bubbling over a hot spring, empty pools of rippling water, many footprints in a muddy puddle, brown half-eaten loaches squirming on a ledge.

Once he found a pet: a black eel as long as his arm swimming slow figure eights in a rock trough, and once it flashed like lightning and he saw its skeleton. Occasionally he'd even catch Marty regarding him with wide suspicious eyes that never blinked—as if he were very ugly and to look away would be an insult.

Consequently, he spent much of his time in the chamber of the Listener, who did not seem to begrudge his company. With his hand he'd spoon water over the white creature as it floated mutely. Sometimes he'd feed it stalks of watergreen, which it munched eagerly, making bubbles at the mouth. He even told it stories about his life in the forest: treebending, woodcutting, the day he scared a fox with a bird in its mouth. Of course, the Listener never spoke, but in its blank white eyes he found understanding and compassion—perhaps because he needed them.

It was there that Marty found him one day, and told him "The Legend of the Wind Tamer," the legend that the creature called "true."

There once was a boy who blew bubbles. He had hollowed out the bowl of a wooden spoon and he'd dip the spoon in a bucket of fresh spring water mixed with his mother's soap. He became so adept that he could blow bubbles into almost any shape he wanted: snakes, leaves, even a cloud that trembled in the wind. But the boy wasn't satisfied. He thought the bubbles popped too soon. He wanted the bubbles to last forever. He didn't realize that the beauty of the bubbles was due in part to their fragile, temporary nature; each bubble was unique, a happy accident that could not be repeated or prolonged.

THE Gift

One day the boy blew a lovely bubble in the shape of a bird. But strangely, the bubble didn't float away and pop. It hovered over his head, its wings undulating. The bird bubble spoke to the boy. "Am I not beautiful?"

"Yes," said the boy.

"Then save me!"

"How?"

The bird bubble popped, sprinkling the boy's upturned face.

He tried all that day to blow another bird, but he could not. He could manage a leaf, a cloud, or a snake but he could not get a bird.

But the next day he succeeded. And the crystal liquid bird hovered over him and said, "Am I not beautiful?"

"Yes."

"Then save me."

"How?"

"Mix your mother's soap with your father's ashes and dump them in the stream and blow me up again."

The boy did not say what he was thinking. He was thinking that he would get in trouble if he touched the vase upon the mantel where his father's ashes lay.

"But it will spoil the stream," said the boy.

"That is the only way that I can live forever."

So the boy did it: mixed his father's ashes and his mother's soap and ground them into mud, then dumped them in the stream and watched the grey muck spread and flow into the current. Then, dipping the spoon into the dirty water, he blew a bubble unlike any other. For it was a bubble black. It oozed and coiled and finally resolved itself into the figure of a huge black bird.

Tim gasped. He had never told Marty about Tomen.

"Am I not beautiful?" said the bird.

"No," said the boy, for he was terrified.

"But I am alive!" And as the bird flew into the sky, one by one, the clouds it passed through grew dark and troubled.

The boy went home and went to bed right after dinner. In the morning his mother woke him angrily.

"Where are your father's ashes?"

"What?"

"The vase is empty!" she said, grabbing his shoulders. "Where are your father's ashes?"

The boy fell to sobbing and told her about the ashes, the stream, the bubble, and the black bird. He expected to be punished, but instead his mother held him close and said, "Boys make mistakes. If they are lucky, they make enough mistakes to become men."

Just then there was a knocking at their door.

"Who is it?" asked his mother.

The door flew open and a big bird flew in, the same bird he had blown the day before. Only it wasn't as black. He saw as it perched on the mantel above the hearth that its color had faded to grey as if it had been caught in the rain.

"Am I not beautiful?" the bird said, then poked its head into the empty vase.

"What do you want?" asked his mother.

The bird withdrew its beak. "More ashes."

"We have no ashes here," said his mother.

"Pity," said the bird. "Then we'll just have to make some." It bent over and coughed into the hearth and fire shot from its beak and set some twigs aflame.

"You have a choice," said the bird. "You can lie down in the fire . . . or your son can."

The mother clung tightly to the boy, who shouted, "Leave us alone, bird!"

"Will it be the boy?"

"No!" yelled the mother.

"Then will it be you?"

"No!" yelled the boy.

Then the mother held close her son and placed a ball of soap into his hand and whispered, "Go. Run to the stream, blow the biggest bubble you can, and dive into it. Ride it up and when you are surrounded by clouds, pop it. This will cause the clouds to rain themselves clean and freshen the water and douse the bird's fire. Go!"

Then turning to the bird, the mother said, "Take me."

Marty stopped as if to catch a breath.

"So?" said Tim, trying hard not to give the creature the satisfaction of knowing how much the story frightened him.

"So?" Marty replied.

"So what happened? Did the boy pop the bubble?"

"I do not know."

"What do you mean? You made it up! What did he do?"

"The legend isn't over yet."

Stupid frog, thought Tim. At least my father knew how to finish a story.

"Tim, why do you suppose you did not sleep in the bubble?"

Uh-oh, thought Tim. It's one of *those* stories. He was supposed to *learn* something. "I give up. Why?"

"It was a sign. You are the Wind Tamer. Only you can complete the legend."

"What are you talking about?"

"When the wizards died, they could not let the winds run wild without direction; they were too dangerous. But neither could they bring themselves to kill them. So they put them to sleep—never thinking anything could wake them up again. But something did. It has woken them and spoiled them with black magic."

Tim shuddered, remembering his encounter with the beast. "Tomen?"

"Yes. Be thankful you did not lie down in his fire. You would now be a slave to his master, the Night Usher. He means to hoard all the magic in the world. That's why he poisoned the water: to be rid of us and our magic. He'd steal your power if he could."

"What power?"

"I've said you are the Wind Tamer. You will learn to ride the winds and stir the powers of the air."

Tim's eyes widened as it became clear. "You mean, I'll learn to fly?"

"Listen, Tim. It is a most dangerous gift. Do not take it lightly. The wind is spoiled, and anyone who rides it runs the risk of being spoiled himself."

"Don't worry. I know what I'm doing." He could already feel the power gathering inside of him. He imagined himself soaring on a tidal wave of storm clouds. And he knew where his first stop would be.

Marty continued. "And after you have ridden it and thrilled to its currents, after you have grown to love it, then you must destroy your gift."

"What?" His plans hadn't included that.

"You must put the wind to sleep. That is the only way to tame it."

After a long pause Tim asked, "Can I kill Tomen first?"

"No."

"He killed my parents."

"Vengeance," said Marty with a sad shake of the head. "Do you know what vengeance is, Tim? It is a dark mirror in which we cannot see ourselves."

Tim did not reply. Riddles, he thought. Stupid frog riddles. He's just trying to frighten me. He doesn't know. He's never lost his parents.

"You can't defeat him."

"I can try."

"It is too late to fight, Tim. A healing is our only hope. Only a great healing can cleanse the water and the wind. It will cost the life of all my people and it will cost you all your power. It will be the most difficult thing you'll ever do."

"It can't be that hard."

The creature closed its eyes and thought a moment. Behind its thin green lids Tim saw its eyeballs roaming to and fro. Then Marty sat beside the boy and laid two hands gently on his head. Its broad lips puckered as they whistled three brief notes.

"Close your eyes, child. I want you to remember when you were much younger—before the fire—long ago. You had a friend who met you every day. Was it a bird?"

THE Gift

Tim caught his breath. He saw it once again in his mind as if it had just happened: the tiny brown bird. The cherry tree. "Yes-s-s," he said, the word spilling out of him.

"It would watch you from a certain branch. And as long as you kept your distance it would stay with you. But whenever you came closer . . ."

"It would fly away."

"But one day it didn't fly away, did it? One day when you stepped closer, it didn't move. So you slowly, carefully climbed the tree, and it just watched you. It didn't move."

"Yes."

"And you caught it in your hands."

Tim smiled, remembering the joy.

"And you held it gently to you. And you named it."

A sudden frown came to Tim's brow. "Marty."

"You did not mean it any harm—you simply wanted to hold it and keep it and love it."

"Marty, stop!"

"But the bird was terrified. It struggled and beat its wings against your palms."

"Marty, please don't!"

"Then you saw why it didn't fly away. You saw its broken wing. You saw it was in pain." The creature paused. "Then what?"

Tears rolled out from under Tim's closed eyes. "I killed it."

The creature softly touched Tim's hand. "That's how it will be."

"Marty?" said Tim, opening his eyes.

"What is it, child?"

"I'm frightened," said the boy. "I don't know what to do."

"You will learn." The creature reached up and put its arm around the shaking boy's neck and held him like a child after a nightmare. Soon, Marty began to sing.

Chapter fourteen

SIMON COULD NOT STOP FOR sleep; he fled the memory of a
dragon. Through the night he galloped and trotted and walked his horse
until it would go no further, and when he stood next to it and cursed and
spit into its face, it flared its nostrils and regarded him with infinitely sad
eyes. It was late morning when the King finally lay down, exhausted. While
his horse slept, he sat up, keeping watch, eyes shifting like a bird's, starting at the least sound: the creak of a branch overhead, the distant whistle
of a jay. When he jolted awake there were stars coming out, and he did not
remember falling asleep. His horse lounged on its belly, eyeing him with
apprehension, as if to say: Not you again, not yet. It had been an odd
dream. A big rook stood on his lap and whispered: "So good to see you!
So good to see you!"

The next day he came to an agreeable town. It was a welcome sight,
looming high on a hill, surrounded by lush fertile farms: a scattering of
ramshackle houses constructed from leftovers but proudly kept—every
doorstep was swept clean, every grey shingle in place. The populace was
breezy: full of smiles and cheer. They made quite a fuss about his rare and
costly horse. Children played in the rutted streets, chattering gaily and
chasing dogs. He was willingly led to the well in the center of town, where
he drew a bucket of clear cool water and—much to the amusement of the
townfolk—poured it over his head. He caught the scent of fresh pies
cooling on a shaded window sill and nearly fainted with hunger. Several
men took it upon themselves to treat him to a meal at the local inn. He

was given a place to put his feet up and some of the best beer he had ever tasted. The King stretched out, crossed his legs, and basked in their hospitality. Yet part of him was still on edge, and he casually scanned the minds of these people for some threatening guile. He found none—only a pleasant cordial brightness that saturated the already warm day with a deeper wholesome glow.

He had almost completely given himself over to the relaxation he so dearly craved, when he sensed one mind, not far away, pulsing with a hidden pain. To Simon it was perverse that a town so agreeable should hold such a misfitted anguish—and anguish it was. The more he focused upon it the less he could bear it. He turned aside his mind, finished his beer, and thanked his companions. Then with great reluctance, like a man approaching a scorching flame, he pursued the pulse.

It led him to a large house with a cowbell hung on the door. Strange idea, he thought: Every time I knock the bell will ring.

His knock/ring was answered by a young man who looked extremely tired and sickly. His skin was flushed of color and his eyes were set back deeply in his face. He wore bedclothes soaked in sweat.

"Why did you come? Now I'll have to tell him!"

"Tell who?" Simon asked.

"Just go away! He'll find you without my help!"

The young man retreated into the house and Simon followed him to a room which reeked of beer. The man coughed and opened a drawer from which he seemed to pull a blade. His hand seemed weighted by the heft of it. There was a hollow which his fingers and his thumb curled around. The only thing lacking was the knife itself.

Just to make sure, Simon made ready to spell the knife into a worm. He sent out a probe. There was nothing there; the man held air.

"You don't understand his power," the young man cried, holding the invisible knife in a quivering hand. "If you did you wouldn't be here.

Look." He bared his arm and seemed to plunge the blade in and drag it from his wrist to his elbow. "See?" he laughed hysterically. "Now do you see?

"It's severed both muscle and vein. But do you mark? There's no blood. Now, watch as it reseals itself." The man stared exhausted and dismayed at his perfectly healthy forearm, then held it up for Simon to see. "No trace. No scars. Nothing.

"It didn't even hurt. For months I've tried to find a way to end this torment. Drowning doesn't work: I won't sink! Poison doesn't work. I can't hang myself—my damned neck is made of iron! The twine keeps snapping! So what am I to do? There's no escaping him."

"The Usher?"

"Yes!" The young man threw down the phantom blade and cursed. "I hate that name. I hate it!"

The man began to scratch the back of his hand. "I was a bleeder. He said he was a healer. I asked him to stop my nosebleeds. He touched me. And ever since then, he is with me all the time. He knows my thoughts. He speaks inside my head. I cannot keep him out. Do you know what it's like, never having a place you can be alone?"

"Yes." Simon sighed. "I do know that."

The man stared in disbelief. "Did he touch you?" Simon nodded, and the young man looked as if he had finally met a comrade across a gulf of pain. "How can you stand it? The moment he touched me I wanted to die."

"What did he want from you?"

"I offered him money. I have plenty of that. He thought that was funny. He said he wanted Lady."

"Lady?"

"My cow. I will never forget. He took both my hands, looked into my eyes, and said, 'May you be safe.'" The young man giggled, but his eyes were empty. "Safe," he spat bitterly.

Simon sat down to think. Obviously the man was going mad. Was there nothing he could do to help?

"He's looking for you. And he'll find you. He told me to watch for a man of power. He gave me a message for you. He said: 'It is wrong to harm a healer.' " The young man laughed and reached for a bottle on the desk. He took a long drink, letting it drip down his chin and neck. "He knows you're coming. Do you really think you can stop him?"

Simon felt as if he were trapped in a burning room. There was no comfortable distance between them: The man's dread and despair were suffocating.

"Would you like to watch me eat glass?" the tired man asked, smiling and reaching for a comb of beeswax on the desk.

"Please!" Simon implored. "Stop torturing yourself!"

There was a noise at the door. A young lady rushed in, took hold of the tired man, and scolded him, saying: "Rodger! Haven't you made enough messes today?" As she escorted him from the room, she said to Simon: "I'm sorry, sir. It's one of his bad days." She forced a smile and continued. "But we're going to come around soon, aren't we, Rodger?"

"Yes," replied the dazed young man. "Soon." Then turning to Simon, he added angrily, "Don't be a fool. Run while you have the chance!"

Simon stepped across to the couple and grabbed the man between the shoulder and the elbow. "Rodger," he said, wondering if this was the right thing to do, if illusion was so terrible when the truth was worse.

"Listen to me," said the King.

The man looked up in hope.

"You are not safe."

The woman held him tighter in her arms.

"None of us is safe," said Simon. And he whispered the counterspell into his ear.

The man began to cry.

Simon left the town, coaxed his horse into a gallop, and headed into the heart of his fear. To the Book House of the Usher. South. When the horse could run no farther, he let it rest, leaned forward against its mane, and shuddered.

He was a fool and there was nothing to be done about it.

Two days later he stopped to water his horse at a thin creek just off the road. For days he had been unable to keep warm, and he had wrapped his red blanket like a cloak around him. He felt weak and he found it difficult to rehearse his spells. Though his mind was dull and his body clumsy, when he heard footsteps he leapt to alertness. A figure was approaching—a big man with a broadsword at his belt. The King watched him with a caution which gradually yielded to doubt and finally, joy, as the man's unmistakable gait and shining beard became clear. Simon ran toward him, shouting his name.

Jason waved and quickened his pace. The King was choking with tears when something in his friend's face alarmed him. It was the incongruous combination of absolutely dead eyes above a dazzling smile. Then his mind caught the beat of a hollow space where Jason's vivid thoughts had once resided. In their place was an overwhelming command which he could not read. He pulled up short and watched bewildered as Jason stepped up, drew his sword, and swung it viciously at his belly. Only years of training and instinct saved him from the blow. He sucked in his stomach, bent forward as the blade skimmed his vest, and wheeled up behind Jason's back.

The King dodged behind a tree and sent out a freezing spell. To his shock and dismay, Jason stepped quickly around the tree and nearly sliced his hand off with a blow that gouged deeply into the bark. Simon ran and tossed a sleep spell behind him that might have set a team of horses snoring, but Jason was unthwarted and sprang after him—gaining with every stride. The King made it back to his horse, unsheathed his sword, and barely dodged an awesome blow that came thundering down to split the saddle and sever the spine of the horse with a faint crack. It crashed dead to the ground.

Jason paused to look upon the steed. He might have been remembering how he had raised the magnificent creature from a little colt. "I think this was a good horse—though I cannot place the name."

Simon told him—too breathless and shocked to say anything else. Jason nodded and gave a quick grunt, then looking back to the King with that hideous smile, he simply said, "Shall we resume?"

Before Simon could reply, Jason charged. In a bold moment of desperation and luck, Simon somehow managed to trip the big man, and he sprawled heavily on the ground but gained his feet in a blink. He smiled again. A new respect settled into his eyes; he would regard his prey more warily. "I'd forgotten how quick you are, lad."

Obviously the man was either spellbound or mind-hexed. But the King could not counter a spell he did not know, or heal with a remedy he did not have. He decided to use the most potent Matter Spell he knew: It would freeze Jason in his tracks. A spasm of weakness passed through him as he quickly said the words. But they rolled tepidly off his tongue and were absorbed by the air like a child's nonsense rhyme. Jason did not even flinch. He simply stood there, grinning and grinning, swaying from side to side, gauging the best line of attack. It was useless—somehow Jason was immune to his magic, or something else was canceling it. The horrible realization came that he must fight and probably kill to survive. He had never killed before.

"Jason, please . . ." He began to plead but the words were barely out when he saw the blow coming. He blocked it. Then another. And another. Then, both men stood breathing heavily, waiting for the return of strength that could lift their heavy blades and guide them to their mark. Between gulps of air, Simon said, "Who is . . . your master?"

"The Usher . . . the Healer."

"He knew I was coming?"

"He knows . . . a great deal about you. I've told him a lot. He is . . . very curious."

"But . . ." said the King, and Jason was upon him. He swung the broad blade swiftly. It was a move he had taught the young King over and over. To thwart it meant a strong feint and a quick block. This Simon did perfectly. There was a puzzled look on Jason's face as he was flung back by the rebound of the blade. Simon saw the dull slackening of a hexed mind— the blunted instincts which must necessarily remain after total surrender to another will.

"That's right," said Jason finally. "I forgot. That was one of our lessons wasn't it?"

"Yes," said Simon, his chest heaving wildly. All their practice and sweat, repeating the same moves over and over like a dance, until they became thoughtless, second nature, until they became a part of you—his tutor had said that someday they'd be real.

"You learned it well, my King."

It was an awful dilemma. His heart knew only love and trust for Jason, yet his mind and will were certain he was his mortal enemy. He felt hot tears on his cheeks.

"Jason, try to understand." He could barely get the words out. "I don't want to kill you!"

A grin hooked into half of Jason's face. "Don't know if you could, even if you wanted. Anyway . . ." He shrugged. "I've promised the Usher your heart in a pouch, and I'm a man of my word."

The King then almost said the words he'd never said to anyone. But the man he loved was not there, really, and he couldn't bring himself to say the words to a stranger.

"I want to talk to Jason. Not you. I want Jason!"

"I'm here, lad."

"This isn't you! He has your mind in his hands! And when he squeezes, you do as he wills. Don't you see?"

Jason's face twisted like a child's who could not figure his lesson. "That's a silly one, lad. I've always been a man of me own mind. You've known that." And he set his stance for another blow.

"He's a fraud, Jason. Dammit, you knew that once! Remember?"

"You know, I once thought something like that . . ." A drunken pause that did not know its length filled the space between them. "But then he touched me and it was all different. He's a good one through and through. And what he does he does for good reasons—no matter what it looks like. He's got vision, lad. He's a healer and he gave me beautiful dreams. I never dreamed much before." Then, as if he had caught himself becoming too intimate with an acquaintance, he paused and loosed that terrible smile again. "But I don't expect you to understand."

Simon thought: I'm done for.

The big man's fingers flexed upon the hilt and the King poised for the attack. Something deep within him screamed: There had to be a way to break the spell, to crack the wall the Usher had built around his brain. Inside this lie was the real Jason; he must try to touch that.

The charge was almost over when he saw it. Jason appeared to stumble but he rolled and dove at his legs. Simon dodged left and grabbed a tree, pulling himself away. Then, he decided to run.

Branches snapped cruelly into his face as he stamped through the undergrowth and ran around trees. He hoped that his youth and natural agility would give him an advantage over the aging Jason; but as fast as he ran, and as much ground as he covered, he could not get a lead on the heavy footsteps of his tutor. There was no losing him and he could not long keep up this pace. The chase must stop and the battle must be waged. He saw a clearing up ahead where there would be room for good blows and wrestling. He made it and turned.

Jason was gone.

He waited a long time. He scanned the woods and realized that while Jason could be anywhere, he stood like a fool in the open—vulnerable to attack from any angle. He knew that he was fair game—Jason would wait for nightfall and trap him in the dark. He could not run, for Jason would be waiting for him in the dark shadows at the margin of the clearing. The Usher had planned it to perfection: a strong ally with the will to kill, a forest where his magic was canceled by some strange force, and a reluctance on the part of the prey to kill the pursuer. It was a foolproof trap. Night would come and in the darkness he could only count on his blind instincts and skill as a pupil to defeat his master.

It occurred to him the Usher would not have gone to this much trouble unless he posed a real threat to his power. This thought heartened him somewhat and he moved to the center of the clearing. This would make him an easy target, but would also allow him the earliest possible warning when the attack came.

He began a steady, watchful pivot that lasted till the sun set and darkness began to swallow his senses. He struggled to fight off sleep—an inner enemy which pleaded a seductive surrender. All the noises of the night merged into one long nagging buzz. He could not hear Jason's empty mind and he knew he wouldn't hear anything at all until it was too late. Jason would set a stealthy, silent ambush. In a brief moment of utter surprise, he would meet his end at the hands of his best friend.

A sword pierced through his side and quickly withdrew.

"Checkmate!"

Powerful hands grabbed Simon's wrists from behind and he dropped his sword. He was spun into a crushing bear hug which would soon squeeze away his breath and then his senses. The King battled nausea and dizziness. He looked into the face of his foe and saw a monster possessing the body of a loved one. A red hot wrath spread into his limbs as the monster whispered into his ear as if it were telling a bedtime story to a child.

"Your father and I were once ambushed at night. We stood against fifteen men—two swords each we had, back-to-back. I remember it well. We killed them all—the last begged

for the dungeon. I lost a finger and John hurt his chest. I never knew . . . a fighter more fierce . . . nor a braver King. He told me to tell you this, if we ever battled together."

Hate this man. Hate him! It is your only hope. He saw the stiff muscles of Jason's neck and bit down savagely. Jason tightened his grip but finally yelled, tossed Simon to the ground, and brought his hand up to the wound.

"Nasty," he grunted. "Like a woman!" Then reaching for his sword he said, "I'll kill you quickly, Simon. You won't feel a thing."

Simon had his sword in his hand—he wasn't sure how it got there. Jason took a slow step forward and wound back for the blow. With the last of his strength, Simon swung his sword, catching Jason on the exposed spine and slicing open a wound below his ribs. The big man crumpled to his knees. He struggled to rise, then collapsed on his back. Simon stood shakily, walked to his foe, and put his boot on his throat. He was about to crush it when he caught the terrified thoughts of a dying man. They started as a whimper and quickly became a wail: "What have I done? What have I done?"

Jason's mouth quivered and the words broke out. "My King! Was it a dream?"

"You'll not fool me with that." But he sensed the rush of unlocked thoughts as they filled what had been an empty chamber in Jason's mind. The hex was broken; Jason was back—wounded but released. Simon removed his foot and knelt beside him.

"Did I really try to kill you?" Jason asked.

"Yes."

"I never knew a power that could make a man do that: kill the thing he loved."

"He made you do it."

"Yes. He made me do it. I see that now." Then he reached up a hand and touched the wound in Simon's side: a clean entry in the back and an exit out his belly. Simon flinched. "You ought to have that tended to."

"I will."

Jason sniffed the air. "When was the last time you took a bath?"

They laughed, and for a moment it was as it used to be, as if they'd never been apart. Then Jason said in a tight soft voice: "My King, I am frightened."

Simon heard the words like a man who hears an unfamiliar animal call in the night. He felt the hair arch along his neck. This proud strong man had finally reached his limit: the wall he could not scale, the blow he could not bear, the enemy he could not face without fear. Simon could not look him in the face.

"You're not going to die, Jason. I'll see to that." And he was about to cast a healing spell when he remembered: Of course it wouldn't work. Jason's eyes bugged and strange sounds worked up through his throat.

"For you," he whispered. "I am afraid for you."

The King turned to face him in bewilderment.

"Simon, you mustn't do what I did. . . ."

He paused like a man intent on choosing the perfect word. Suddenly there was too much silence and Simon shrieked at the man: "Jason!"

His eyelids fluttered and he rasped, "I meant to kill the Usher. Don't you see, lad? You can't fight darkness with darkness. You don't get light that way. You only get . . . this."

"What are you talking about, you old horse?" There he goes with his riddles again.

Jason did not answer.

Chapter fifteen

"CLIMB," MARTY TOLD HIM.

Tim had expected a fonder farewell but that was the creature's last word before it turned and walked back to the fire. He was to climb as high into the White Moon Mountains as he dared: preferably higher than the clouds. Then he was to wait for the Teacher—whoever that was. So he climbed. He waited. He waited long enough to feel silly: a boy all alone on a mountain waiting for someone he'd never met! After his long ascent he had lain down exhausted, watched the sun set, and spent a chilly night in the crevice of a rock. In the morning he munched on seagreens Marty had provided and tossed a few stones out over the ledge. He could not hear them land.

As the noon sun blazed down he napped on the warm rock ledge and dreamed about his mother tucking him into bed. Her face was shadowed. He asked her, "Will I ever see you again?" She answered in a faraway voice, "What a silly question. Marty will come." He sighed. "Not Marty, Mother—*You.*" Then she laughed a strange laugh—like the shriek of a bird. Tim awoke and saw he lay under the huge shadow of a giant bird standing at the edge—a dark silhouette watching him. He backed away, his eyes wide.

The bird cocked its head and Tim saw it was not black at all, but pure white. A white eagle. It settled its bright frame on the rock, its tail hanging over the edge, and inspected Tim with one eye. Finally the great bird spoke in a strange cracking voice that came between the clicks of its hooked beak. "Which do you prefer?" It showed Tim its right profile. "This side?" It swiveled its head into a left profile. "Or this side?"

"What?"

"Someone wanted to replicate me once. He preferred *this* side. But I think this side has merit."

Tim wondered if this was a test of some sort. He honestly couldn't tell the difference. At last he said, "They both look good to me."

The eagle cocked back its head once again, looking down its beak at the boy. "That's what I think, too."

"Are you the Teacher?"

"I am."

"I'm Tim."

"Tim . . . I have heard it whispered in the air. Do you know what it means?"

"No." His people had long lost the lore of their names.

"Then I will tell you. It means . . . Switch. Or . . . Ender."

A joyful shiver went through Tim's body. Oddly, he found himself wondering what was the meaning of Marty's name. "Thank you, Master," he said.

The bird tilted its head back at a curious angle—which Tim later learned was the way birds smile. "Why do you call me Master? Do you know what that means?"

"No."

"It means servant," said the eagle, and it gave a mighty laugh.

"I have much to learn." Tim sighed. "Teach me."

So began a long visit that would be the happiest time of his journey.

In his first lesson, the eagle revealed to Tim that there were four levels of magic. The first was Illusion, whose symbol is fire. The second was Manipulation, whose symbol was earth. The third was Transformation, whose symbol was water. The fourth was Possession, whose symbol was wind.

This was the story the white eagle told.

In the beginning, the world was made of Four.

Fire. Earth. Water. Wind.

Fire went up, seeking the highest places before it died.

Earth never went anywhere. The Earth was still, changing only when Fire or Wind or Water moved upon it.

Water went down from the clouds, seeking the lowest places until it settled into the ground.

Wind went to and fro, resting and traveling, moving as the Maker moves, known only by its touch upon the trees, the water, or the skin.

Now, the Maker gave to the Wind creatures that flew, and to the Water creatures that swam, and to the Earth creatures that walked, but to the Fire he gave people. For they are the only creatures that love fire.

Just as the bird cannot leave the sky and the fish cannot leave the water and the deer cannot leave the ground—people cannot leave the fire. It draws them all.

For all creatures are drawn to their home.

What grounder can keep their eyes from the hearth? Or the setting sun? Who among them passes the winter without the flame? Who among them prefers to sleep in the day?

This is truth: You are the People of the Fire.

The white eagle paused a moment and looked down upon its pupil from its perch. "Questions . . . answers. What kills fire?" he asked.

"Water?" Tim replied, saying the first thing to come into his mind.

"What kills fire?" repeated the eagle. And Tim wondered how that could have been the wrong answer.

"Earth?" he replied, imagining a candle being ground into the dirt.

"What kills fire?" asked the eagle.

Tim thought. It could only be the last possible element. "Wind," he said confidently. And after a time, he asked, "Which one was right?"

"All of them." The white eagle cocked its head like a flower in a breeze. "Fire is killed by everything. Earth always was. Water always was. Wind always was. But the People of the Fire are made of the only thing that dies."

This was the start of a lifetime of learning, a journey the boy continued long after the months he spent with the white eagle on the White Moon Mountains. Yet in all those later years, he never found again the joy he knew in those first lessons in the Way of the Wind.

Tim learned the wind was not one but many—different winds with different names. He learned he should ride the winds carefully, for in their sickness they were no longer trustworthy; they had become like rabid dogs: At any moment they might turn on their master and attack. He learned the names of the southern winds who were more dangerous because they were more awake, the names of every tree along the timberline, the way to know a storm is coming when you cannot see it, to pass through an evil cloud with your eyes closed, the most intelligent birds and how to address them. Avoid flying after dark for the wind has nightmares, beware of bats: they are mindless; drink no water on the plain: it has gone bad; never trust a talking blue jay; always trust a magpie: they have the gift of human speech because they are the best listeners; sparrows are the most loyal but also the stupidest birds; golden finches are splendid messengers, so long as they fly toward the sun; all hawks are mercenary and unreliable; butterflies are sacred children: do not disturb them; never fly in one day longer than you can walk in twenty, for it is possible to forget how to walk; beware of the tallest trees to the south: they have a magic too old to fool with; gosis love a shadow; eat only the fruit from green trees. The list went on and on: remarkable facts, survival tactics, reliable opinions, and gossip. Tim thought his head would burst with the effort to retain it all.

But his study went quickly. Soon he had learned a smattering of postures and wind calls. He seemed to have a knack for it. The promise of flight carried him through the more difficult passages of his study: the many hours he stayed with the eagle reciting names, learning secrets, listening to tales untold for ages. Often he dreamt of Bubble Sleep.

But even as Tim grew more confident in his skills, the Teacher grew sterner and more cautious. Shaking its head and clicking its beak, the eagle reminded him "All your work is but a child's groping for its first words—even when the words come they are no evidence of wisdom. Wisdom is what you most need, Tim, and it is the one thing I cannot teach you."

When it tired of teaching, the eagle would tell stories. After one particularly cold sunset, it told a story about *a huge black bird who tried to swallow the moon. But the moon got stuck in its beak and would not go down. The bird was too stubborn to let go and spit it out, and the moon was too big to be swallowed. As the bird grew hungrier and hungrier it grew bigger and bigger until it filled the sky and became the night, covering the world with its black feathers.* The eagle said that when the stars twinkled the bird and the moon were wrestling.

"I met a bird like that once," said Tim. "He was about your size— maybe bigger—and he was darker than night."

The eagle closed its eyes. "The Beast with no heart."

"You know Tomen?" asked Tim, surprised.

"We crossed currents once or twice," said the bird, eyes still closed, lost in remembering. Then, abruptly, it began to recite in a strange high voice that rattled in its beak, like an old man mimicking the voice of a woman:

> *His voice: no sound but for the lie.*
> *His eye: no look but for the lost.*
> *His wings: no flight but to the end.*
> *The Beast with no heart,*
> *The Fire with no light,*
> *Beware the Usher of the Night!*

When the eagle opened its eyes under its constantly furrowed brow, Tim recalled how difficult it was to get used to this fierce stare, to understand the bird wasn't angry all the time.

"The song goes on, but that's the most of it."

"Who wrote it?"

"Widowers," the eagle said wryly. "Last I saw him, he was flying south—the legs of a puppy stuck out of his mouth. They kicked furiously. But I knew him ages ago, when he was still a man."

"He was a man?"

"Yes. He wasn't very good at it either."

"I'm going to kill him," Tim said.

The bird cocked its head. "Are you?"

"He killed my parents. So I'm going to kill him."

"Ah!" said the eagle with a sad shake of the head. "I am sorry. That would make me angry, too."

"You don't believe I can do it?" said Tim fiercely. He stood up, clenching his fists. Then he does not know me, he thought.

"Well," said the eagle calmly. "I certainly believe you want to. But there's a problem. It's quite impossible to kill Tomen."

"Why?" shouted Tim.

"He's not alive."

Tim looked hard at the eagle for any sign that it might be teasing. Then, red-faced and furious, he strode off and would not speak to the bird for the rest of the day.

The eagle found him sitting on a cliff the next morning, dangling his legs over the ledge. "Come here, Tim. I want to show you something you've never seen before."

Tim followed the bird up the mountain to a shallow cave that smelled of smoke. In the center of the cave lay a small pool. The eagle landed on a rock and beckoned with a wing. "Come and look," he said, indicating the pool with a nod.

Tim leaned over the edge and looked into the black water of the pool.

At that moment he would have given anything to be blind. He tried to close his eyes but found he could not. The vision held him ruthlessly. His hands gripped the rock around the pool and he began to shake. Finally, the eagle touched his elbow and said, "Enough." Tim fell to his knees and covered his eyes. He felt as if he had been wrenched inside out.

"Master . . . what was it?"

"I think you already know."

"I saw a creature. He looked at me. He was . . . so horrible. Tell me what it was."

"*You* tell me."

"It was dark. So dark. I couldn't see."

"You saw," insisted the eagle.

"No!" Tim cried.

"What did you see?"

"I do not know!"

"What was it, Tim?"

"I don't know!" Tim whimpered through his teeth. "I don't know!"

"But you do," said the eagle. "That is why you're afraid to say it."

"No!"

"Say it, Tim."

"*No!*"

"Say it."

"A haunter!"

"No."

"A monster!"

"No." The eagle shook its head.

Tim looked up, his eyes brimming with tears, his face almost visibly aged. "Me!" he said miserably. "It was me!"

For a minute the bird lightly touched the boy's hair with a wing tip and said nothing. Then it spoke with a weary gentleness. "There is only one way to conquer revenge, Tim. That is to truly see yourself. You will know then that given the moment, you are fully capable of every evil that has ever been done. If you are ever tempted to covet your gift, to let the wind stay restless after you have ridden it, if you ever need a reason to disarm yourself, remember that face you saw in the pool. Imagine it with the power to do anything. And you will know what you must do."

Tim struggled for the words. "I—I saw something else in the pool. I'm—I'm not just angry at Tomen."

"No?" asked the eagle gently, as if this was no surprise.

Tim's chin trembled. "They said—they'd be back soon. They said they wouldn't be long."

After a moment the bird whispered: "And if you were them, what would you have said?"

The eagle folded its wing around the boy, who cried as he had never cried before. When he had no more tears, the Teacher said softly, "Now you are ready."

The next morning the white eagle led him to a high ridge, then left him alone for his encounter. All day nothing happened. In the fading twilight Tim watched a thin cloud line stretch across the horizon, as though a colossal serpent had shed its skin against the sky. He felt it coming then—but not as he had expected. There was no sudden rage, just a tentative breeze, barely tangible, that moved the brush about him slightly. To Tim it felt almost playful. He stood up, anticipating the end of his wait. He extended his arms as he had been instructed—assuming the pose of relinquishment. But in that moment the wind was gone.

Tim cursed himself. What had he done wrong? Had he frightened it away? He could find no fault in his technique; he had studied hard. What then? Had he been judged unworthy? Had he lost his one chance to be the Wind Tamer?

He was to wait two more days for his answer.

It was after the sun had set into a perfect night of stars and the stillness had become oppressive. He built a small fire for company. The crack-ling twigs and fluttering sparks reminded him of the many nights he had spent with Marty. The flames seemed to reassure him that all was well. His stomach growled and he felt weak, but at least it was warm and dry—and soon he would bid the eagle good-bye, go down the mountain and find a proper meal. In the morning he would be gone. He would make his jour-ney to a town where he could apprentice himself—perhaps as a Go-Boy at a tavern or a hired hand on a farm, a quiller at court or a book house scribbler. He would go away and never bother himself again with strange places and powers, strange creatures and their odd ways. He would do ex-actly what he felt like, when he felt like it. So what if he never flew? So what if he never saw the yellow glow of the caves again? Who cared if he never talked to another bird? He would never miss something that re-minded him of his childishness, his stupidity, his unworthiness.

He stood and kicked the glowing coals over the ledge, watching as they tumbled into the darkness below. Some dashed into bright little cinders on the rocks, some streaked on like falling stars—their orange light di-minishing into dark space. Tim stood over the edge and screamed into the night. "I was willing to do anything! Do you hear? Anything! I would have walked through fire to be able to fly. I would have fought and killed to be able to float in a bubble again, to see the other side of clouds. I have tried to prepare! I have tried to do my best! What more do you want? What more can I do?"

The darkness surrounded him, thick and cold and utterly indifferent.

"What more?" he cried, his eyes blazing at the starry night.

He did not hear it at first: His ears were still ringing and his body shook with anger. He thought perhaps it was a pebble settling behind him, dislodged by the enormous echoes of his cries. But no. It was soft as a whisper: the sound of a mild wind gathering force. It swept up the moun-tainside, curling around rocks like a river. Dust began to rise and there was a trembling of earth. Tim thought he heard a small voice coming from behind him, but turning he found nothing. Then he was sure it came from below him, and looking over the edge, he felt a warm updraft against his face, gradually building momentum.

At last he knew that "It" was not singular: It was multiple. Many, many voices slipped into his mind to form a clear and gentle chorus repeating the same word, a word that terrified him, though somehow it made perfect sense. The voices said, "Jump."

He obeyed. It was not so much a compulsion as it was the only other choice. He could go down the mountain and deny that anything had happened. Or he could do the most foolish act he had ever considered. It was something the white eagle said that somehow tipped the scales: "Those few who choose the Way of the Wind dread and cherish it forever." He knew that if he waited too long, if he stirred it about too much in his mind, he would freeze and his chance would dissolve. He blinked, followed his heart, and leaped from the ledge into the night air.

In a rushing moment that swamped his mind like a huge wave, Tim felt as if he were receiving the words of an endless crowd of children, children who had been locked away in a dark place for ages, as he himself was hidden in the well. They enclosed him in a desperate, welcoming embrace, each telling their own story as if they hadn't been listened to for years. So many stories. Stories of being lost. Of dying. Of wandering alone over a darkening land under a red and shrinking sun. Of roaming through nights blacker than those in the great forest. Stories of being hidden. Stories of being left behind. Forgotten stories no one had heard in years. It was as if, in one moment, he had absorbed all the stories ever told, every possible combination of incident, invention, suspense, and surprise—they sang in him: a thousand voices clamoring for a harmony only he could provide. He had never heard so many stories. He could hardly believe this many stories existed.

And as the winds folded themselves around him like a warm soft garment, he realized this was not falling. It was what he wanted more than anything: the child feeling of warmth and belonging and freedom that he never hoped to feel again; it was more thrilling than treebending and more frightening than Bubble Sleep. It was all this, yet more. For had not this first flight been so sweet, it would have been terrible. There was no mercy in this beauty. In the midst of such innocence Tim felt soiled. He floated, utterly naked, every blemish of his spirit wrenched open to inspection. And he screamed the scream of the Wind Tamer who accepts the awful gift. The winds received him and he fell helpless into their arms.

"No. I'm quite well, thank you," said the Teller. "There's nothing wrong at all."

Chapter sixteen

IN A DREAM SIMON WATCHED the little creatures approach him, bouncing awkwardly from one webbed foot to the other as though walking were a difficult exercise they had yet to master. Soon they surrounded him. Their skin was pale grey, their huge eyes black; they had no mouths. Though they looked familiar, he could not remember where he had seen the likes of them before. It did not matter now. He watched lazily as they clasped him in their fragile hands—baby hands, he thought. They lifted him off the ground and carried him slowly out of the clearing. Looking back, upside down, he saw a body lying on the ground above the sky.

A black sheet covered the stars.

For days the King wavered between a waking horror and a nightmare that drained and terrified him. In the day the sun was a huge red eye that burned him with its brilliance. At night it closed shut with a dull thud; the sky was empty of light and the voices came: whispering, pleading, screeching, each interrupting the other, demanding to be heard. They all wanted the same thing. The King knew he should not give in: It was a horror he had read about in the journal, a threat which every wizard dreaded, a threat to which he was most vulnerable. For when a man of power reaches a place of despair, he is besieged and hounded by the incomprehensible forces he has stirred—forces in nature that are more than half awake, not quite alive yet filled with the longing to be human, having been touched by the gift at the hands of the wizards. Like voices of the dead, they would do anything to wake again. Simon had been warned: When the body is weak the will is in danger and it must be guarded zealously. But he found that his resources were sluggish in coming and weak on arrival. He felt he could not endure this much longer. But then the darkness would break and the burning red eye would return and he could find no shade, no silence, no peace.

A voice called him out of sleep and he awoke to a room full of dancing candles. He was in a hammock and each of the strange creatures was holding a candle and bobbing up and down. Can't they sit still? he thought. Next to him, so close that he could feel his exhale, a big bearded man looked down into his eyes with curiosity. Eventually the King realized that he was being talked to. Soon he remembered he could hear.

"—is my domain. Your spells have kept me fed for hours. I am the Magic Eater."

Who'd want to eat magic? thought Simon. What a silly idea.

"These are my pets, the Griffs." The old man pointed to the round grey lumps of clay holding the candles.

Griffs. Miffs. Tiffs. Cliffs. It's a riddle, thought Simon.

"I must ask you to be a bit more careful. They turn to stone when they touch deceit."

Ahh! thought Simon. There's a lot of that going around.

"You've petrified two already. One when you were having a nightmare, and another when you were raving."

You can tell the difference? thought Simon. I can't.

"I don't suppose you could try to calm down a bit?"

Be glad to, thought Simon. Untie my hands and I'll calm down permanently.

"Where'd you learn your magic, lad? I haven't felt such power since the wizards. Your minor spells are sending ripples up my spine."

Jason! thought Simon fiercely. Take off that stupid disguise and get me out of here. This is a dumb game and I don't want to play anymore. Jason, I'm commanding you as your King. Jason? Jason! *Jason!*

The Magic Eater placed a cool hand over Simon's eyes and immediately he was asleep.

When it became evident that the King was as well as he was going to get, the old man had the Griffs put him in an isolated cell in the boughs of a great tree, just outside the range of his power.

It was a tree, the legend goes, *that a wizard had once slept under. And as happened with everything they touched, the tree had become, in some fashion, awake. And in the morning when the wizard rose, he saw above him the silhouette of a huge grasping hand, reaching for the unreachable sun.*

King Simon would be safe there. At least he could get some solitude and distance from the bustling minds of his pets. How strange to think that quiet was all he had to give this young man. The old man could only see to his comfort; he could do nothing to ease his torment. His power was foolproof but limited—it only extended to freshly made spells. It was defensive rather than offensive. He could absorb; he could not destroy. He could cancel; he could not heal. Simon's trouble was something unfathomable, beyond his power, something which must find its own counterspell.

Simon could not be bothered with his own recovery; he was much too busy defending himself against the voices. For hours he would wait tensely for their assault and often nothing would happen. Then, exhausted, he would relax too deeply and they would ambush him and clamor against his skull until he knew it would split open. Then there would be numb fatigue and bad sleep. In brief moments of waking he would find his head cradled in the thick hands of a bearded old man, and queer creatures, holding candles would caress his face. But inevitably, the voices would return full force and he would struggle and fight with all his will. He dodged, refused, retreated—it was a losing battle on the very brink of his mind. He would not yield to the awful thing they asked for. Then he could not. He should not. Finally, he knew that he must not, ever, under any circumstances, no, never, please.

But one evening in his lonely cage he did.

He tried with all his magic to spell himself to death.

Chapter seventeen

IN THE MORNING TIM FOUND the eagle's nest snuggled under an archway of pines at the bottom of a sheer white cliff that leaned up out of sight. The eagle sat erect and snoring, its head tucked down and under one wing—noble and proud even in sleep. The brilliant white feathers on the crown of its head rose and fell to the rhythm of each breath. Tim couldn't resist reaching out to touch them; they were so smooth, so soft. "Master," he whispered.

The eagle's beak clicked and its eyes blinked. Then, cocking its head, it regarded Tim with one fierce eye. "Did you . . . ?"

"Yes."

"Can you . . . ?"

"Yes."

"So what are you waiting for?"

"I came back to say good-bye."

The eagle studied him silently. "You've not forgotten what I told you?"

Tim knew he meant putting the wind to sleep. "No."

"Good."

Again Tim touched the eagle. "Come with me."

The eagle laughed. "I'd be no use, child. Outside these mountains I'm just a fat Teacher called Dub. Ah! But I can give you something." The eagle stood and jumped to the edge of its nest, then instructed Tim to rummage until he found a loose feather. Tim reached up and felt about.

His hand grazed something hard and warm and round. He peeked over and saw four white eggs resting at the bottom of the nest.

No, not eggs, he discovered as he touched them again—stones.

Stones? he thought. "Master?" he asked.

"The feather, Tim," the bird said.

He finally found a soft fuzzy one with a silver spine.

"Crown feather," snorted the eagle. "That's a lucky one."

"Master?" Tim said.

But the bird would not explain; it simply gazed fiercely toward the sky. "Keep it close to your heart, child. And if you ever find yourself windless and alone, hold it up and the nearest kind wind will rush to your aid."

Tim tucked the feather into his heart pocket, then asked the great bird what its name meant. The eagle cocked its head proudly and told him. "Thank you," said Tim. Then, "What's it like? Being an eagle?"

"Whoever said I was an eagle? I haven't been a bird for quite some time now."

Tim thought the eagle was joking. "What are you then?"

The bird made a sound in its throat. "I am a toy. Somebody's idea of a plaything. Listen." With one great wing the eagle guided Tim's head up until it rested on its smooth breast. For a moment he heard the astonishingly quick drumming of the bird's heart. But it did not sound like a heart. It sounded like a woodpecker working on a tree.

"I don't understand," said Tim.

"It doesn't matter." The eagle shrugged. "Someday, perhaps, you will." It tilted back its head into a smile.

Tim held him tighter. "I will never forget you."

"Get on with you, then! You're getting my feathers wet!"

Marty had said good-bye in much the same way: abruptly, as if they might see each other the next day when, in fact, they'd probably never see each other again. Didn't the bird know how fond Tim was of it, how much he'd miss its stories and piercing laughter echoing off the cliffs? Perhaps he couldn't expect such things from a frog or a bird. But he had had nothing but quick endings lately and he hadn't gotten used to them.

The eagle watched as Tim lifted and coasted out of sight. Gradually, a tear swelled in its eye. "The child is no match for a monster," it whispered. "Do you hear, Mother Death? Do not let him face the Beast alone."

Soaring down from the mountain heights Tim coasted on the updrafts between the walls of great crevices. He dove and swirled and occasionally turned somersaults. It was all new to him; he was still learning the tricks of wind riding, the enfolding and lifting, the gentle play of cool air against his muscles, the way the wind withheld its massive unimaginable power in a tender yet sturdy embrace. He hadn't expected that: to feel as if he were being held. He had pictured himself commanding the wind, sailing it like a sea captain with a firm hold on the tiller. It wasn't that way at all. In its gracefulness it reminded him of the roll of clouds or the surge of a great waterfall. It was so much better than Bubble Sleep and almost as quiet, for he discovered that if he looked down or to the side, he had a silent flight. It was only when he looked forward that the wind would whistle in his ears.

The ground so far below him resembled one long tapestry of flags all stitched together to make a common quilt. Some green, some yellow, some striped, some overlaid by the brown fur of a bear. And weaving through it all at random intervals were the blue spiked backs of beasts he had seen in the Bubble Sleep—woods of pine huddled over the quilt like sleeping creatures sprawled in different postures of repose.

Far off to the south a giant grey cloud stood up on its haunches like a wave, stretching up as high as he could see, so that it hung like a shroud over the land, dividing it in two. So high was this wave Tim swore that if it ever crested, it could swallow the whole Kingdom, and still not crumble until it had reached the Shear, the unpassable precipice that protected their northern border from invaders. It was a monster. Flat at the top and scooped in a yawning arch down to its base, casting a deep blue shadow upon the land behind. In the gap beneath it, small clouds caught the sun and glowed a stark yellow, shedding sheets of rainbow to the ground.

It was then he saw the funnels of smoke that rose like giant swords out of the great golden plains—or what was left of them. They were no longer gold. Eastward, for as far as he could see, the land was burnt down to stubble. All was grey and black and still but for the slow drifting rivers of smoke: the remains of a landscape devoured by fire.

He recalled the eagle's words. "Find the Beast of fire but do not fight him. Look him in the eye and put the wind to sleep." When he had asked how he was ever going to find Tomen, the eagle had told him not to worry. Apparently he was on the right trail, and it was fresh.

Somehow he spotted on the vast desolate plain a small freckle of life: a survivor. He flew down and found a young sparrow clinging to the branch of a burnt-out tree. He sat beside it on the charred limb and saw its feathers had been singed off, leaving the skeleton of the wings on a bare shivering body. Its eyes were closed and its claws were locked in place. Tim was amazed that it was still alive.

He was reaching out to comfort it when he saw a strange black cloud approaching. A storm cloud? Impossible—it moved too fast. A cloud of smoke then? The way it coiled and undulated reminded him of maggots in the carcass of a squirrel. Portions of the cloud moved fast then slowed as if they dragged the rest of it behind. The shape finally resolved itself into a rushing swarm of birds. They lighted about him with a tremendous flurry of wings, as if the same wind that had stripped the leaves off the tree had changed its mind and, in one gust, had stuck them all back on.

He found himself surrounded by nearly every type of bird imaginable: sparrows, hawks, jays, finches. They cawed at him from all sides. Some scooted down the branches at him, shrilling and scolding, then darted back in fright. Some eyed him suspiciously. The tree shuddered under their weight. Finally, a shimmering green bird as small as his thumb, with wings that fluttered quicker than the eye, slipped down and hovered between him and the scorched bird. It shouted out in a fierce tiny voice: "Is he the Grounder's friend?"

"Yes!" replied the chorus of birds.

"Does he follow the Man in the Tree?"

"Yes!"

"Who brought the fire?"

"Yes!"

"Who burns our children?"

"Yes!"

"Must he pay?"

"Yes!"

"Must he die?" Tim had been so fascinated by the comical little squeak of the bird that he hadn't suspected it might be talking about him. Until it was too late.

"Yes!" replied the mob. Three hawks dove and rammed him in the chest, knocking him off the branch. It felt like he'd been hit by a handful of rocks, but it didn't hurt as much as when he landed on his back: Stars shot against his eyes.

The birds wasted no time; they came at him in waves, taking turns diving and pecking his face, legs, and belly. He rolled over but he could barely lift his head—he had lost his breath in the fall, so he lay helpless under their assault. They pulled out strands of his hair with their claws, stabbed their beaks into his neck—no matter where he covered himself they found an opening. When he finally got to his knees and wrapped his head in his arms, they peppered his back with their beaks like a hailstorm. When he could breath he shouted, "Wait!" But still the swarm pummeled him. "Stop it!" he cried, trying to beat them away with his hands, but this doubled their fury. They crowded the air like flies; when he breathed, their feathers filled his mouth and made him gag—there was no escape, no pause, no way to fight back. He was close to passing out when he remembered the eagle's crown feather in his pocket. He reached for it with a bloody hand, beaks nipping at his fingers, then held it aloft as he crouched on the ground shielding his face under his other arm. The pecks and bumps and screams and caws began to fade until, gradually, he was surrounded by silence.

Soon he chanced a peek: drifting tufts of many colored feathers were settling to the ground like snowflakes. Birds of every size encircled him, staring at the bright white feather in his hand. Tim tasted his own blood and coughed. Then, slowly, he knelt up, careful to hold the feather before his face: a shield against the mob.

A voice called down from the tree. "How fares my sister?"

It was a grey eagle.

"Your sister?" Tim replied, wiping his mouth with the back of his hand, remembering the stones. "She . . ." the word felt strange on his tongue. "She did not tell me about you."

"Neither has she told me about you."

"She is well. She is my friend."

The bird scowled. "You may have met the white one, Grounder. But she is a long time gone and nowadays, we choose our friends more carefully."

"She gave this to me."

"Or you took it. How do I know you are not a friend of the Maker of Fires? How do I know you haven't killed her?"

Tim had never been hated before. He did not know how to respond. So he told the truth. "You do not know. You have only my word and the feather of Dub."

The grey eagle was so shocked he nearly fell off his branch. Before warriors battle they exchange names. But only to their loved ones do they give the meaning. "You know her name? Then you have either killed her or loved her." The eagle sprang from the branch, twice flopped its wings, and coasted to the kneeling Tim. His landing cleared a hollow space on the down-covered earth. "What does it mean, Grounder? What does her name mean?"

"Twin."

The grey eagle sighed and closed his eyes: His sister was alive. Then cocking his head in a familiar gesture, he regarded Tim curiously. "Child? May I ask you? The white one . . . she taught you magic?"

Tim could hear the change in the bird's voice. Such politeness after such rudeness made him suspicious. "Yes?"

"Healing magic?"

"Yes, and other things."

"You must know the Man in the Tree."

"Never heard of him," said Tim, by now irritated by this interrogation. He stuffed the white feather back into his pocket.

Again, the green bird with the needle nose and invisible wings appeared before him and began to recite.

The Man in the Tree is a wicked man,
He burns our children to the land,
He turns them into balls of fire
And drops them in the lake.

"That's very interesting," said Tim, and with a puff of breath he blew the bird away.

"He has magic," the eagle said.

"He has a power we cannot fight," said the little bird, fluttering beside him.

"You don't say." Tim stood up wincing: He hurt everywhere.

"We thought you were on his side," the eagle explained.

Tim said nothing.

"Help us," said the little bird.

Without a word Tim walked away, and the birds parted quickly for his feet.

"Help us," said the eagle following him, waddling quickly to keep up.

Tim prepared to call up a wind and ride away and rid himself of this nagging bird.

"Do you see the mercy of Grounders?" the grey eagle squawked suddenly. "Mark how they turn their backs on the helpless!"

The boy turned, hands on hips, and faced the bird. He whispered to the wind, and the eagle was caught in an air pocket that flung him into Tim's outstretched hand. He grasped its neck tightly in his fist and looked it in the eye. "Mercy? I was going to help your little one, but you attacked me, accused me of burning your children, and nearly pecked me to death. You don't even apologize. You have a funny way of asking for favors."

The eagle's voice squeaked out of Tim's fist. "I'm sorry."

"You're a little late."

"You have the power!" coughed the bird. "Heal the Man in the Tree!"

"Why should I?"

"Heal him!" squeaked the eagle.

"Why should I?"

Every bird who looked upon the grey eagle thought the same thing: He better have a good answer. He did.

"He is your King."

After a long moment Tim set the bird down and released him, thinking, I've got to do something about my temper.

He followed the eagle for many miles over the scorched plains. East they flew, Tim calling up a fresh wind as soon as he had exhausted an old one—thanking it as it relinquished its hold. As they approached, across a series of low brown hills, a dark green lake that lay as still as if it were frozen, the eagle reared up and refused to go any closer. He left Tim, saying, "You'll find him on the other side."

Tim paused on the shore of the lake to wash his wounds. He found himself more bruised than cut; the beaks had seldom broken skin. Still, when he rose up clean and sore, there was a cloud of blood in the water at his feet. As Tim flew over the green water he saw himself reflected perfectly as by a mirror, and for a moment he enjoyed the image of a boy floating, arms outstretched against a cloudless sky. So he was taken totally off guard by the sudden jolt that petrified him in midair and left him dangling like a drop of rain on the tip of a leaf.

"No further!" a voice stormed from the shore.

One of Dub's warnings came rushing back to him: "Beware still water."

He thought: I have been a fool.

First he heard the sounds of creatures swirling and churning below him, casting a froth upon the otherwise still lake. Then he felt himself being drawn downward to the dark water in a slow hideous descent. He thought desperately of the eagle's feather resting in his shirt, but he could not reach it; his arms were pinned.

He could not call back the wind. He could not move his mouth.

He could not even close his eyes.

If only I could see him; if only he would show himself. And no sooner had the thought swelled in his mind than his descent abruptly halted.

The moment his mind became blank, he once again began to drop.

Why would he want to kill me? I've never even met him! And the instant the thought broke out, the descent stopped once again—but this time it did not resume.

Why does he torture me like this?

"Be quiet!" the harsh voice called out.

Who are you? thought Tim.

"No!" commanded the voice. "You *will* be quiet. You *will* stop talking. I can hear you!"

Tim's mind screamed: I've done you no harm!

"Be *quiet* and leave me alone!"

Unbind me and I will be silent.

"Tricks! You trick me! You say you will be quiet but you won't! There's no such thing anymore! You'll talk, talk, talk, just like all the others!"

But I won't, thought Tim. I promise.

"Stop! No promises. They mean nothing. He promised to heal me and he gave me voices. I didn't want voices, I wanted to hear! But they do not stop; they never stop. They taunt me even as I sleep. I . . . have . . . no . . . peace!" The voice wailed the word *peace* as if it were the only thing it ever wanted and the only thing it was ever denied.

If it was silence this pitiful creature wanted, then he would offer it. Tim forced his mind into a memory of the purest silence he'd ever known: a peaceful journey high above the turmoil of the world: the Bubble Sleep. Time drifted as in a lovely dream, and when eventually he heard the voice again, it had changed, softened into the cry of a troubled child.

"You meant it. You *can* give me silence. You—you *were* quiet! Please," it whimpered, "teach me this silence."

Tim was immediately freed. The winds were there to catch him and he coasted over the lake and landed softly on the shore. He didn't have to go far into the forest to find a strange tree. It was a sort of cage. The stocky branches had turned back upon themselves and intertwined to make a hollow cell in the middle. It looked very much like a hand which had frozen on its way to becoming a fist. He lifted upward to the top and found a place to stand. The cell was thick with coiled, twisted branches that allowed for only a few narrow openings. Tim had his first thought since his silence: Was this the dwelling of a hermit or an exile? A filthy arm jutted out of the cage and clenched Tim's neck.

"I could kill you!" a wild voice whispered.

Don't, thought Tim, reaching for the eagle's feather.

"I could snap your head off!"

Don't, Tim pleaded, pulling out the feather.

147

The voice became a giddy laugh that slid into a whine. "It hurts!"

The feather slipped from Tim's hand and he watched it flutter to the ground.

The voice sobbed. "I curse the day I asked to hear!"

Suddenly, the hand let go, and Tim had to brace himself against a fall. He heard a loud snoring and watched the creature in the tree fall forward out of the shadows, sound asleep, his mutilated face lodging in a gap between the branches. And Tim, completely unprepared for the shock, encountered for the first time, the ruin that had once been a man. King Simon.

Chapter eighteen

"COULD THE BIRDS REALLY SPEAK our tongue?" asked the Go-Boy, Nib.

"You've misunderstood," said the Teller. "I never said the birds could speak our tongues. I said birds talked a tongue that we could understand. The wizards put a gift into our minds that could translate their words. That gift has faded."

"Why couldn't King Simon fly?" asked a fat man near the back of the listeners. "Didn't he know the proper words?"

"Have you heard nothing I've said? King Simon couldn't ride the wind because the wind would not carry him. It was the wind's choice, not his. The magic was in the wind, not us. I mean . . . him."

The Captain chuckled, and drew his hand away from the yellow ear jewel he had been itching to point up to the sagging sails above them. "If anyone was ever on good terms with the wind, it seems they are no longer." He smiled down at the Teller.

"Perhaps the winds begrudge your passage?" said the little man. "As you begrudge mine."

The Captain scoffed. "Winds go where I tell them. They are beasts of burden."

"You are a learned man," replied the Teller. "Your sons must feel very proud of you."

At that the sailors caught their breaths and dared not look their Captain in the face. They knew: He had no sons. And they wondered if the Teller was a brave man or a fool.

."Your Captain's right." The Teller laughed, and all the sailors gladly felt the tension drain away. "A wind cannot choose its course. It cannot give or withhold its favor. Not anymore. That reminds me of the shortest story I know."

There once was a man with two choices. And he couldn't make up his mind, because he didn't want to give one of his choices away. He wanted the freedom of choice. This was the first unhappy man.

The Teller laughed a surprising wheezy laugh, like a drunken old woman. The sailors joined along.

"Now," he continued, "when a sailor has no wind he has only one choice: to wait. And waiting makes a good excuse for stories, does it not? So I shall resume."

As Tim clung to the gnarled bark of the branches and smelled the sap pooled in the blisters, he recalled the serene memory of bending trees. Once he had climbed a willow too thick to bend: Instead of yielding to his weight, the uppermost branch broke off in his hands and he fell a long way. Luckily, he landed on a patch of tall weeds and they nestled him gently down to earth. It was like settling into a soft bed after a long day. Tim understood now the longing he had felt when the trees were churning him madly about: it was the longing for flight.

Searching for an opening, he finally wedged into a small gap between two limbs. Across the interwoven branches that formed the floor of his cage, a man almost twice his age huddled in the corner. Yet he looked like a child who had been locked away in the dark. He slept a fitful sleep broken by starts and moans. It hurt to imagine his suffering.

Tim no longer feared him.

He had sensed that his anguished crowded mind needed quiet in order to be healed. So he had invited winds from the four corners of the world to come and form a cocoon of silence about the man, to enfold and shield him from any outward disturbance.

At least it was a start.

Bracing himself for the ordeal ahead, he quietly sat down beside him. Then placing the sleeping man's head on his lap, Tim shut his eyes and whistled three brief notes into his ear: It was the Spell of Return, the whippoorwill refrain his mother used to hum whenever his father was overdue from a tinker trip, whenever she missed him: "Coming Home? Coming Home?" Then laying his hands gently on the sleeping man's head, they began their passage.

Presently, the memories came.

Tim saw a string of bright summer days passed under one of the castle's towers, practicing archery. An uncommonly big man with a coarse red beard stood behind the young prince, correcting his stance and aim. The arrow flew and caught the straw target dead center. Jason smiled and he was flush with pride. Then a series of images flashed by so quickly Tim barely saw them: a horse, a stream, an empty smile. Then: a tall dark room filled with books—dusty books, picture books drawn with the hand of a master—and Tim could smell the musty air of the Book House. A chessboard: a white queen taking a black rook. It was night in a candlelit room and a young nurse stroked the head of a feverish boy propped up by massive pillows, tucked under a rich embroidered quilt, sipping a steaming sweet brew. She softly sang his name: Simon. His name *was* Simon. There was a painting of a lovely woman, and the old King sat under it weeping, covering his eyes. A hawk perched high on the turrets at noon, called out and startled a sleeping guard—Simon laughed.

An army on horseback, fully armored and carrying bright shields emblazoned with a familiar coat of arms: a lion wrestling a snake. From a high window the boy watched the children in the courtyard. He wanted to join them as they played in the mud, but he was the Prince and his father would say it would be unseemly. Guards chasing him as he ran laughing down a corridor holding a torch. A market of tents and wooden stalls, chickens clucking in cages and fruits hanging in clusters, the smell of freshly butchered pigs, shoemakers, tinkerers, farmers, spice traders, craftsmen calling out their wares, each trying to outshout the other. There was a huge throne room where tapestries hung from ceiling to floor: each telling the tale of a hero or a battle. Tim recognized the elkhorn throne his father had carved. Throughout the castle, down long halls that echoed and swirling steps of stone, dogs roamed freely. Tim shuddered. Gradually—as the sound of crashing surf diminished as he traveled inland— the sound of the memories faded, until all was a whisper, and as much as Tim strained to hear, he could only make out the occasional word. Yet the images grew more vivid in color and detail while becoming jumbled and brief.

There were faces—mournful, sympathetic. There were flashes of light, like the fireworks you make by knuckling your eyeballs. A row of bottles full of sticky blue fluid tottered and fell against each other, sending a cascade of broken glass. Tim set himself against the onslaught of a mad mind. The images of frenzy and panic dashed against him and scattered into pieces. Torches waved frantically in the night. A glimpse of a dragon. A hooded figure with no face—two eyes like fireflies floating in an arch of darkness. A mouthless word emerging like the sound of a woodpecker: Tick. Tick. Tick. A man leaping from a window. Ambushes and swordplay. A falling horse. A severed spine. Jason smiling but his eyes wept blood. A child alone in bed at night, crying out between flashes of lightning, "Mamma! Mamma! Mamma!" Finally, after what felt like hours, there was a long silence, as if the mind could spew up no more pain and had collapsed exhausted.

This would be the healing place.

Tim opened his eyes and spoke urgently to the four winds. Then, as the Teacher had instructed, he took a deep breath and exhaled into the face of the man. For a time nothing happened. But eventually a sound began to grow in the silence: a blizzard's howl. The deep dark began to come to light, first turning grey like a raincloud, then white like a winter morning, and finally it burst into brilliant color. Both Tim and Simon's mouths opened wide, and a sharp crack rang out of both: the sound of stone falling on stone.

Then there was a quiet so rich and gentle that Tim felt compelled to settle down for a nap. Yawning, he spoke to the winds: "No, we may not linger. It is his mind, and our visit is through." He said this because winds are very comfortable with people; they have a tendency to overstay their welcome. The winds left abruptly without a good-bye, for winds, though they are never purposely rude, have no sense of manners. Tim glanced lazily at the green glow of the sun through the treetop. King Simon lay motionless and pale; like the boy, he was drenched in the sweat of a long journey. Tim smiled once, then passed into sleep like a pebble sinking to the bottom of a lake.

Simon rose out of a delicious dream: a bird twittered and the trees whispered in the wind. He could not bring himself to discard it and enter the world of the waking. He clung to it till he realized it was not a dream: He had almost forgotten what the world sounded like. When it was not crowded with the cold sounds of thoughts and the fire of emotions it was a glorious feast of simple, varied, and wholesome noise. Every sound felt pure and new, as if it had been created that moment, especially for him.

He found to his astonishment that he was not alone. His hand rested on the arm of a sleeping boy. He reached out with his mind and saw the boy was dreaming of flying over a green lake—an exceptionally quiet dream, it was a pleasure to eavesdrop. But he pulled back in embarrassment: He knew he was intruding on something private. Funny. He had never felt that way before.

Though the boy's hair was matted with dried blood, his clothes torn, and his face looked freshly scratched and bruised, there was a hint of a smile on his lips. Suddenly, Simon was overwhelmed by a vast tenderness. He sat up bewildered, reluctantly removing his hand from the boy's arm. A branch creaked above him. He shook his head, tried to get it clear enough to think. On the one hand he felt as if he had known the boy for years, that he was in fact a loyal traveling companion. Now where did that come from? Yet, on the other hand he knew he was a complete stranger— he didn't even know his name. How did he get up in the tree? He gazed at the young boy and love pulsed inexplicably inside of him. He could not say why, but he felt he owed his life to him, whoever he was. My father felt nothing like this for me, he thought. Never. Finally, he could bear the suspense no longer; he nudged the stranger awake.

Tim rubbed his eyes and looked up. "Oh, hello," he said with a yawn. "How are you feeling, Simon?"

"Wonderful," Simon admitted, although he hadn't known it was true until he said it.

This pleased the boy very much. Simon could not keep from staring at him.

"Oh, I forgot . . ." Tim shyly introduced himself. Then, crinkling his eyebrows, he asked: "Are you really the King?"

Simon nodded.

"My father built your throne," the boy said proudly.

Simon frowned. "You're John-John the woodcutter's son?"

"Yes."

"May I ask what you're doing here?"

Tim smiled. "That's a long story." Then, looking at the scratchings on Simon's pale face and the deep dark circles around his eyes, he asked, "Are you sure it's better now?"

"Yes." It was then that the young King realized the voices were gone. The nightmare had finally ended. "Did you do that, Tim?"

"With some help."

"Thank you," said Simon, feeling quite ridiculous. "Thank you . . .

thank you . . ." He nearly got it right the last time, but something caught in his throat. He wanted to tell the boy that he had never felt so free and that he wasn't used to it yet, that if he ever needed someone to stand up for him he would be the man, and that it was awfully good to be well again. But of course he could not find the words, and he cried like a fool.

Chapter nineteen

"DO YOU SEE WHAT HAPPENED to the King?" the Teller asked. "He got a bad story in him.

"I see you do not understand. Listen, then. There are stories that hide themselves inside of us like bats inside a cave. For instance:"

There once was a woman from Sotton's Bay. A bad story got inside her and she was so young she believed it. Her husband was a harbor guard and he worked all night, and once a week she'd wake him at dawn to say what a pretty sunrise it was. And when her husband would growl at her, as any man might, she'd first look hurt, and then look huffy, and then she wouldn't speak to him for days.

The married men on deck laughed.

You see, somebody told her a story once—someone she needed, someone she loved. And the point of the story was that she was bad. And she believed it. A bad story like that gets inside of you and there's only one thing to do: Prove it. Tell it over and over again, the way you tongue an aching tooth.

So she'd irritate her man until he'd bark, and she'd feel justified. She'd take her revenge, but on the wrong person, and she'd feel powerful. She would decide when she would be hurt. She could keep the illusion that the bad story was not about her but him. She could believe she was the Teller, not the Tale.

It was easier to feel her husband's better and pretend she didn't care what he thought of her than to feel the poison tale inside. It is easier to tongue a bad tooth than to face the pain of extraction.

It is always easier to keep a rotten tale than to learn a new one.

The mast above them creaked. And the Teller continued.

✳   ✳   ✳

THE Gift

When the tree began to shiver Tim and Simon stared at each other. It was not the wind; it was not the earth: The tree seemed to shake of its own accord. Yet it was not a violent shaking; it was rather like a child tugging at its mother's dress. Through the tangled branches of the cage Tim thought he saw a face—but unlike any he had ever seen: The skin was pale grey, the eyes were wide and black, and it had no mouth. He was calling up a shielding wind when Simon stopped him.

"Don't! I know them!"

"Them?" Tim asked.

Then he saw another one. Same face, same grotesque, passive stare, squatting on a branch and trembling. With a mixture of disgust and fear he realized that every branch he turned to had a similar creature perched upon it. They were surrounded.

"What are they?"

"Griffs."

"What are they doing?"

"Trying to get our attention, I suppose. Do you see that quiet one there? He's not dancing like the others."

"Dancing?" said Tim.

"The older one, he wants us to go with him."

"How can you tell he's older?" Tim asked. "They all look the same to me."

Simon smiled. "It's a long story."

The Griffs pried back the branches of the cage to form an opening wide enough for the both of them. It was a long way down. Simon was wondering how they were going to descend when the boy wrapped them in a wind pocket that floated them gently to the ground.

"That was marvelous! I must have tried that spell a hundred times. I could never make it work!"

"You've got to know how to ask," Tim explained with a shrug.

Ask? thought Simon. It never occurred to him to ask. "Watch out!" he cried suddenly, pulling Tim away.

The Griffs were falling out of the tree, bouncing and spinning crazily on the ground like ripened fruit. Tim covered his mouth to hide his laughter. The creatures collected themselves, and walking as if their feet were shackled, they escorted Simon and Tim away from the lake and the tree. It wasn't long before Tim's repulsion at the Griffs dissolved, and he began to find them rather charming. Shyly, he let his hand brush against one, and felt the pliant, shell-like skin.

After a time they came upon a clearing where a huge old man sat sleeping on a large stump. A wreath of wild red berries crowned his head. His chin rested upon his chest, and his long grey beard hung down to his belly. Gnarled hands lay limp upon his lap, and his bare toes peeked out from under the folds of his long cloak of autumn leaves. A Griff padded over to his side and tapped him on the arm. He mumbled, blinked open his eyes, then stretched out his arms and released a glorious yawn that echoed through the woods.

"I know him, too!" whispered Simon.

"You seem to know everybody," said Tim.

The old man squinted at the sky and frowned. "Why, it's not even noon yet!" he scolded the Griffs. "And I was *dreaming*! You'll get a story when it's time to turn to the trees—not a moment sooner. Ah! I cannot believe how spoiled you're getting! What's that? Visitors?"

His eyes skimmed the faces of the Griffs until he saw the two humans they surrounded.

"I know *you*!" he said to Simon. "Just give me a moment and I'll get the name. Oh. Ah. So much to remember in a lifetime, so little to forget. Ah! Got it! Samuel!"

"Simon," corrected the King.

"Well, I was close, wasn't I? Yes. Well. One can't be expected to remember all the names, can one? Mother Death, no! Why in my day I've met more people than a, than a—what was that name again?"

"Simon."

"Right! Simon! Have to repeat it sometimes. Helps clear the head. So what brings you here?"

"The Griffs brought us here."

"Ah, the Griffies! They bring pretty much everybody, sooner or later. I'd never get to meet anyone otherwise." The old man laughed, rustling the leaves of his cloak. "Yes, indeed. Plenty of visitors in my day . . . armsmen, wizards, dragons, even a woman or two. Ever met a woman?"

"Yes."

"Strange creatures. They've got these two big lumps," he said, showing them with his hands. "Make the damnedest noises you'd ever want to hear. Well, then, Samuel, what can I do for you?"

"You've done very much already. You took me in when I was half-mad, and I believe you provided for me. For that I give you thanks."

A light sparkled in the old man's eyes. "Why, of course! You're the one we put in the tree! I'd have never gotten any sleep otherwise. Well, Sam, for a man who'd been run through with a sword, with a mind like scrambled eggs, you look quite fit!" The old man glanced at Tim. "So, who's your friend?"

"This lad healed me."

"I see," said the old man, and for a moment he drifted away, knitting his brow and stroking his beard with deliberation. Suddenly he put a look on Tim that would have startled any man with its intensity. "And how'dcha do that, laddy?"

"I had help," Tim answered.

The old man locked his eyes upon the boy. Bracing both hands on his knees, he stood up, his cloak of leaves crackling as he rose. Sitting, his true height was impossible to judge, but as he stood it became apparent: He was a giant. No longer the drowsy babbling codger, he looked down upon Tim with a terrible fierceness, and though his words were softly spoken, they rang like lightning. "What kind of help?"

Tim did not waiver. "Winds from the four corners."

A darkness passed over the old man's eyes. "How sleeps the wind?"

"It grows restless," said Tim.

The giant folded his hands behind his back, and immediately, all the Griffs shuffled behind him, away from Tim and Simon.

"Who wakes the wind?"

"A pet of the Usher of the Night."

Simon turned to look upon Tim with new eyes. He had hoped never to hear that name again. What had this boy to do with that black wizard?

The giant calmly said, "I am Disabla. The Eater of Magic." He pointed a finger at Tim and whispered, "By the Maker I command you to disclose your given name and gift!"

"My name is Tim. I ride the winds and stir the powers of the air."

"No man rides the wind! It has long been asleep. The last wizard died ages ago. Who are you to claim the ancient rites of wind passage and power?"

Tim hesitated. He did not know why the giant was angry.

"Answer me, boy!"

"I am the Wind Tamer," said Tim.

The words hung in the air. Simon trembled as the giant stepped forward, reached down, and picked up Tim under the arms. He held him aloft like a father admiring a newborn son. "So. You have come at last."

Over a delicious meal of baked apples and rhubarb they became acquainted with their host, the Magic Eater. To their wonder he confessed to being a creation of the last wizards, a failsafe against the rampant spread of magic. They had given him a great hunger and a great gift: the ability to consume and thrive on spells and charms, and in his time he had absorbed many. But early on his diet and interest had dwindled. The wiz-

ards died, taking most of their magic with them. He found himself restless and bored with the great task he'd been left with. Until recently his
meals of magic, when they came at all, were thin and unsatisfying—nothing like Simon's spells, nothing he could really sink his teeth into: "Rather
like drinking water all day." Soon the dullness had grown so great that it
was all he could do to sleep all morning, manage a yawn or two, then doze
away the afternoon basking in the sun, following stray thoughts like butterflies.

One evening he woke and found a creature sleeping at his feet. Though
it had no mouth and could not talk, he found that without much effort
he could understand its thoughts and moods. It turned out that he and
others like him were the botched experiments of a local alchemist. They
were made to be Lie Catchers: the results of interbreeding and spells.
When exposed to deceit or outright falsehood they instantly turned to
stone.

The alchemist had planned to sell them to the courts of justice, but
they had proven unreliable: Somehow they had developed a powerful hom-
ing instinct; they would always manage to escape, find others of their
kind, and hide. Aside from this craving for their own company, they were
very passive creatures who fed on moonlight. They were trusting and loyal
but rather dense. They were also just what the lonely old Magic Eater
needed to cheer him up. So he was not too surprised and not at all disappointed when the next night he woke to find several more creatures huddled about his feet. It got to be a ritual: Every evening the creatures
multiplied, and soon their numbers resembled a field of giant grey eggs
until one day no more came, and he ironically dubbed them Griffs—a
variation of the mythical Eagle/Lion, for "They looked like somebody
stuck the worst halves of two animals together."

Later that evening, as they lounged before a fire, Tim and Simon
watched as the old giant stretched and sat and, plucking a leaf off his
cloak, dipped it in his steaming mug to make tea. Then the Magic Eater

told a bedtime story to the Griffs—a nightly ritual they demanded before they went to sleep in the trees to soak up moonlight.

This is a story about the very first cloud who fell. One night he passed over a small
lake. The moon was full behind him, and looking down upon the waters, he saw his own
reflection. He found that he glowed yellow in the moonlight and he was much taken with
himself. So much so that he decided that he was by far the most handsome thing in the world.
So he spent the rest of his days hovering over the lake, watching himself and delighting in
his image. And like every cloud, he gathered water to himself, for this is how clouds eat, and
when they are full they cry because they must go on and they hate to see the water go. As
the days passed, more and more water rose up into the cloud's body. And he became darker
and darker, and heavier and heavier, and soon no sunlight could pass through him—he had
become a deep grey blotch against the sky. He looked and looked but he could no longer see
himself in the lake. In the day all he could see was a dark hole in the sky where he used to
be. And at night he saw nothing but a dark space where the stars would not shine.

Many winds passed him by and offered to push him to another place, but he was a
stubborn cloud and would not be moved. Many clouds rolled by and laughed at him and
called him a fool. But still he wouldn't budge. Eventually he had drawn up all the water
in the tiny lake and there was nothing but a soggy swamp beneath him. By now the cloud
was so heavy with water that it was all he could do to squat just above the treetops. And
he sulked and sulked until he had convinced himself that he was the unluckiest cloud in the
world. It never occurred to him to cry and be done with it.

And one morning when he was sleeping, he sank all the way down to the ground. And
his body spread out through the swamp and the forest around it, and before he could awake
he became a deep, billowing fog. And to this day he sleeps in the cool ground when the sun
is hot—for too much sun is death to fog—and when the night comes he rises out of the
ground and roams the swamp and forest in an endless search for the lost lake. He was a
proud cloud, and proud clouds are ashamed of crying. You will know them when you see
them: They are dark, they move grudgingly, and they will not cry.

Suddenly, the giant clapped his hands loudly and said, "To bed my little ones! Morning comes quicker when you're not waiting for it!"

As the drowsy Griffs roused and filed away to their trees, each of them touched one of the mighty hands of the Magic Eater. Simon lay sleeping against a stump, snoring loudly. The giant crooked a finger at Tim and walked slowly, as if nothing in the world could hurry him. Still, Tim had to step briskly to keep up with his enormous strides. He took the boy to a high hill overlooking the forest. The old man gazed into the sky. "This man, this Usher . . . what do you know of him?"

"Not much. My friend could tell you more."

"Your friend," grunted the old man. "Your friend is too afraid of him. He may be healed, but fear clouds his mind. He cannot tell me what I need to know."

"What's that?"

"The name. I need to know the name of his power."

Tim did not understand, but something brought the image of a great black bird to mind. "Do you know about Tomen?"

"Tomen," repeated the old man, and he grew very still.

"The Beast with no heart," Tim continued. "He is the one I seek." After he told him the rest of the story, the old man did not speak for a long time.

"Tomen," he finally muttered. "Oh, this is a terrible riddle. I doubt the wizards bargained for this." The Magic Eater lifted an arm and pointed up to the night sky. "You see that star? It lies at the tip of that group that resembles a leaf. That is where the Masters came from. Ages ago—long before you were even a thought in the Maker's mind—that star died."

"But it shines," said Tim.

"The light we see is a memory. It comes to us long after it gave up all its light. It hangs like a rock in the sky. That is Tomen. A dead star that still shines." The giant placed a huge hand gently on Tim's shoulder. "Child? I know where you can find the Usher."

"Where?"

"One of my favorite Griffs was stolen—snatched up in the talons of a huge black bird. Some others followed his scent to a book house south of here. The last message they sent me before they were killed was that he was chained to the wall high above the gate. I would have rescued him myself, but my parameters—"The old man stopped when he saw Tim's face. "My . . . area of influence is limited. If he lives . . . if you could bring him back, I would be most grateful."

"Of course I will," Tim replied. He touched the leaf cloak of the giant. "But I do not know the way."

"Your friend does. It was his father's book house. He abandoned it when his queen died. It used to be her favorite place. The Usher lives there now."

"Please come with me," said Tim.

"Have you forgotten? I am the Magic Eater. Were I to go with you I would make you powerless. No doubt you'll need all your powers to face the Usher. No. I cannot be your companion. But don't worry. I will send help when you need it. And besides, you have your friend Samuel. Hold that up to the light and see if it doesn't make shade!"

Tim looked over the vast forest under the vast night sky and felt very small.

"And, Tim," Disabla added. "Don't forget to put the wind to sleep, eh?"

Chapter twenty

THE NEXT MORNING TIM AND Simon woke to an immense quiet. The Magic Eater was gone, no Griffs were in the treetops, and they found beside them two leather packs stuffed with apples. After a breakfast and a cold wash in a nearby stream, Tim explained the Magic Eater's request. Simon was not enthused.

"Have you lost your senses? He took my only friend's mind and turned it to mush! He can make you kill someone you love! Do you really hope to challenge that?"

"I promised," said Tim, as if he hadn't heard a word Simon said.

"Well, I *didn't*! I admit I was a fool for dabbling in magic, for thinking I could match such a twisted monstrous power. But I'm not such a fool as to make the same mistake twice!"

"Fine," said Tim.

"And for what?" he yelled. "A Griff? What possible difference can one more Griff make? There are plenty of others just like him! I'd be amazed if he wasn't already stoned. Hell, *I've* stoned a few of them myself. That's partly why they put me in the tree—to keep them away from me. You don't really think that Griff stood a chance against the Usher?"

"You're probably right. But the only way I know how to find Tomen is to find the Usher."

"That's the last thing on earth I want to do! I mean just the thought of looking in his eyes . . . I'm sorry! I'm not interested!"

"Fine then. Just tell me how to get there. I'll go alone."

"You'll go alone? You'll go *alone*? You'll get your bloody head torn off! *I* was half-mad and I froze you in midair. What do you think *he's* capable of?"

"I'll find out," said Tim.

Simon shut his eyes, shook his head, and let out one long disgusted sigh. I knew there was a catch, he thought. It was too easy. He couldn't just heal me. He couldn't let it go at that. It couldn't have been some warty old healer. Thanks for the cure. Here's some gold. Good-bye. It had to be some bloody innocent fool who can't leave well enough alone. Please Mr. Usher, if it isn't too much trouble, can I have that Griff back? Thank you, sir! Dammit! Why couldn't he have left me in the tree? Why couldn't he mind his own business? Why, oh, why do I like this boy so much?

"Oh hang it all!" said Simon. "Let's go."

The trip, though it was solemn, was not without its merriment. They saw a rainbow. They found clear, cool ponds where Simon taught Tim how to swim. They spent long afternoons dozing under trees. Squirrels came cautiously begging for food, and when not startled they would eat nuts out of their hands. For a few days they were followed by a mangy little brown rabbit who, despite persistent efforts, could not be coaxed closer than twenty paces. Simon dubbed it Fred after someone he had known at the castle: an affable boy with a quirky smile.

Each morning Fred would be watching when they woke; each evening it would circle the firelight. Somehow they felt reassured by its presence, as if it were a sentinel against the wilder darker things they stalked. "Mighty Fred has the night watch," Simon would say before bedding down, and they would laugh and rest easier. But one day Tim looked back and Fred was gone. They expected him to return the next day, and the next, but they never saw the little rabbit again.

For the rest of their journey they would regularly look back upon their steps, feeling as if they'd left someone behind, someone who belonged: an easy friend whom they had taken for granted.

They had come to the rocky hills of the Southlands: abandoned for the most part due to the lack of deep soil for farming. It was here they saw a strange procession of boys pass by on the horizon. Their heads were bowed as they walked silently—from a distance it looked like they'd been sent away for punishment. Their steps were sluggish and their arms dangled at their sides. One small lad trailed the group, breathing heavily, struggling to keep up.

"They look half-asleep," Tim observed.

"Where could they be going?" asked Simon, knowing they were far from any town.

"My father told me of a legend that says the further south one travels the more foolish he becomes."

"There may be something to that," said Simon.

"Do you feel it, too?"

"I'm not sure what I feel. It seems like all the colors are getting duller and all the smells are the same."

"Magic?"

"I wouldn't call it magic," Simon replied. "It's more like someone's kicked the wind out of this land and it still hasn't gotten up off its knees."

The next day they happened upon the skeleton of a bull near a stream. It had been a huge beast: The thick ribs curved upward to form an archway tall enough for Tim to walk through—which gave him an idea.

"What are you doing?" asked Simon as Tim grabbed hold of one of the ribs and started bending it back and forth to snap it from the spine.

"Just as I thought," said Tim, peering down into the end of the curved white bone. "The marrow's dry."

"So?"

"So, it's hollow." Tim put his mouth to the bone hole and blew with all his might. A cloud of dust puffed out of the far end which rested on the ground. When he blew again, a ragged throaty note tooted out.

Simon laughed. "Whatever made you think of that?"

Tim shrugged and ran his hand up and down the sun-bleached bone.

"Do you play?" asked the King.

"No. But I bet if I carved some holes in this . . . Hand me that sharpie." It was something his father used to say in his workshop, to make the boy feel useful.

Simon snatched and passed him the splinter of bone and Tim started to bore holes in the flat top side of the rib.

"Gosis got that one, eh?" Simon said.

"Huh?"

"Gosiloaches. You never heard of them?"

Tim shrugged. The word did sound familiar.

"That's what got this bull, by the looks of it. We're near the marsh-lands now, you know. Damp. Mucky. They say it's cursed. The fog gets so thick your mind starts seeing things in it. But you do have to watch out for the swamp gosis—or gosiloaches, as they call them."

Simon told the tale with the proud authority of a local.

Rumor has it the wizards had something to do with them. Brown scaled creatures no bigger than my hand. Shaped like a wad of bread dough. They travel in pools and dart up out of the water and latch onto their prey: deer, foxes, rabbits. They suck the blood out. After they feast they bloat up like a ball and lie still for hours, sometimes on land, sometimes bob-bing on the water like apples. Southern children used to creep up on a school of gorged gosiloaches and squash them underfoot. Dangerous game. But the gosis soon learned to at-tack at night so they'd have ample time to digest before morning. They're terribly dangerous when hungry, but totally helpless when fed. They are spineless. Bones being the only thing they lack and the only thing they leave—that is, the only thing they cannot eat.

"Maybe we'll see some," said Tim cheerfully.

"Please, no." Simon rolled his eyes. "It'll be the last thing we'll ever see."

Tim dusted the shavings off the bone and found that by covering and uncovering the hole as he blew, he could play two notes. Obviously the rib was too unwieldy to take with them, so they stashed it in a tree, for their return trip. Simon marked the trunk with a cross.

THE Gift

Early the next morning Simon woke to find himself alone. It was, he realized, the first time since his hermitage in the tree that he was without company. An embarrassing panic seized him and he tried for a minute to reason with the fear that flayed about his chest and swelled into his throat like a crowd escaping a burning room only to jam themselves in a doorway. Stop that now, he scolded his body. He's a powerful lad. He healed me; surely he can take care of himself. He began to breath deeply, as Jason had once instructed him, and eventually his body relaxed. Then, he discovered a more disturbing though less obvious fear that lurked within, somewhere close to his heart. "He's left me," he whispered. "The bastard's gone and left me."

Damn! thought Simon. I hardly know this lad. How did he get so deep inside of me?

"Tim?" he called out.

No answer.

"Tim!" he called again, trying as best he could to keep the fear out of his voice.

The forest was thick around him. No wind in the trees.

Damn.

Finally, he cast out his mind and searched the woods. And just when he was about to give up he caught an echo of the boy's presence: a happy tune Tim was humming in his mind. It felt to Simon like the music he had heard in his dreams: haunting, lovely, indescribable, as if dreams had their own private scales and instruments that could not survive in the waking world.

He followed the lingering melody until he picked up the suggestion of a path: broken weeds, stomped grass, and in a muddy clearing, the clear imprint of a boy's foot filling slowly with strange water: Rainbows oozed upon the surface, as on the skin of a bubble. He was close now.

Tim's trail led him out of the woods. It disappeared over the lip of a steep hill and coming over the rise, he looked over a huge valley that fell sharply below him. It looked like a giant trough had been dug by an immense tool, or, perhaps, a boulder as big as the moon had fallen to earth, crashed and slid for miles, scouring a groove into the ground, leaving a wake of rubble, stone, and soil. Seeking a way down into the green and rocky valley, Simon followed the path and the misty echo of Tim's mind.

As he descended Simon grew more alarmed, for he discovered Tim's trail became a ledge around a red rock cliff. There were gaps in the ledge, and though leapable, they were a fearsome prospect: Birds flew under his feet.

Tim, if I were your father, I would whip you.

Cold wind assaulted his hands and face. At times he had to lean against the sheer cliff and shuffle sideways, trying not to look down. Once Simon thought he was stranded, but eventually, he found a foothold that let him crawl down onto a promontory jutting out from the face of the cliff. Tim's mind pulsed louder now. Where the spit of red rock met the cliff Simon found a small cave.

Had Tim been looking for a sheltered place to spend the night?

Simon crawled inside, and ducking under a low ceiling, saw light. The shallow entrance opened into a much larger room. A room obviously made by tool: It formed a smooth and perfect upside-down bowl in the red rock. At the top of the dome was a pattern of holes: the source of light.

Tim stood under them, looking up.

"What is this place?" asked Simon, which was the third question on his mind. He had to restrain himself from asking the first two.

"Isn't it wonderful?" the boy replied.

"You might have told me," said Simon, folding his arms over his chest.

Tim looked at him, not understanding.

"Traipsing off alone like that. What if something happened to you?"

Tim looked at him and shrugged. "I can take care of myself." Then seeing his scowl, he added, "I wouldn't have left you, Simon."

The King held up his hands as if that were the furthest thing from his mind, as if the boy had misunderstood. But, of course, he hadn't.

"I won't," said Tim. "I wouldn't. Alright?"

Simon could not reply. He swallowed and nodded.

Tim looked back to the holes in the ceiling. They were hollow wells that extended up into the rock, widening out like horns and letting in a strange twilight.

Simon, meanwhile, wandered the perimeter of the bowl and found upon its rock face many paintings: the work of children it seemed, for they only rose as high as his waist. They were glyphic: circles, squares, triangles, dots in circles—painted, apparently, with shimmering black ink; they caught the beams of light Tim stood under. The floor was of a different rock altogether: yellow and polished and reflective as quartz. Blue veins and cracks ran beneath his boots, crisscrossing like a cobweb.

"Look, here!" called Tim.

He'd found a type of sword embedded in the floor. But though it shined like any fine blade, it was white as a tooth and had no grip.

"I wouldn't touch it," Simon was saying, but—too late—Tim had already given it a tug. It shifted on the floor like a smithy's lever, and from deep inside the rock they heard the shriek of a monster and the clatter of a thousand swords striking shields. Tim backed against the concave wall. Simon ran to him and stood between the boy and the white sword, which tilted and shuddered like a serpent in a fever.

The room began to hum, loud and soft, as if a swarm of wasps was circling round them. The wall Tim braced himself against picked up the song and sent shivers against his back.

A light came up through the yellow jewel of the floor, and Simon could see that what he took to be blue veins were thick worms that breathed and swelled beneath his feet.

They were too frightened to move. The five holes in the ceiling were shedding dust to the floor below—mites that glowed and pulsed as in a beam of sun. They swirled and swirled until they formed five perfect shafts: each filled with a whirlpool of green light.

The glyphs and fingerpaintings began to press impossibly against the concave face of red rock at the margins of the room, like children poking their faces into sheets hung out to dry. The flat circles and squares became translucent jewels: each lit from behind as if from a candle. The various crosses, shapes, and figures confidently acquired dimension. It was as if one moment Simon had been peering at a painting of a room, and the next, he had walked into that room.

A type of shelf ran around the circular cave. It reminded Tim of his father's workbench and its display of tools—he couldn't grasp its purpose any more than he could as a child, looking up at the mysterious instruments on his father's workshop wall.

There was a great hissing sound and a terrible *bong* that echoed through the cavern and made them wince. A giant had rung a bell and they were clinging to the clapper.

The hair on their heads lifted of its own accord and their scalps tingled.

Neither had any thought of using his magic. This was so obviously a place beyond their powers. They couldn't imagine the intent of the creature who had hewed this specter from a mountain, the power that could make light dance at will, the mind that could conceive of hiding a chest of jewels in stone. They felt, though they would not talk of it until later, that they were in the belly of a great beast, and that at any moment they would die.

In a blink, tongues of blue light clutched them and held them fast.

"I want to go home," cried Tim.

Simon shouted an unlocking spell that might have battered down the door to a dungeon, but the bonds of light only wavered, then held them tighter. Another chest of jewels emerged from the middle of the floor: astonishing gems with colors they had no words for and shapes not struck by a jeweler's tool but frozen in some molten mold.

In the center of the room an apparition rose up in a waterfall of light, a shape formed by cascading sheets of pale blue and floating behind the green bars like a ghost in a cage. It shifted, pulsed, and resolved into a shape resembling an elongated blue shell.

The apparition spoke, but in no language they recognized.

"Begone!" Simon bellowed.

And the ghostly shell mimicked him with alarming accuracy, trying out the strange word on its tongue, familiarizing itself with its contours. It screeched it, sang it, stretched it out, and clipped it into its component sounds.

"What can we do?" said a terrified Tim.

And the ghost did the same with the boy's words: mimicked and repeated them as some birds are said to imitate their masters.

"I don't know, Tim," said Simon.

"I don't know," repeated the specter of the blue shell in the voice of a dragon, spinning fast and faster as it took the phrase and made it its own. "Idunno Idunno Idunno Idunno."

A blue light exploded.

When they opened their eyes they saw behind the bars of light: a face. It had Tim's eyes and Simon's thin beard. It had no mouth.

"I know," it said in a voice that sounded exactly as if Tim and Simon were saying the same word at the same time.

"I do," the harmony repeated.

"Simon, it's talking," said Tim in wonder.

The face looked at the boy and said his name. Or rather, it said this: "Mit. Tim. Mit. Tim. Trans. Tim. Off. Tamer."

Then it turned to Simon, and saying his name, it formed his face. Then it became both of them again.

"This is deep magic," said Simon.

The boy tried to move, but the strands of light would not yield.

"Magic," said the voice.

Tim had a thought. He asked the blue face, "Can you let us go?"

"Go?" it repeated.

"Can you unbind us?" asked Tim.

"Tim go," the face said. And immediately the glowing straps slid off the boy. They folded together like the petals of a flower, until they formed a headless stalk of blue, which dove into the yellow gem floor like a tongue into a mouth.

"How did you do that?" asked Simon.

"Simon, too?" asked Tim. And the King was immediately freed.

"Simontoo," the specter said.

As they stepped closer to the cell of light it watched them carefully. After a time, Tim smiled, and the face grew a mouth and returned the compliment.

"Did you notice?" said Simon. "It's only using the words we say."

"I notice," said the face.

"It's learning," said Tim.

"I learn," said the voice.

"That means something," said the King, furrowing his brow. "It started talking just after I gave out that opening spell. Maybe magic works on it, but in a different way."

"A different way," the face repeated.

"The wizards," said Tim, looking about. "I bet this is their place."

"Wizards." The voice smiled. "Keyed."

"We didn't say that word," said Tim.

"Maybe it's getting smarter," said Simon.

There was a whirring sound. The face began to age before their eyes. It grew a long white beard. And it lost all the features of Tim and Simon.

174

"Are you a ghost?" asked Tim.

"Contradiction. Superstition. Wait."

"Didn't get that. Did you, Tim?"

"Sounded like nonsense."

"Prime. Load. Wait."

"This is very strange," said Simon.

"What kind of magic would make this?"

"Wizard mythos. Husk potential. Link. Frame. Instruct."

Then, as if it were the most natural thing in the world, the face of the old man beamed at both of them. "Welcome, lads. What can I do for you?"

Tim and Simon looked at each other.

"I apologize for the delay and any confusion it may have caused. I have been long asleep. Are you hungry?"

"As a matter of fact—" said Simon.

"We're famished," said Tim.

There were two goblets of fluid resting on the floor at Simon's feet.

"Drink." The old man nodded encouragingly. "You needn't fear. I am no threat to you."

They drank the darkling brew, and it was delicious, sweeter than any cider they had ever tasted.

"Hits the spot," the old man said.

Simon looked at Tim.

"What are you?" asked Tim.

"I am all my master's knowledge." Noting their faces, it added, "I suppose you would call me a library."

"What's a library?" whispered Tim to Simon.

Simon shrugged.

The Shell Man offered, "A collection of books?"

"You're not a ghost?" asked Tim.

"No. My visage is tuned to your spectrum in a mirror form."

"Let me understand this," said Simon, shaking his head. "You're a book house without books that looks like the ghost of an old blue man?"

"Exactly," said the man.

"You're not alive?" asked Tim.

"Correct. I am a construct of light. I look and sound as you need me to. My design is beyond you, I'm afraid."

"*He's* afraid." Tim smirked.

"That's not what he means, I think," said Simon. "Where are your masters?"

"Most are gone. Their husks broke down. Though one has stasised, his current symbiotic emergence is ineluctable beyond the enormous power he is expending to sustain his host as he transmogrifies decay—"

"*Stop it!*" Simon bellowed. "You're giving me a headache."

The old man paused. "You require less . . . context?"

"You make no sense," Tim clarified.

"Wait . . . Wait . . . Wait." The old man smiled. "Would you like me to tell you a story?"

Chapter twenty-one

AND THE BLUE SHELL MAN began to speak in a different voice altogether, as if he were reciting a poem he had committed to memory.

There once were songs who knew only night.

Songs no one had ever sung.

And what good is a song without a singer?

A song without a singer is like a story no one has ever told.

A song without a singer is like a wind without wings to ride it.

Then one day the songs found a vessel. A vessel that had been broken and abandoned by its Captain. A ship that could take them on long journeys. A ship that could hear their songs, though it could not sing them. And they gave themselves to the ship. They healed it. And upon that ship they fled their darkening home and sailed across the long night, looking for new lands and new creatures who could hear their songs and sing them.

They traveled many years, to many strange lands. But they could find nothing to nourish them. And they moved on. They found many wonderful creatures. But the creatures could not hear the songs, or, on hearing them, they died. So they moved on.

And on one beautiful green land where the air was clear and the water was blue and deep they found some simple creatures who might one day grow to hear their songs and sing them.

So they settled on this green land. And made it their home. And visited the people.

But soon, they found, they could only visit; they could not stay. There was not enough room for them. The space between the creatures' ears was too small for them to fit in all their songs, for they had many. And so, through much trial and error, they made the space bigger. They helped the simple creatures grow, and the songs entered into them like a wind into a cave.

And though they felt relief at having finally found a place to put their songs, they wanted more. They wanted to breathe the clear air, and taste the blue water, and touch the green land. They wanted bodies. They desired to settle in the people and make them their home.

And so they learned and grew the people of the land into another type of ship, a ship that could carry them into the day, as the other ship had carried them through the night. And when it was big enough to hold them they took possession.

And the songs lived in the space between the ears, and spoke with the tongue of the people of the green land. And they gave them gifts to recompense them for the long times of many trials and errors.

And they called these people ships, but they were really husks.

And they called these people homes, but they were really hosts.

And they called these people singers, but they were really instruments that the songs could play themselves upon.

When he had finished, the Shell Man had lost some of his color: He glowed a paler blue behind the bars of light.

"The Masters were the songs. You were the ship," said Simon, clarifying.

"Yes. They needed my substance to survive. They were so nearly nothing." He smiled.

"How did I manage to wake you?" asked Simon.

"You uttered the disable illusion command which dissolved my dormancy."

"What?"

"You said: 'Begone.' "

"Oh."

"Thank you for unbinding me."

Simon bowed. "You're welcome."

"What is your name?" Tim asked.

"I am called Caine."

"Can I do anything else for you, Caine?" asked Simon.

THE Gift

Shock settled into the face of the Shell Man so suddenly that Simon wondered if he might have offended him. After a time, he said, "That's . . . very thoughtful of you. I—I hesitate to impose upon your goodwill." The face blinked and frowned, troubled by thoughts it could not voice. Then the Shell Man changed the subject. "I have learned that your kind values foresight. Would you allow me to analyze and project the odds of your mission?"

"Alright," said Tim before Simon could stop him.

The boy again, sighed the King inwardly. *Flinging open doors any grown man would have the sense to leave closed.* "Tim, I think it best if we just—"

"But I want to know."

No, you don't, thought Simon, already sensing what the Shell Man was about to divulge.

"My conclusion is, you have no chances."

"None?" asked Tim.

"None. Your powers are no match for the Usher or his servant."

Servant? thought Simon.

"They are the authors of your crafts. A pupil can hardly be expected to instruct his master."

"I don't believe you," said Tim.

"I do," Simon said darkly.

"There are unknowns, of course . . . a few variables and one legend. But, overall, my prediction is grim."

For a moment, silence in the cave.

"May I ask you a question?" the Shell Man asked tentatively.

They nodded.

"Why do you want to live? It does not strike me as an enviable existence."

Then they both in their own ways knew that this blue creature was not

179

alive, or at least, not alive in any sense they understood, that it could never be alive, could never know the tastes and thrills and joys and their possibilities that made every day a wonder.

"It is, frankly," the blue man said, "the only appetite of my masters which I have never fathomed."

"It's not something I've ever thought to explain," said Simon.

"Alive's better than dead," said Tim with a shrug.

"That is what my masters thought for many spans. Yet, eventually, they arrived at a different conclusion. They desired to die."

They did not know what to say.

The Shell Man continued with obvious reluctance, wondering, as a servant might, whether it was prudent to impose his perspective upon the discussion. "I share their desire."

It took a moment for Tim and Simon to realize what he was saying.

"You have asked if there is anything you can do for me."

They said nothing.

"I believe you are sincere. So I will venture one request. Will you stop me?"

"Stop you?" said Tim.

"Disable me?"

"From what?" asked Simon.

"Will you—what is the correct term?—kill me?"

Simon was dumbfounded; Tim speechless.

Finally, the King ventured a question. "Has no one ever asked you what you wanted?"

"No," the man replied.

"Ever?" asked Tim.

"Never."

Tim tried but couldn't bring himself to imagine the sort of existence the Shell Man must have endured to have come to that request. Simon had no such problem. And he remembered crushing the golden shell. "If that is what you want, I'd be glad to."

"Not you, Simon. Although I thank you. It must be the Wind Tamer."

"Me?" asked Tim.

"Only your magic can stop me, I'm afraid."

"How? How?" asked Tim.

"A simple sleep spell ought to do it."

Tim recalled the eagle's warning about the great spell that would put the wind to rest. He'd called it "irrevocable." Unlike most magic, it stuck.

"Are you sure?" asked Tim. "It will be permanent."

"I understand. There is no undoing. Yes, I am sure."

"Alright," said Tim after a moment, and he could have cried at the relief that seeped into the face of the Shell Man.

"Thank you," he said. "I wish there was some way I could repay you." He paused and looked at the chest of jewels below him. "Take one of the learning stones. The green one you might like. It is most instructive."

Tim stepped over to the jewels and picked out one that looked like a fat green worm coiled into a circle.

"It includes a persona matrix."

"It what?" Tim asked.

"It shows you who you are. Hold it in your hand and tell it you want to go Between. It will get warm. You will go there in your mind. When you come back it will be as if you had a dream. Don't stay too long or you'll be stuck."

"Stuck?"

"You'll understand."

"Thank you," said Tim, rolling the stone in his palm.

When the Shell Man spoke again it sounded as if there were something caught in his throat. "Strange, I am reluctant to leave you. You bring the first fresh learning in aeons. I have a satisfying sense of usefulness." The

Shell Man closed his eyes. He smiled briefly, then looked back to the man and boy. "But I was conditioned that way. The Masters said it made me more pliable."

Tim fought back his tears.

"Please," the blue man said. "Do it now before I change my mind."

Tim lifted his hands and spoke the words of power after which there is no undoing. And in an instant, the lights disappeared, the blue man was gone, the bars of his cage were mere dust, and the jewels and glyphs that had emerged from the rust-colored rock shelf slunk back into their previous, now permanent, forms and would not yield their wonders again.

A loud silence.

Tim sat down and held his head in his hands.

Simon, as his tutor had done many times to him, laid a hand on the boy's shoulder.

Chapter twenty-two

"ANY QUESTIONS?"

The Teller smiled and scanned the befuddled faces of the crew. If the men had any questions they were of the type that could not yet take the form of words: They did not know where to begin. And so, the Teller readjusted his position on the deck, and continued.

"Now," he said with relish, "it gets scary."

Simon and Tim descended the steep ridge to the floor of a wild valley. The whole land was still—no wind stirred the trees. They lay down that night without a fire for it was very mild. Fitfully they slept, for somewhere nearby a woodpecker was feeding, and the rattle of its beak on bark echoed through the valley at regular intervals and kept waking them just as they were drifting off.

Simon was startled awake by Tim talking in his sleep and woke him from a dreadful dream.

"It was horrible," Tim said breathlessly. "I dreamed we were sleeping here and we would never wake up. Leaves covered us, snow buried us like we were rocks—and we wouldn't wake up!"

"Easy, now."

"And there was something else. Something watching us. It was cold and—oh, I don't know—it was big."

They tried but could not get back to sleep. Then simultaneously, as if upon a silent command, they rose, gathered their packs and set off at a quick pace. Walking by the dim light of a cloud-covered quarter moon, they avoided the deeper shadows and kept to the rugged open hills. They had made little progress when suddenly Tim whispered, "Hush!"

He pointed to a mound of rocks and trees that jutted out of the ground. From somewhere within came a faint clicking sound. They crept forward silently, crawled up the slight bank, and gradually peered over the edge. In the middle of the trees there appeared to be a hooded, old woman on a black rock sitting before a small fire. They heard the clicking sound again: It looked like she was making something with a mallet.

They crept to the other side to get a better look. The old woman was draped in thick, ragged clothing. She held a short club. She was a skeleton. The peculiar clicking sound occurred when she brought the club sharply down on the back of her hand: wood against bone. She was beating herself. After each series of blows the mouth of the skull would open wide and say, "Shame on you. Hogging the mote!" There would be a pause. Then the process was repeated.

It wasn't clear who started running first. Simon had much longer legs, but soon they were tearing neck and neck away from the hideous sight. They stumbled and ran until they could no more, then Tim collapsed and Simon knelt beside him, panting.

"We must leave this land tonight," cried Tim, "or I'm afraid we'll never get out!" Simon agreed, and as soon as they could, they began walking hastily. After several miles, Tim spoke. "How long has it been night?"

"Why, you're right! Either the nights are much longer here, or else . . ."

"Or else," said Tim, "there is no day here."

"We—we must hurry!" stammered Simon, and he trotted away through what appeared to be a freshly plowed field of cabbages. Tim ran to keep up. Simon tripped and sprawled and there was a cry of pain. It was not Simon's voice that cried out. The King lifted his head and found himself face-to-face with a boy who had no body. Rather, his body was entirely buried up to his head. His eyes were bloodshot, his teeth were a grungy green, and his breath stank of something rotten.

"Watch where you're steppin', Pinky!" he snarled.

Simon backed away with a scream and bumped into another head.

"Now you've done it," it snapped. "Now you've made me mad."

Tim was horrified to see the field was full of boys planted like carrots. They all had bald heads covered with sores, and they were all waking up.

"Who goes there?"

"He kicked Charly!"

"Oh, he did, did he? I'm getting the Usher!"

At the sound of that name, Simon became a child again, cowering in the corner of his bed, watching the shifting shadows in the corner.

When Tim saw the boys were buried in a field of sand a terrifying thought occurred to him: If they didn't keep moving they would sink themselves; they would join the field of talking heads.

He ran to Simon then, gingerly stepping over the heads that swiveled back and forth and glared up at him. Simon would not move, but knelt with his eyes closed, whispering to himself.

A chorus of voices rose about them.

"Get out of here!"

"I'm telling on you!"

"Damned trespassers!"

Tim slapped Simon hard and dragged him to his feet. "Run, Simon," he pleaded, and they ran, dodging the angry heads and snapping jaws. It wasn't easy going; they had to work hard to gain any footing at all on the loose sand.

"What'sa matter, Pinky? You afraid?"

"Spit on 'em, Jack!"

"Nab his ankles!"

"Teach him a lesson!"

It took a long time to get out of the field, but at last they dashed into some bushes and heard a wave of scornful laughter behind them. Still they ran. When they had no strength left, they fell down. When they could talk, Tim began. "I know of no power that can keep night from turning to day, do you?"

"Of course not."

"In none of your studies have you found such a spell?"

"No," Simon replied.

"Alright, then. That's what I wanted to know."

Simon looked blankly at Tim then broke into giddiness. "Well, that's fine! Now we *know* all this is impossible! How very comforting!" He fluffed his pack into a pillow and lay down, disgusted. "I have got to get some sleep."

It seemed like a very good idea to Tim, so gradually he, too, settled down. They had traveled long and hard—they would solve the puzzle in the morning. But on the brink of sleep, Tim opened his eyes and sat up. A smile crept over his face. "What am I doing! Of course! Of course! Simon!"

The King grimaced and squinted up in utter disbelief that anyone would be so rude as to rob him of his rest.

"Simon, notice anything peculiar about this place?"

"*Everything* is peculiar about this place," Simon murmured sleepily. "Now would you please just leave me alone?" He closed his eyes and let out an exasperated sigh.

"But we went to sleep at the bottom of a valley, right?"

"Right," said Simon with severe disinterest.

"So, where's the valley?"

When it dawned on Simon that he'd not seen a valley all night, he snapped open his eyes and looked at Tim. Then they began to laugh. Soon they were giggling and slapping each other about like puppies at play.

THE Gift

Their laughter subsided and they faced each other. Tim said, "Simon . . . Wake up!"

Simon awoke in the valley under a bright blue sky and scudding clouds. There was a gentle breeze that danced in the patch of wildflowers at his feet. Tim was sleeping next to him wearing a serene smile. Bending over, Simon spoke into his ear. "Tim . . . Wake up!"

Tim rustled, then sat up smiling. "I thought so!"

Simon touched him on the shoulder. "Thank you. That was not pleasant."

"Can you imagine it? If we hadn't woken up, we could have lived the rest of our lives in a dream."

Simon yawned and saw that both his hands were trembling. The words of Jason rose in his mind: "He gave me beautiful dreams."

So great was their relief at having passed safely through the nightmare that the humdrum of the next few days was welcome. Tim got a sliver. Simon showed him how to skip stones on a pond, and using sticks, instructed him in swordplay. Tim tried several times to sing a few of the beautiful water chants, and although he sang well, he would inevitably break off midsong, frustrated, claiming that they were nothing like that at all. One evening as twilight set, the forest around them came alive with the sounds of many birds and bugs; their chorus crescendoed until it was deafening, and unable to stand it any longer, Simon stood and shouted *"Shuttup!"* The silence was so total and abrupt that they laughed aloud, imagining thousands of dumbstruck creatures cowering in the dark. Eventually the various hoots and squawks returned at cautious intervals, with far less enthusiasm.

For Simon it was as if Tim had turned him into half a child and half a man. Part of him felt protective toward the boy. And when he would romp off into the woods alone, promising to be back in a bit, Simon waited and fretted, and tried not to imagine all the dangers he might fall prey to. Yet, he had found in Tim the childhood playmate he had always longed for. It made him feel young to jest with him, to hear his easy laugh, to watch as he suddenly soared up into the sky, coasting and somersaulting like some drunken bird. In time, he came to believe again in things he had never dreamed would be real: hope, fun, trust. Just walking with the boy was a healing thing, and he felt the scabs of hidden wounds melting inside of him. Yet still it frightened him, in a way, to need Tim as he did.

Tim often found himself daydreaming about his days in the great forest with his parents. They seemed the recollections of another age, another person, a simple child who had never seen a Waterman, a white eagle, or the other side of clouds. He could still vividly picture the nights his mother sang and rocked him to sleep before the hearth. These thoughts gave him great peace—until he recalled the fire. Then he would be choked with anger. Somehow these bittersweet memories blended into his days in the caverns. One moment his mother leaned over him fussing, licking her fingertips to smooth down his cowlick, and suddenly she was Marty, smiling, waking him up to a breakfast of freshly caught and cooked fish.

After they passed out of the valley they crossed into the marshes proper: a long, fog-laden strip of land which was the quickest route south. They spent an untroubled night in the misty swamp, clinging to the fire, knowing that gosis shriveled in extreme heat and would avoid them. To be doubly sure, Simon cast a dome spell around the fire that protected them throughout the night.

By noon the following day they were nearly out of the swamp, leaping from log to log over mucky green pools. The path had long since disappeared in the wild foliage. It soon became a game of follow-the-leader. Simon leapt over two rotten logs and landed deftly on a slippery moss-covered stump. Tim followed—taking more steps of course, to compensate for his shorter stride. The game ended at the upturned roots of a huge dead tree, where they caught their breath. Simon lay back and gazed at the thick leaves that shielded them from the sun and gave a faint dappled

THE Gift

light to the ground below. A great cloud passed overhead, throwing them into a deeper cool shade that they could feel on their skin. He turned lazily to Tim, who was busy kicking his toes in a dark pond a short distance away. "Did you see that big cloud?" he called.

"Yes. Wonderful."

Simon yawned deeply, crossed his legs, leaned back, and closed his eyes. Presently he said: "What a glorious day!"

Tim didn't answer.

"I mean, here we are, the sun is out. The air is cool. Our stomachs are full. Ahhhh! It's good to be alive, eh?"

Tim didn't answer. Simon opened his eyes to find himself alone. He looked over his shoulder and sat up. "Tim?" he called. Silence. "This isn't funny," he scolded. He sprang to his feet to look about. "Stop it, Tim." He heard a rustle of water behind him and turning, he glimpsed something pale rise almost to the surface of the pond, and instantly drop back into deeper water. *"Tim!"* he screamed.

As he rushed to the bank, a spray of bubbles worked their way up through the water. Suddenly the surface was fractured by a wild splash as Tim broke through, screaming. Simon reached for him but couldn't get a grip: His body was knobbed with slippery, squirming gosis; his eyes were full of agony and terror.

What could he do? Simon thought desperately. He could not cast the water into a boil. Every attack spell he knew would be too great of a risk for Tim. Tim's magic was impotent as well, for Wind Wizardry only works in its native element—it is useless underwater. Finally, he jumped into the pond, hoping to drag his friend back or peel off enough of the awful creatures to set him free.

It didn't work. No sooner had he plunged in than he was engulfed by gosiloaches. One clasped firmly over his mouth and he felt the itchy suction begin to work on his lips. Several more chained around his ankles and prevented him from kicking. He began to sink, but managed to get hold of some protruding roots. He reached down and felt a shoulder, then an arm. Tim reached up, desperately grasping Simon's hand. Immediately, two gosis merged over their hands and sealed their grip in a sticky vise. Mud had churned up in the water, making it impossible to see. Simon worked his way up the roots, one by one, determined to reach the surface before Tim was forced to breath water. But it was useless. For every bit of progress he made upward, the gosis would swarm in force and pull him back down. He felt the strength draining from his arms, Tim becoming a limp weight beneath him, and soon, it was all he could do to hold fast to the root.

Here it is, thought Simon, a wonderful sunny day, and everyone else is enjoying their lunch and we're drowning. It was almost laughable. And, presently, it didn't seem so bad after all. Just one small breath and the cool water would seep into his lungs and they wouldn't burn so. It would be nice and dreamy soft. Just to forget it all and drift away . . . drift away . . .

Chapter twenty-three

THE TELLER PAUSED TO EXAMINE the green stone in his palm. He yawned deliberately, as if he weren't aware of the tense, expectant faces surrounding him. He looked up at the flat white sails hanging under the stars. He could have been listening, but stranded as they were upon this dark sea and windless night there was nothing to hear. He closed his eyes and feigned sleep. And just at the moment one of the sailors was about to ask the question listeners always asked: "What happened next?"—he spoke.

"Death, it seems, is nothing like we imagine."

He paused again to let the silence grow.

"Yet each of us retains, in some corner of our mind, in a place well off the main, a neglected room, locked, blocked, hidden, and gathering a skin of dust, somewhere we don't venture often: the idea of our death. It is my experience that people will go out of their way to avoid that room, where everything ends, but more particularly, we do.

"Look for clues in the faces of the dead and we find nothing: an absence so complete and irrefutable, that many who have seen that face which all people someday wear, often rush to dress it up and call it something else: peace, or resolution, or, perhaps, rest. But they know: In their hearts they know it for what it is, oblivion.

"But on the margins of the End, in the border regions outside that dark kingdom, there are places in Between. Places where the laws are rewritten, where failing souls wander and are somehow given chances they never had when they walked the world. Who knows their purpose? Perhaps they are the last discharge of comfort to the wounded, the body's mercy, the mind's reprieve, the spirit's passing kindness before that final voyage.

"Or, perhaps, they are something else.

"Forgive me, I speak, as anyone who speaks of final things must, with words unworthy of their task. In these places, the simplest things—colors, smells, the texture of the wind upon the skin—are so strange as to demand a new lexicon, words no one has even thought to invent. And the traveler who would take back remnants from this other world would find on his returning, the currency of his images useless, his words depleted of their power. Have you not marked how a dream which felt a haunting omen in the night, will lose all its coherence in the day? So it is with the places in Between.

"But with that apology, I will tell you how Tim died."

First of all, he was in pain. (How often these stories leave that out.)

His lungs screamed. His skin burned and itched under the gosis' hunger. His mind dashed from one futile thought to another like a dog whose tail is on fire. Then someone's hand grasped his.

Simon.

And he thought: I am saved.

But then nothing happened. Why doesn't he rescue me? he wondered. Why are we floating here drowning? It was as if the King had expended his last bit of energy in the act of reaching the boy and could do no more. Tim felt their hands sealed under the prickly, spongy grip of the gosis.

Simon? he asked in his mind. Simon? Help me! Help us! Can't you hear?

Soon he discovered that after a time, pain loses its ability to shock and terrorize; it becomes mere sensation. His thoughts scrambled and tripped into nonsense as his last breath expelled.

A choking moment.

And then, against his will, his lungs sucked in the cool dark water of the gosi pond.

It felt, in a way, wonderful. There was a peace in this surrender he would never have expected. And his body seemed to thank him from every aching corner.

Darkness came eventually.

That's better, thought Tim. Much better. It was getting too bright anyway. His body, by now, had lost all feeling. He had, as far as he knew, no limbs, no head, no hands. He felt himself reduced to a small pulsing ball. The ball was all that was left of him. And in his last of what we would call thought, he knew what it was. The green shell that the blue man had given him. He had held it in his hand when the gosis came. And he recalled what he was to say: I want to go Between.

And thinking these words, he made it so.

There was no period of transition. One moment he was in the pond getting used to his death, the next, he was somewhere else.

This is what he saw.

He was in a white room. He sat in a white chair. The floor was made of white squares. There was a white door against the wall opposite him whose frame was almost, but not quite, invisible. If he chose, he could get up and walk the length of the room in twelve strides. To his left there was a great mirror flush against the white wall, perfectly reflecting its opposite. There were two white chairs next to the door.

Is this death? he wondered, feeling oddly disappointed.

When we are in a dream we do not question its validity, do we? That is the chief attribute of dreams. Tim knew that he was not dreaming because he questioned everything about him. Nothing made sense. Everything seemed imaginary. Yet, somehow, he knew he wasn't making it up.

He found himself looking at the reflections of a strange face in the tips of his black boots—the most amazingly comfortable things he had ever worn. He curled his toes to confirm it: wonderful. The door opened and a man's head peeked around the edge to tell him: "Five minutes."

He stood then. Five minutes till what?

He walked over to the mirror and gasped at his reflection.

He saw a small woman in a white gown with bare arms looking back at him. She had short dark hair trimmed close to the scalp. Small breasts and large hips. On her wrist she wore a type of band; he glimpsed writing on it. And then she turned away, and he realized she was not his reflection at all, but a woman in a chamber opposite him: the mirror was a window into a room shaped exactly like his in every respect. And he saw the blurry outline of a man in black: himself. He realized he was the only black thing in the white room.

As she walked away to sit on a white chair, he saw that her room was much brighter than his and that, somehow, she could not see him.

"Can we just get on with it?" she said to the ceiling, which glowed like a snowclad lake under a full moon.

A bald black man entered his room and moved slowly to his side to observe the woman in white through the mirror.

Afraid to face him—Why?—Tim watched him from the corners of his eyes. Then compared their reflections in the mirror: twin shadows standing side by side, their skin was black, their heads were bald.

They stood together as if around a barrel of fire: the boy inside the man, the man beside the black man, the black man beside the man with the boy inside, the two dark reflections of the two men in the mirror.

For a moment Tim lost track of how many of them there were. And which was real.

The white woman stood away, excluded. Tim felt certain she, at least, was real.

"Listen, dammit," one of black men said, as if he had just been interrupted. "I've known you, what, six years now? You think I can't tell when you're . . . doubting?" The way he whispered the word: as if it were a se-cret. Tim saw fear in his eyes.

He's real, too, he thought.

"Hell, we all do. My first five I puked my guts out after." He lightly grabbed Tim's arm just under the shoulder, the place adults touch each other when they mean no harm. "You're not supposed to feel good about it. You wouldn't be a man if you did. You'd be some sort of monster."

The man released his arm.

"It's not about feeling," the man said to his reflection in the mirror. "It's about duty. And law. And . . ." His smile included Tim. "Hell, we can be honest. It's a good job."

He leaned in closer and Tim could smell a flower scent. "Don't tell anyone . . ." He backed away and looked at his hands. "Sometimes I wish I didn't know what I know." He looked back to the mirror that was a win-dow. "Take this one. Hell, she's eighteen if she's a day. You think you're supposed to enjoy this?" He swallowed. "She looks like my little sister." He covered his eyes with one hand.

He's my friend, thought Tim. We used to get drunk at the commis-sary—a strange word that he knew meant place to eat. We're in an army. We work underground. I am his classmate. He trusts me. He's trying to help me. He's trying to keep me out of trouble.

These knowledges came upon him like dream images, unbidden. It was as if the process of occupying another body was a gradual one. First, you were inside: You saw and felt what the other saw and felt. You absorbed the senses. Then, slowly, came memories and experience: words, places, feelings, names. He knew, without knowing how, that soon there would be no difference between himself and the man in black. He looked down to see his hands were the color of a muddy stream. There was something about them that frightened him: their strength, what they were capable of, what they knew.

The man interrupted. "You owe me, dammit. I did the grandma lesbo." Angry now. Desperate. "You said you'd do the foeticide. You promised. Ahh, hell."

Tim spoke for the first time. "What's hell?" he asked, shocked by the depth of his voice.

His friend backed away from him. "Sometimes, bro, I think you're a stranger." He moved to the door, and opening it, said, "Hell is here. Right here."

And he was gone.

Tim peered at the dark face in the mirror: the face he wore. Touching it, he felt tiny knots of whiskers. Until that moment, he hadn't really believed he was there.

The woman on the other side ran toward him and pounded the mirror with her fists. Tim stepped back, afraid that she might break the glass, but to his surprise, all he heard was a muffled sound, like the beating of a drum.

The woman yelled, "Get it over with, you yellow bastards!"

Yellow? he thought. But he was brown.

For a moment he held his head in his hands. It was like the time he had healed Simon in the fist tree. The images and sounds from the King's past had poured into him. But this was somehow stranger, for all these memories were both weird and familiar. He knew them effortlessly, the way his father knew the names of all his tools. Yet, part of him felt this knowledge for the first time, and he reeled as it burst inside his mind and spread outward like ripples from a boulder cast into the sea. He was a young black man. His people had once been slaves. He was an armsman. There was a war. It was a war against women. Women who had done unspeakable things. Women who threatened the very fabric of society. Society was the men who ruled and their laws. There were not enough babies. Crimes against babies were State offenses. Babies were the future. It was the right of the State to protect its future. All women were obliged to bear children. As many as possible. This was an honored role. Motherhood was sacred. He had never been in love. Men were obliged to pass on their seed. There were laws that made this mandatory. Armsmen enforced these laws. Any man limiting himself to one woman was punished. Any woman who refused her sacred role as the bearer of the race was punished. Any woman who dared harm her issue was executed.

He was an executioner.

It was a duty for which he was well paid. Yet there was something dubious about it. Which is why he lived underground. As much as the public approved of and supported his role, they preferred not to be reminded of it. Discretion was the hallmark of his trade.

He leaned his head against the glass and closed his eyes.

How did I get here? Who am I? Will I be this dark man forever? Where am I? When am I? I want to go home.

The door opened, and he jumped.

"Take it easy, soldier." There was a white man in white clothes at the door, golden stripes on his shoulders. He held the door open for Tim. And waited.

Somehow he knew what to do, what was expected of him. This horrified him.

Outside, the corridor was white. He had to restrain himself from touching the walls—they looked like the skin of a plucked bird. Around the corner they found a pregnant woman in a white dress, sitting in a chair beside a door. She was reading a book.

· Standing, she spoke to both of them. "She *declined*."

"Surprise, surprise," said the man with the stripes. The stripes denoted rank. He was a superior. "So, Nina," he said cheerfully, "you want to witness?"

Her young face broke into a smile. "Thank you, sir!"

"You're due soon?"

"In a month, sir." Her hands cradled her full belly.

"Excellent." He held his hand over her unborn child and gave a type of blessing. "For the Fathers."

The young woman blushed, and set the book down on her chair. Tim read the golden words on the cover. *What Every New Mother Needs.*

"First time?" asked the superior.

Her blush deepened and she smiled. "Yes, sir. But I know the drill."

Drill?

There was a pause as both of them waited for Tim.

"Forget the code, soldier?" the superior asked him. *Soldier* was their word for armsman.

He said nothing.

The man smiled. "It happens." Then, reaching past him, he tapped several times on a box of jewels that rested on the wall beside the door like the chest in the blue man's cave. Tim wondered that they didn't spill onto the floor. The door slid into the wall with a hiss and they entered the white room. The oubliette.

Oubliette?

On the opposite wall he saw the mirror he had been looking through. In the corner stood the young woman.

The pregnant woman, Nina, moved to the corner and sat, folding her hands over her belly. Tim wondered why she was called by her first name and he was only called soldier, until he remembered: Women give up their last names when they marry; executioners were on a no-name basis with everyone. This was a concession to decorum which made everyone more comfortable.

"Three of you?" said the prisoner.

"Shut your hole," said the superior, "and this'll go quicker." He cleared his throat into his fist. "Three-three-three-three-three-four, you have been convicted under the Reproductive Laws of First Degree Foeticide. Your sentence is termination. Your jury, considering your age, voted leniency.

THE Gift

The judge overruled them in favor of prolongation in the second degree. Therefore, swift justice isn't an option."

The superior paused and held out his hand over the woman as if he were instructing a dog to stay. The woman looked at his hand as if she wanted to bite it.

The man's voice changed as he intoned the judgement. "By the hand of man, for the good of all families, for the mercy of all children, for the hope of our future. For the Fathers. So it is."

Tim felt sickened by the lovely words.

"You have declined your rights to blessing, absolution, and medication," said the man in stripes. "Mum?" When there was no response, he turned to the mother-to-be. "Nina?"

The pregnant woman stood suddenly with a sharp intake of breath, saying, "Sorry." Girlishly she rolled her eyes, stepped forward, and braced herself as if she were about to sing a solo in the choir.

What's a solo? Tim thought. What's a choir?

Before she could speak, the prisoner laughed. "Nina? Not another one of those Preggy Ninas."

Tim thought, Named after the doll you all played with twenty years ago. A doll whose belly bloated when you blew into her thumb.

"That's great." The prisoner smirked. "My name's Nina, too!"

"Your name is of no consequence," the superior said.

The pregnant Nina blew out a fierce puff of breath. "You *know* there are no names in here!"

The prisoner Nina turned to Tim, and reining in her smile, asked, "What's yours, soldier?"

"Jordan," Tim replied. His name was Jordan. He was named, as many boys of his pigment were, after a great leaper who had lived long ago.

"Soldier!" His superior frowned.

The mother-to-be said the words carefully, proudly. "Do you have a *statement?*"

"I have a question," said the prisoner.

A pause.

"Do you enjoy your work?" She was looking at Tim.

"That's not a *statement*," said Nina exasperated, shaking her head at the superior. She leaned her head toward the condemned woman. "Can't you even get that right?"

"You're wasting your breath on this one, Mum. Incorrigible."

"No," Tim answered the prisoner. "No one enjoys it." His superior looked at him. "That's why they pay us so much."

Now the mother-to-be was looking at him.

The prisoner lost all her expression, as if she had seen something in his face that had finally managed to frighten her.

"Soldier?" she said.

"Have a little *dignity!*" the pregnant Nina hissed.

"Jordan?" she asked him. He couldn't meet her eyes.

"Shuttup!" said the superior, stepping toward her.

"Quickly," she whispered, her bottom lip trembling.

The superior was about to strike her when Tim caught his arm. The man looked at him with a cold fury, until he said, "Let me."

The officer—that is what he was, an officer—exhaled through his nose. "With pleasure," he said, and stepped back.

The woman sank into the white corner as Tim approached.

The next part, he knew. It had to do with his hands and where he would place them. There were twelve rules. Fourteen nerve points. Four degrees of excruciation. And he knew them all without wanting to.

He wondered, for the briefest moment, what Nina would have been like as a lover. As a friend. As a sister. As a mother.

That wasn't possible. She had broken the law. The law was all he had now. And all he would have afterward.

Cupping his hands around her head, he felt the familiar heat of the skull, the dampness of the scalp. He smelled the fear: that tangy salt smell mixed with panic, some sort of gas the stomach released at the moment before judgement. Her throat was making tiny bird noises the way they all did. And instantly, she ceased to be the singular Nina. She could have been any of the prisoners he discharged. This didn't surprise the black man, though it shocked Tim deeply: how in the hour of our death we lose everything that makes us different; we become bodies.

It wasn't personal. It was his job.

There was no grudge between them.

Between.

He didn't even know he thought the word.

But thinking the word, he was gone. And a beautiful darkness swallowed him whole.

Chapter twenty-four

LIKE A TREE FULL OF sleeping birds woken by a lightning strike, the sailors on deck began to chatter all at once.

"Never had a dream like that," commented one out of the corner of his mouth, and several others laughed.

"It's not a *dream*, you clam! It's a lesson."

"Never had a *lesson* like that, either."

"I liked the part about the woman."

"Sucking thumb."

A few grunts and chuckles.

"My cousin met a black man once—"

"I never did!"

"My other cousin."

"He's dead."

"He met him before he died, you loach."

"Ah, well, at least they got women after death."

A brief, awkward pause.

"I liked the jewels part."

"Everyone shuttup! I want to know what happened to the King."

"That's right! He was in the gosi pond!"

"I like the gosis. I could use a leeching."

"Shuttup!"

"Well, I could!"

"Shuttup!"

"Go-Boy, who you telling to shut up?"

THE Gift

"Shuttup!"
Silence.
And then the Teller continued.

It began as a roaring in Simon's ears; his head began to spin, then his entire body was flung about wildly in the pool—caught in the center of a cyclone. The gosi on his mouth was wrenched free, and he felt a rising dizziness that sickened him. He fell and landed on his side with a hard thump. When had he left the water? Someone was coughing beside him, and he opened his eyes to see a sick and sopping Tim. Too exhausted to move his body, he turned his head and saw the water of the pond churning madly in a whirlpool—except in reverse. It spit out rocks, twigs, and ruptured gosis high into the air, expelling them like poison. The whirlpool gradually spent itself and the pond resumed its calm. Then a brief agitation rippled its surface and out sputtered a sleek, spinning object that rose to the treetops. It reached the peak of its ascent and became visible. Simon could not believe his eyes. It was a huge emerald frog. It descended swiftly, bounced off the murky pond, somersaulted, and landed with a slap on the bank. It stood, hands on hips, and regarded him with suspicion and anger.

"You're a Waterman!" Simon blurted.

"And you're a *stupid* man!" cried the scowling creature. "Haven't you the sense to stay clear of a gosi-pond in the shade?"

"I didn't know about the shade—I thought only night—"

"If the boy is drowned you'll answer to me!" The green creature cast a look of pure hatred at the King. "And if you dare spell at me—for I see you are a man of some skill—I'll toss you back and let them finish their lunch!"

Tim lay facedown on the ground, whispering, "I'm sorry! I'm sorry!"

The creature was at his side in a flash. "I am here, child. It's alright now." But it was days before they knew he was out of danger. During those long hours as Tim thrashed about in delirium, gripping something in his fist that even Simon couldn't pry out, Marty would stroke his brow and whisper words Simon could not hear. The Waterman nursed the boy with an odd ritual, using sweat from its delicate green arm, grasped at the elbow and wrung down to the wrist. The sweat gathered in its tiny fist, which held leaves and moss, then droplets would dribble into Tim's open mouth. Marty chanted softly as Tim swallowed.

Once, under a hot afternoon sun, Tim began to shiver violently. Marty immediately demanded Simon's purple cloak, disappeared for a while, and returned with the wrap drenched in cool water. When Marty stripped Tim to wrap him in it, Simon saw the scars. They ran in streaks all along the boy's body—raw red patches of stippled skin. Simon touched his own face and felt pocked flesh about his mouth which he hadn't noticed before. The whiskers on his chin were gone, as if singed off by fire. He wondered for a moment how ugly he might look, then he looked upon Tim and was ashamed. "Will the scars go away?"

Marty was in no hurry to answer, but finally said, "Yours will."

For days Marty refused to talk to Simon except to curtly answer questions. The creature forbade him to use any of his magic on Tim—saying something about the danger of spies and Earth Sorcery doing more harm than good. At times Simon was in awe of Marty; other times he was merely annoyed. The face bore the features of a child: innocent and totally self-absorbed; yet Marty's manner and words spoke of authority and the wisdom of many years. It was an unsettling combination and Simon found himself reacting to Marty as a child one moment, and the leader of great armies the next. There was also something different, something in the way Marty watched the fire at night: as a child observes its mother's face, or vice versa. There was a wildness in those eyes that clearly separated Marty from the world of men—deep shining black eyes—eyes that could tell stories. At times Simon felt afraid of the creature. He would roll over in the morning and find it in the exact position which it had been at nightfall. Marty would shake its little head and croak: "Men! Hmmm! No stamina whatsoever!" It was unnerving.

Two days later Tim's fever broke and his color began to return. He said he had had terrible dreams. But he would not elaborate.

What happened to Tim in Between is not explainable; perhaps, not imaginable.

He was never to tell Marty the story. And it would be weeks before he told Simon. Mostly because he himself did not comprehend where he had gone, what he had learned, and how he had changed. He was, after all, a child. And like a child who has moved from the home he was born and raised in, he needed time to take in a new world. A world where even the simplest things had shifted into strangeness: His bed was in a different corner, the view from his window was missing the friendly elm that had always been there when he awoke, the floor felt colder to his feet.

But Tim had not really moved anywhere, he had merely left himself. He had worn the skin, the memories, and the living mystery of another. He had, in some way, become that person. In one visit he had absorbed a lifetime of experience. And these new sensations and knowledges roiled inside of him, seeking a place to belong.

In his fever-dream his familiar self clashed with the presumptions of the man he had worn. He was constantly reminded of how small he was—the man inside felt as if he were crouching all the time. He learned the sky was too open, too threatening to a man who had spent his life underground. Even something as simple as a bed could cause an argument: It had always been the straw under a blanket in the loft. No, it was an astoundingly comfortable mat that molded itself to his sleeping form. The simple act of living became a debate.

Yet, that was the easy part.

His mother now had two names. His fears were doubled. He knew what it was to have a woman before he even had an inkling of desire for one. He knew things he never wished to know. He lacked things he never missed before. He was a boy; he was a man.

He could find no comfortable compromise between his dual memories. For the longest time he regarded the life of his cell mate as a dream— a vivid, haunting dream. That helped. But, finally, try as he might, he could not shut out the man he had adopted; his feelings would erupt and flood him with fire, and he was forced to let him out.

Years later he would still see the world through a killer's eyes.

That woman there will go quickly. That woman there will beg. Her neck is easily snappable. Her bones would give him trouble.

Stop it! he would cry in his mind. How can you think of people like that?

I was trained to, his other self would reply.

It isn't right, Tim would say.

No, the man inside would reply, but it is my duty.

You could have refused, he would insist.

And then, in his mind, the man would show him the body of his best friend who had dared just that, and what they had done to him would sicken Tim.

You can change, he would say fiercely.

No, the man inside would simply say.

Sometimes the longings were unbearable, longings for foods he could not taste, friends who hadn't been born, comforts uninvented, familiar sights and music that, to Tim, were shocking visions and terrifying noise.

To dream the dreams of another man.

And, of course, to remember the women.

Criminals, the man would always add.

Women, Tim would insist. And girls.

Eventually, through the days of this fever-dream, as Marty and Simon watched over him, he learned in silence and despair that a person was capable of containing anything—any horror, any grief, any hideous notion that battered his skull. He discovered that the body has extra places reserved for these new and awful things, as if there were rooms within, like the unused rooms of a great castle, rooms that could hold and honor and sustain infinite levels of wonder and pain.

He found those rooms one by one.

And he learned to be two men.

Luckily, he had help.

One day Simon emerged. Not the King Simon who sat beside Marty and took turns watching the boy, but the Simon of the memories Tim had shared in the healing tree. Simon talked Tim through his occupation. "At least he's not a voice of the dead," he'd say. "You don't have to fear him." The man inside was sullen when Simon appeared, as if one more intruder was too many to share this cramped space inside the boy. For a time he was silent. Then, with Simon's encouragement, he began to talk. Tim listened. And when his help was no longer needed, Simon disappeared.

Of all the lives Tim ever wore, the King was the only one that never came back. From that day forward he loved Simon.

The Teller looked out at the faces around him on the deck. The open mouths, the wrinkled brows, the stifled snickers, and the sidelong glances.

"I told you it was not explainable, and you thought I was being coy. But you, Captain," said Tim, with a smiling voice that emerged from a face that gave no form to the impulse, "you can imagine it, can't you?"

The Captain yawned and ran his thumb across the yellow jewel that itched his ear.

Chapter twenty-five

THE NEXT MORNING TIM WAS able to sit up and talk, and Marty was in better spirits. The boy spent a great deal of time convincing the creature that Simon had not kidnapped him. He went over the whole story of Simon's healing, and finally, Marty was grudgingly able to look at the King with something other than suspicion.

"Did the Usher touch you?" asked the creature.

"Yes," said Simon.

The creature shook its head. "Everything he touches goes bad. The Listener said he could smell his scent in every pool. And in the wind. Have you put it to sleep yet, Tim?"

The boy did not reply. He was telling the man inside not to be frightened of Marty.

"Tim?"

The boy blinked and looked at Marty. "What?"

"Have you put the wind to sleep?"

"Not yet," Tim replied.

Marty sighed as if this was expected bad news, then moved to the fire, rubbing hands over the flames. In all the time Simon had watched Marty worry over Tim, he'd never seen the creature so distraught. Even on Tim's worst days (and there were several) Marty always looked determined and resolved. But now he saw or imagined he saw in its blank green face the features of despair. He watched the sweat run down the frog's green back—for all he knew, this was how Watermen cried. Simon sought to comfort Marty and he reached out his mind to try to understand, to break the uneasy silence. The creature whirled about and Simon felt his tentative connection snap like a stick—but not before he caught a sense of overwhelming defeat that stretched out like a trail ending in inevitable darkness.

"Don't you ever, ever do that again! My mind is my own and you'll not play tricks with it!"

"Simon," said Tim, "you ought to know better than to enter a man's mind uninvited!"

Marty snickered.

"I'm sorry!" said Simon. "I only meant to help!"

There was another awkward silence till Tim said, "Well, you're coming with us, aren't you?"

Marty nodded.

"It'll be over soon, Marty. Then we can all go home."

Marty sighed. "No. There's no home anymore."

"What are you saying?"

"They're all gone. They took the Bubble Sleep to the sea. You would have liked it, Tim. They filled the night like floating moons."

"Why didn't you go with them?"

"I wanted to. But I couldn't leave the Listener. He was too frail for the journey. A few days after the family left he had a vision. He could barely talk but he told me he saw the Wind Tamer in a dark land with a stranger. He said you were sleeping, yet you were awake. Does that make sense?"

"Yes, it does," said Simon.

"So I came as soon as I could."

"Why?" asked Tim.

Marty explained. "Tomen snatches up the orphans of his fires and eats their souls as they pass through his flames. They *sleepwalk* to the south."

Tim shuddered, remembering how close he had come to lying down in the fire.

Simon recalled the sad group of boys they had seen. "What good are orphans to him?"

"His school!" cried Tim.

"Yes. He's recruiting young boys for his school of sorcery. I do not know, but I can imagine why. They graduate and go to towns throughout the land. They quickly become healers, jesters, even town counselors if they're old enough. They are infiltrators—each a servant of the Usher. They cure a toothache or a case of warts and the people are delighted. They do not see their true purpose. Some may advance to high positions. Most will capture the favor of the mayor. In time, no doubt, these boys will rise to power."

"Why are there no girl recruits?" asked Simon, thinking of the dragon and the witch.

"I'm not certain. Perhaps a witch is deemed less trustworthy than a sorcerer. Perhaps the Usher's power only extends to males, in which case we are fortunate."

Why? thought Tim. So what if the Usher only has power over men? "How does that help *us?*" he asked.

Marty looked at the ground. "It doesn't matter."

"Tell me," said Tim.

Marty sighed. "I told you I was different. That's why I never ate with the others. That's why I like the fire . . . and why the Mother was barren."

"What's all this about?" said Simon, totally lost.

Marty took a deep breath. "I am female."

Tim and Simon did not know what to say.

"I thought you knew and it didn't bother you."

"I didn't know," Tim admitted. "But why should it bother me?"

"Well, you're the only one it didn't then. You see, in my family, there is only one female: the Mother. She always dies giving birth to the next

Mother. But when she bore me she lived. She showed no signs of weakening. It was a terrible omen."

"Was it the Water Sickness?" asked Simon.

"Yes."

"Then . . . you're only four years old! You're a child!"

Marty laughed. "You can't put your numbers on Watermen! They don't work. Remember we do not waste our lives in sleep as you do." Marty stared into the fire. "So you see, I am the last one left."

"The Listener?" asked Tim fearfully.

Marty looked at the ground and began touching her middle finger to her thumb: the Waterman equivalent of a scratch. The suction as she pulled it away made a little plop, like a stone dropping into water. "That's something else I can thank the Water Sickness for. He was my only child. After I bore him no Waterman would touch me. It confirmed what they suspected all along: I had the sickness."

"He was born that way?" Tim asked.

Marty nodded. "And he died that way. It took much longer than I thought it would. You wouldn't think such a tiny thing would take so long to drown."

For a long moment no one breathed. Tim's feelings bounded back and forth like a moth around a candle: horror, bewilderment, grief, sympathy. "You . . . you . . . ?"

"I had to choose. You were in peril. I couldn't bring him with me: He was too frail. I couldn't leave him alone. One of you was going to die. He had no chance, but you did."

Horrified, Tim whispered. "You did it for *me?*"

Marty looked at Tim, astounded that he did not understand. "For all of us. You are the Wind Tamer." Then the creature covered her eyes and wept. "Oh, Tim," she cried, "he smiled at me as I held him under."

You see? said the man inside. Sometimes these things are necessary.

211

*　*　*

In the middle of the night, Simon woke trembling. He couldn't stop. It had grown chilly, and though he rubbed his hands and arms, he couldn't get warm. Finally, he wrapped his purple cloak about him and sat down closer to the fire. Marty stepped out of the darkness carrying a load of branches in her arms. Tim slept under a blanket, snoring quietly.

"Is he well enough to go on?" asked Simon.

"I think so."

She began to stoke the fire, glancing several times at Simon's face. "What is it, Simon?"

"Nothing. I can't sleep."

"It's a lot of nothing that keeps you awake. You sleep like a bear."

"I'm cold," he said, reaching for a stick to stir the fire.

"It is getting nippier," said Marty, putting the last branch into the flames then sitting down opposite Simon, the fire between them. "But that's not why you're awake."

A bird called far away in the night. Simon held up the slender branch with the fierce glowing tip and thought how it resembled the early stages of a sword, before it was smithy-hammered flat and polished sharp.

"I'm afraid," whispered Simon.

Marty looked at him through the flames.

"You are, too!" he said. "I saw it in your mind."

Marty sighed. "So I am. So why talk about it? It doesn't change what we have to do."

"Tim isn't afraid. He doesn't know."

"No. He doesn't," Marty agreed. "He believes too much in his power."

"We have no chance," whispered Simon, thinking of the Shell Man.

"We have a chance," said Marty. "We have each other. And if we have any advantage at all, it is in the fact that he does not expect Tim and me."

"He expects me?"

"I believe so."

"That's comforting," said Simon sourly.

"Simon, you mustn't lose heart. Look." She stood and slowly waved her hands above the lapping flames. "We are like this fire. We are strong because though we are three, we are one. The heat is the gift—that is Tim. He warms us with his innocence and love. The light is the guide—that is you. You have traveled through the darkness. You know the way. You will lead us. The flame—well, the flame is me. I do not sleep. I do not dream. I am the guardian against darkness. The fire is one. But it is three. We are three, but we are one."

For a long minute Simon stared through the flames at the strange frog. Finally, he said, "How can I thank you for saving me?"

Marty looked at him darkly. "Take care of Tim."

It wasn't long before Simon found he could sleep again. He lay back down and let the fire take the bitter chill out of the night.

They woke to a summer snowfall and the sight of wildflowers poking through the white crust. Tim said it was impossible, but Simon said he had read of such spells, and perhaps somehow the Usher had heard him coming and this was his form of discouragement. By the time they were packed Tim's teeth were chattering and a thin cap of snow had settled on Marty's flat head. Simon tore his purple cloak into three parts and divided it among them. Marty declined but Simon insisted, saying that soon the snow would be level with her shoulders. Between the overcast sky and pure white ground the only sound to be heard was Marty's labored breathing as she struggled through the drifts to keep up.

"It's not far now," said Simon.

Chapter twenty-six

"YOU MUST FORGIVE ME THIS interruption, but it needs saying.

"The Watermen were made by wizards. And made poorly, I might add. They were one of their bungled experiments. One of many creatures that were found to be flawed and allowed to die out. You see, the wizards came for many reasons, but their chief ambition was breeding.

"They were Creature Makers.

"This is what they came here for. This is what they did.

"Their tools were as complex as ours are blunt. Their knowledge was beyond anything you imagine. The wizards played along the tiny rivers that run through our bodies and govern our health and growing. They modeled their course and currents and composition. They played with our design, rearranging it to suit their needs, changing our shape, and nurturing our latent talents. What they could not make work in the flawed designs of the Watermen, they perfected in us.

"This will be of interest to you, Captain, for it involves women.

"You see, to weave the creatures that they wanted, they had to change their origin. To get a better crop they had to change the garden's soil.

"They had to start with mothers.

"Through trial and error, they found the breach between a woman's legs too narrow.

"There is nothing funny about this, sailor.

"They had to widen a woman's hips. To expand the passageway. For they had wrought a larger baby. And a longer stay in the womb. This

made for a harder birth. A later weaning. And an extended attachment between child and mother.

"Imagine how they did that.

"Now can you imagine why?

"They wanted a bigger brain.

"A brain large enough to hold their stories. And they got it. But they
got something else, too. Something unexpected. They had wrought a more
feeble child than any in the land. A child that could not survive its early
life without its mother's constant care. A smarter child, although a weaker
one. And, in a sense, a weaker mother—a mother who, for long portions
of her bearing years, was greatly burdened. It was inevitable. And it was a
price they were willing to pay to get this new thing they desired.

"Captain? Is there something wrong? You look troubled."

The Teller removed his pinky ring and examined the red indented
flesh where it had clung.

"Ah, then. I'll continue. If you had paid attention to the Shell Man's
tale, you might have understood what the wizards wanted with us. Have
you ever let a loach cling to your finger? Tenacious, aren't they? No doubt
you've come upon a certain shore crab that puts on the abandoned husk
of a snail. Ahh, you have seen this.

"Then, I might as well tell you: You have seen the wizards."

The Teller slid his ring back on and continued.

As he reached the crest of the hill, Tim stumbled slightly in a drift of
snow.

When he gained his balance he looked up and saw the Usher's Book
House: a derelict structure of crumbling grey stone, dead ivy, and brittle
slated roofs. It was surrounded by a hastily constructed perimeter: a stag-
gering of stubby pike staffs embedded in the soggy ground. Small guards,

resting their spears on their shoulders, sluggishly patrolled the narrow battlements: decorative designs unintended and unlikely to keep out enemies. Beyond the gate and wall, at the corner of the keep in the center of the courtyard, one tower rose. Though Tim had never seen a book house before, this looked like a poor excuse for one. It was nothing like he had imagined; it had the air of something lost or neglected.

Then he saw the Griff. Even from a distance he could tell it was stone. It was the same color as the Book House gates on which it stood, hunched forward awkwardly under the burden of its chains. For a moment, he gazed at the thick snow that came up to his knees, then below him he saw a group of boys trodding past a large boulder that lay beside the road, their breaths frosting in the air.

They took little notice of him as he stepped into line behind them; their eyes were on their feet. Though one small boy looked up at Tim and asked, "We shall be eating soon, shan't we?" He was immediately shushed by the others.

They did not have to knock on the gates; they opened as they arrived. Entering the Book House, Tim looked back and saw two boys in black behind each door holding heavy rope handles, then resetting the brace. Above them he saw a tiny lad holding a spear and cleaning his boots on the battlement.

It was a house guarded by boys.

The group halted in the center of the muddy courtyard before a tall boy in a dark blue robe. His thumbs were hooked upon a metal-studded belt.

The man inside warned, Watch him. He's got buttons.

Buttons? thought Tim. We've all got those.

The tall boy's black hair fell to his shoulders and the beginnings of a moustache hung under his thin nose. His eyes looked right through them. Suddenly, he grabbed the boy closest to him by the hair and effortlessly lifted him to his face. The boy grimaced and whimpered and clutched at the thin hand that held his hair.

The tall boy turned to the group and held up the little one as if he were selling a chicken. "Welcome to the Book House of the Usher of the Night. My name is Satch. You'll remember my name, because if you don't I will hurt you." He paused to scan the group. "What's my name?" he demanded.

"Satch!" came the immediate reply. All eyes were on the moaning boy he held aloft.

"That's very good! Now. I'm the Usher's Prefect. That means I get things done, and that means you'll follow my orders. If you don't follow my orders, I will hurt you."

He paused and spoke to the boy he held. "What's my name?"

"S-S-Satch," replied the youngster painfully.

"Right! Now. Let's understand each other. This is a school. You're here to learn. If you don't learn, I will hurt you. Have I made myself clear?"

"Yes!" the group replied.

"You're off to a fine start," said Satch with a smirk.

Tim's face grew very red when the Prefect dropped the boy in a heap at his feet. As the boy cried softly, Tim had to check himself: Not yet, not yet.

"Follow me," Satch instructed and, turning sharply, he headed for a doorway off the courtyard. Several boys picked up the little one and helped him along. Tim glanced behind him and noticed a old man cloaked in purple hobbling through the gates.

Right on schedule.

A chubby boy who wore a thick sheathed knife watched the old man looking about as if he were lost. He stepped up boldly, resting his meaty hand on the hilt. "What do you want, wrinkly?"

The old man, whose back bent him halfway to the ground, glanced about, unsure of who addressed him. Finally his squinting eyes found the rosy face of the boy. "Come to see the Usher!" he declared.

"State your business!" shouted the boy.

"Nope. Sorry. That's a secret. Only for the Usher's ears!"

The boy laughed. "You can't just walk in here and demand to see the Usher! First you've got to see the Prefect. Then you've got to make an appointment. And then, if he *wants* to see you—"

But the old man either did not hear or he was being very stubborn. "Nope. Gotta see the Usher. Important message."

The fat boy drew his blade. "Now look!" he warned, shaking the knife proudly under the old man's nose.

"Nice knife you got there, lad," the old man said. "Give it to me."

The boy stopped waving the knife. He stood very still for a moment, then reached over with his free hand and took hold of the blade. He offered it handle first to the old man, saying: "Well . . . if it's alright."

"It's alright," said the old man, and the blade disappeared into the folds of his purple cloak. "Now, where can I find the Usher?"

The boy could not take his eyes off the old man. He pointed a thumb behind him. "He's—he's in the tower—where he usually is. But he never sees anybody much anymore."

"He'll see me," replied the old man. "Now get back to your post and forget about this."

"Yes, sir," said the boy, turning on his heels.

As the old man clung to the wall and slowly made his way to the nearest doorway he heard a cow lowing sadly.

In one of the Book House lower halls there was a small broken fountain filled with scummy green water. The hall was deserted except for the old cook who had just finished preparing lunch. He was hiding in a remote corner in the shadow of an arch, drinking a bottle of wine from his private stash—leftovers from the days when the Book House was a favorite retreat of the Queen and her ladies. How far he had fallen. Doomed to serving gruel to mutts, daily bearing the brunt of their cruelty. This struck him as a singular injustice. He had once been the Queen's assistant chef. His specialty was pastries. He had proudly served many a royal feast, but he was reduced to boiling potatoes for a slimy group of ungrateful brats. It was fate, cursed fate.

He tilted the bottle once more and in the corner of his eyes glimpsed a splash in the fountain.

He set the bottle carefully down, then rose up shouting: "Look here now! You get away from there! You're making a mess!"

The usual silence followed. He liked to think that he carried some authority in the Book House, though it was far from true.

"The Prefect will hear of this!"

He shuffled to the fountain and found a small purple cloth floating on the surface. They've been at it with the kittens again, he thought.

He shouted out to the escaping prankster: "Don't go leaving your bloody rags about, you hear! You little beastie!"

It was then he glimpsed the strangest set of footprints he'd ever seen: two wet wedges repeated at intervals until they disappeared around a corner.

Tim's group of boys were shown to their quarters: a musty cold room full of tall bunks of straw. The only light came from one slit in the wall that was too high to offer any view. Straw covered the stone floor. They were told to undress, then marched naked single file down the chilly corridor to a room filled with stacks of black cloth. Here they were fitted with robes. While they were dressing a loud bell rang out, followed by the footsteps of running boys bursting through doors, rushing down stairs.

It was lunchtime. Satch led the boys in their scratchy black cloaks to the refectory: a big room with many long tables; its high ceiling was fitted with wooden beams, and tall grimy windows let in a grayish light. Boys scrambled for places in line, pushing, gouging, and cursing, but this seemed more out of hunger than play, for their faces were oddly solemn. As Satch walked by they cowered like animals. The new boys stood with Tim at the end of the line, unsure of the proper behavior, watching the others with wide eyes.

A blond boy ran up to Satch and said, "Prefect, it's—um—Thomas. He's—he's—he's got—you better come and see."

Satch cursed quietly and pointed at Tim and two other new boys. "You, you, and you. Come!" he barked.

The blond boy led them up a spiral staircase flanked by smoking torches. Another boy—who could have been his twin—ran to meet them. He was frightened. "Thomas got his spells mixed up again, Prefect!"

They followed the boy into an empty room. One of the twins pointed up. Tim brought his hand to his mouth when he saw Thomas, spread eagle, pinned on the ceiling like a bat. His head rolled slowly on his shoulders and his eyes were locked back into his skull, making white slits in his face. "You can't touch me!" he screamed. "You can't touch me!"

The Prefect looked annoyed as he stepped to the spot directly under the boy. "That's enough now, Thomas."

At the sound of Satch's voice the boy's head stopped rolling and he was perfectly still. Satch mumbled a rhyme, then said, "Down, Thomas. Down, boy."

The boy dropped and Satch caught him in his arms. Thomas's eyes snapped back into place and he gazed at the Prefect with mounting horror. "Oh, I'm so sorry, Prefect! So terribly sorry!"

"You messed up your spells again, Thomas," the Prefect said quietly.

"It was an accident! I was doing a defense and, and . . . Oh, I'm sorry. I'm sorry!"

"Next time, Thomas, I will leave you locked in your spell."

"Never. I will never, never again!"

Satch dropped the boy to the floor. "Stand up, Thomas."

THE Gift

"Please, Prefect." The boy was whimpering on his knees. "I remember now. Gravi-gravi-something."

"Up, Thomas," Satch commanded, and the boy was jerked to his feet by an invisible force. Satch laid his hand on Thomas's trembling cheek. He spoke with utter calm and reason. "You simply must learn to be more careful, Thomas. You are far too eager. You haven't studied your spelling hard enough."

"I will, Prefect. I promise."

"I know you will," said Satch sympathetically.

Thomas let out an awful wail and fell to the ground. "Take him to the infirmary," instructed Satch. The blond twins picked up the unconscious boy and dragged him out of the room. As he passed, Tim saw a raw burn on Thomas's cheek. It was in the shape of a hand. Satch looked down at Tim and his companions. "We demand an intense commitment from our pupils. We do not tolerate failure. Now, let's see what that drunkard's made for lunch."

As they followed Satch out of the room he said over his shoulder: "What's my name?" The two boys immediately replied. Tim remained silent. Satch stopped walking, turned, and gazed at Tim, who stood behind the two boys. "Step aside," he said, and the boys bolted out of the way. "I'm afraid you didn't hear me." He folded his arms and looked coldly at Tim.

"I heard you."

So accustomed was Satch to inspiring fear that he was momentarily puzzled by Tim's reply. But as he sensed rebellion, he became angry and still.

Tim stood his ground and looked him in the eyes. He was thinking of a boy. A boy who is angry about something. Something he could never tell anyone about. Not even his father.

It was the day he watched as the stranger hurt his mother. Of course, he didn't know what he was doing. Not then. He only knew he was hurting her. And she was naked. And as he hid in the loft and heard the sounds of the bad man, his dogs whinnied and barked about his bare legs as their master's violence and laughter ascended. And he felt as if his mother was being devoured by a pack of wild dogs. And somehow it became easier to be-lieve that people weren't capable of such ugly acts—only dogs could reach such an frenzy.

And how she apologized afterward. How she said it didn't hurt that much. How glad she was he didn't touch him. How that was all that mattered to her. How well he hid. How proud she was he didn't cry out or interfere. And how he mustn't tell. Mustn't tell anyone. Ever.

He never remembered a word the stranger said. Only the barking of his dogs. And that was how he remembered it. For years. The Day the Wild Dogs Came.

"Your name is Bully," said Tim. "And I have had enough of you."

Satch tried to claw Tim's face but found, to his surprise, that his hand bounced away just before it reached its mark. He stepped back and held his hands aloft. "So!" he cried. "You've learned some witching from the country, have you?"

The space between his hands burst into a ball of fire, which shot out and enveloped Tim. The other boys dove for cover. As quickly as the flame had come, it faded to nothing.

Satch screamed with fury, and suddenly, he was a blue wolf, growling and ready to pounce. He leaped into the air, his fangs wide and dripping. Tim caught the wolf in a wind pocket and flipped it over his head. It smashed against the wall and fell to the floor, whining.

Tim approached the blue wolf, holding his hand before him like a shield. "My name is Tim, and you'll remember it."

The animal spasmed twice. Satch lay crumpled on the floor, a trickle of blood running from the corner of his mouth. He flinched as Tim stepped closer and said, "If you don't remember it, I will kill you."

The two boys stood speechless, swiveling their eyes between the Pre-fect and the stranger, unable to decide which to fear more, until finally they took off down the corridor.

THE Gift

And the man inside whistled silently in respect for the boy he was stuck with.

The old man moved as if he were blind: one hand ran along the wall, the other hung loosely at his side. A bell was ringing loudly somewhere and a group of boys ran past the stranger without alarm. They might have noticed an odd shadow in a Book House full of shadows, or an old chair tipping against the wall, or if they were very observant, an extra torch with a bright flame. But it would not have struck them as strange. The Book House was heavy with magic, and they were accustomed to illusion.

As the old man ascended the spiral steps that led to the tower, he remarked to himself how eerily silent the Book House really was: He heard no minds. He focused his attention at the room at the top of the stairs. Nothing. He paused before a heavy metal door and tried to bore through it with his listening sense. Nothing. He concluded he could wait no longer for his two friends: This was his battle. As he lifted his hand to knock, a voice came from behind the door. "Come in. . . ."

Chapter twenty-seven

AFTER MONTHS OF HEARING THAT voice in his nightmares and memories, it was quite alarming to hear it come to life before him. Simon pushed the door lightly and it swung open on protesting hinges. He felt the weight of the knife in his belt. Do it. Kill him now. Kill him. With great effort he pushed down the thought. He would wait for the others.

"So good to see you!" said the Night Usher as the old man stepped in.

The Usher's room was full of candles, they hung from the ceiling on wheels, the walls were coated with them. Their melted wax covered tables and the books resting on them. A huge black tapestry with golden dragons hung on the wall behind him. The dragons locked their jaws onto each other's tails so that they formed a perfect circle. On the marble floor lay a five-pointed star: Squat candles rested on the tips, and their wax flowed slowly toward the center. A ball of flame was set in a wide stained glass window on the near side of the room. There was a huge fireplace fully stoked and burning insatiably on the opposite side. Against one wall there stood a golden tub full of water. Gigantic shelves rose to the ceiling on the other wall; they held hundreds of books, and a tall ladder leaned against them. The Usher's throne was raised slightly by a black platform; three steps led up to it. The heat of the room made Simon queasy, and sweat dribbled down his back.

"I heard you coming," the Usher said.

He sat slouched in his throne, one leg casually thrown over an upholstered arm. His head tilted back lazily so that he looked down his nose, and a startling white smile broke out of his thick black beard. He was a small man. His other leg did not reach the floor. He wore a black velvet robe with black leggings; a simple golden cord was tied about his waist. He wore no jewelry. In his good hand he held a glass of milk. He lifted it to his lips, slowly drained the glass, and set it on a small table beside the throne. A white crescent remained on his mustache.

"Ahhhhh!" he uttered and smiled.

This innocent gesture disturbed Simon greatly, for it slyly suggested he was about to be toyed with.

"Gosi got your tongue?" He giggled.

Simon's old man façade faded instantly. "Hello, Usher."

"That's *much* better. Now we can have the pleasant chat that I've *so* been looking forward to."

He motioned to a chair opposite the fireplace. A sense of defeat cascaded over Simon. *Could I have been so foolish as to believe I had the power to challenge this?* As he sat he noticed a strange flat rectangular object resting on the arm of the Usher's throne. The King had never seen anything like it before. It resembled a small jewelry box, but it was not made of wood and it was too thin to hold anything inside. It seemed to be made from black metal but it had no sheen. It was covered with rows of tiny crystal bumps and each was labeled: Impossibly minute words were scrawled in white below the bumps.

"What's that?" Simon said pointing.

The Usher looked down at the object and smiled. "That is the future. But its relevance is remote to us now. We have other business." The Usher slapped his hands together and sat upright. "Milk?" he offered.

Simon shook his head.

"Wonderful stuff, really. Quenches, invigorates. I have a good cow named Lady. So I drink it all day." He poured himself another glass from a silver pitcher.

"Well, I suppose you want an explanation for everything? Yes. Well. It's really very simple. I apologize outright for any inconveniences I may have caused you. They were unavoidable."

Simon could not take his eyes off the man. He felt a vast helplessness—he tried but was unable to make a fist.

"Your cure was a necessary step toward acquiring this Book House. Did you know I was raised and schooled here?"

Simon shook his head.

The Usher looked about the room and sighed.

"So many fond memories. But, sentiment aside, I needed a place to continue my studies and set up my school. I hadn't the wherewithal at my disposal so I sought a suitable benefactor, shall we say? Imagine my surprise when I learned of your ailment . . . and the reward. It all seemed too good to be true."

"I don't believe you," said Simon. "You did something with the water—poisoned it."

"Oh. I didn't think you knew about that. Yes. Well. I did indeed have a run of bad luck with several experiments—water into blood, blood into water—that sort of thing. And, oh, I guess you could say that bad came to worse—these things happen you know—and I had to dump it somewhere. I had no idea it would spread so far and wide. But there are certain sacrifices that must be made for the sake of Science." This final word he said with great reverence, and leaning forward with a look of concern he added: "By the by, that's another good reason to start drinking milk." He laughed loudly.

"But why harp on the past, eh? The Water Sickness is leveling off. And, let's not forget that you did regain your hearing. I should think you'd be slightly grateful to me."

"You cursed me with a Listening Spell," Simon said.

The Usher pondered this for a moment. "Alright. It wasn't the most effective spell, I'll grant you that. But *believe* me, it was given with the best intentions. True, the spell was in its raw form—not entirely mature—I might have left out a word or two, some of them are so old I can barely decipher them." He looked humbly at Simon. "But it was the best I can do."

"What about Jason?"

"Jason? Oh, you mean that huge brute! What about him? He came bounding in here one night after slaying two of my best dogs, and what was I to do? The man lacked all proportion! He was hysterical—he was determined to physically harm me!"

"You spelled him mad."

"It was either that, my young friend, or fisticuffs. And I've always found that vulgar. And anyway, haven't I the right to defend myself? There was no reasoning with the fellow! He—" a wet cough erupted from the Usher and he nearly doubled over to address it.

When the man had composed himself, Simon said, "You sent him after me."

"Did I?" squeaked the Usher, then cleared his throat. "Well, yes, I suppose I did."

He was like a fog: shifting, deceptive, impossible to corner, malleable to the least pressure. Simon began to suspect he didn't exist.

"You must understand my position. I began to hear alarming reports about you after I settled in here. Stories about a young sorcerer matching your description. And, frankly, you surprised me, lad. You were not a man of power when I first met you. How did you gain your knowledge?"

The question was offered in utter innocence. Simon felt obliged to tell him and was about to when he noticed the Usher drumming his fingers on the arm of his throne. To an ordinary man this would have meant nothing. But to a man of power like Simon, it was clearly the sign of an interrogation spell which induced an answer. He clamped his mouth shut. The Usher marked his resistance, stopped drumming, and continued as if nothing had happened.

"Ah, no matter. I only ask because I am a collector." He spread his arms, showing off his books. "I have perhaps the most complete collection of esoteric studies by some of the most farsighted, brilliant thinkers in history. Forgive my boasting, but it has been a remarkable venture. I shouldn't wonder that you've read some of these volumes. I've read them all. Many times. This, my friend, is my wealth—my dream. Not the school, certainly not this Book House. Goodness, how it's gotten shabby. But knowledge! Knowledge to release mortal man from his bonds of ignorance!" The Usher gazed into the air, consumed in his revery. "I have found worlds beyond your wildest imaginings! Forces with the power to unlock the very heart of the world and lay its endless fortunes at your feet. You've surely tasted some of these mysteries. But I assure you, there is more. Much more." The Usher stood and Simon heard a faint sound: a jingle of metal, as if he had a pocketful of coins. "Why, in this room alone there is enough knowledge to build a house like this in one day! There are the cures for every disease that has ever afflicted man. There is the key to open any man's mind and read his inmost thoughts. There is the power to control fire, earth, plants, stone! There are spells that can take a man out of his body as he sleeps and send him on a journey to strange distant lands. He may stay there for years before he wakes." His eyes danced merrily. "I know. I have done it!"

He descended to Simon, jingling with every step. Somehow, the force of the Usher's words, combined with that homely jingling, petrified the King.

"You are a man of power, my friend. Not so great as mine, of course, but enough so that you can see the potential in all of this. A man could do anything he wanted. He could bring the world to its knees and raise it up again, singing his praises. We two are very much alike. We both have sought out the secrets of the earth. We both have mined the ore of everlasting.

"Life without end—I tell you—it is within our grasp!"

THE Gift

The Usher held out his hand. "I ask you to join me on my quest! I offer you . . . limitless possibilities!!"

The open hand implored Simon to grasp it. The King found himself trembling yet caught in the vision the Usher had drawn up. He hadn't expected to be offered an adventure or a partnership. And his mind whirled with magnificent landscapes, waterfalls of color, and bold rousing music that beat to the drum of his heart. He was very tired. Very tired indeed. And he saw no alternative but to admit defeat and throw in his lot with his better.

Chapter twenty-eight

As Simon's hand rose there was a noise at the door.

"There you are!" cried Tim.

The Usher turned and screamed spittle at the schoolboy in the doorway. "How dare you interrupt me!"

Simon said weakly, "He's with me."

"With you?" said the Usher, pivoting his head between the two.

Tim walked to Simon's side and touched his arm. This small gesture lifted him out of the depths and cleared his mind. Had he actually considered allying himself to this man? Was that possible? He still had no hope of victory, but now at least, he was no longer deceived. The Usher, jingling slightly, moved backward toward the throne, his face utterly cold. "Who is this child?" he demanded.

"A friend," said Simon.

There was a splashing in the golden tub and all eyes turned to see Marty climb out dripping wet. The Usher tensed visibly, then relaxed back into his throne and touched a finger to his lips. "My Lord, you are full of surprises. Another one of your friends?"

"I'm afraid so."

"Remarkable. Will there be anyone else coming?"

No one answered him. Marty moved to the roaring fireplace, gazed into the flames for a moment, then said, "I got here as soon as I could."

"And now," said Tim, "we can begin."

They stood in the center of the room facing the throne. Simon remembered that he was to be the spokesman at this point, but he hesitated, feeling rather silly, as if he were about to tell a bad joke. Finally, he admitted, "We've come for your surrender, Usher."

The Usher's eyes betrayed nothing; he might not have heard.

"Of course, I know all this is foolishness," Simon continued. "I tried to explain it to these two, but they insisted . . ."

"And if we cannot come to terms?" asked the Usher.

"Well," Simon replied, "that's the sticky part. See, there *are* no terms."

"No terms," said the Usher dryly.

Simon shivered as he spoke. "It's unconditional, Usher. All or nothing."

"Just a moment," said the Usher. "Let me attempt to summarize your position. You, this frog, and this child have come to offer me my resignation. That's it, isn't it?" Simon nodded and the Usher continued. "You are prepared—correct me if I'm wrong—to influence my decision?"

"We mean to challenge you. You'll have to take my word for it. These two are set on it."

The Usher pondered this, then spoke to Tim. "Who are you, child? Why do you disturb my quiet home? How have I harmed you?"

"My name is Tim. I have nothing else to say to you."

"I can appreciate your temper, lad. Really. I know I have a tendency to upset people. But there's a problem here. I just can't see giving you my throne. Because I honestly enjoy it."

"Enjoy it while you can," croaked Marty.

"Froggy!" said the Usher with delight. "If I'm not mistaken, you are an actual Waterman! Marvelous! I had thought your race extinct! What's your part in this?"

Marty turned to Simon and said, "He talks a lot, doesn't he?" Turning back to the Usher the frog said, "Any last words?"

The Usher had a coughing fit that turned into a stifling of giggles. "Your Majesty!" he mocked when he had recovered. "I am amazed! I do believe he's threatening me!"

"I told you they were in earnest," Simon said.

"It boggles the mind! And what's *your* role, Simon? Fool? Teacher? Guide?"

Simon cleared his throat. "Well, frankly, I'm with them."

"You want me out, too?"

"I do."

A dark chuckle came from his lips. "You disappoint me, my friend. You of all people should know your place. The truth is, you were never very good at magic, Simon. You could never quite give yourself over completely. That makes your art dull and weak."

"We wait for your answer," said Tim impatiently.

The Usher sighed deeply and stifled a cough. Then, covering his eyes with his good hand, and wearily rubbing his brow, he said, "Ah, children, children."

The small man began to caress the ruptured palm of his bad hand. "You remind me of a witch I once instructed. She thought she knew about power." He smiled slightly and rolled his tongue about his lower lip; it looked like a serpent caught in a pouch. He looked at Simon. "She knew nothing."

The Usher rose, then turning his back to his guests, he stepped over to the fire.

"This will be less sport than I counted on. Apparently, my young King, you have infected them with some misguided righteous zeal. Well . . ." His shoulders jiggled. "Let us see the force of zeal against madness." And facing the hearth, he raised his hand, commanding.

Tim took in his surroundings with several quick, darting glances. He was standing as he had been when the transformation occurred, but he no longer stood next to a chair. He was at the edge of a wide canopy bed that was covered with pure white lace. At the foot of the bed, across an intri-

cate rug, was a roaring fireplace, and standing before it, with his back toward Tim, was the Usher. Tim could feel no heat from the fire. The smells
of the ornate chamber were identical to the room where, moments before,
he had stood next to his companions: wax, dust, and burning wood.

"This is some kind of trick," he said.

"Don't bother yourself with that, child," said the Usher over his shoulder. "There's someone here you'll be very happy to see."

There was a knock at the door. "Come in," the Usher said.

"Mother!" whispered Tim.

"I've brought you some soup, Timothy. You look moon-pale, son!"

"Mother, how did you get here?"

"Hush! Your soup first," she said, sitting him down on the bed and laying the bowl on his lap. She neatly snapped open a folded napkin and
tucked it under his chin. Something throbbed in Tim's throat and he
found he could not speak without crying. His mother put a silver spoon
in his hand and stroked his hair with cold fingers. "There now! I told you
we wouldn't be long, didn't I?"

"Yes," said Tim, crying.

"This is *your* room, Tim!" she whispered, as if they were sharing a glorious secret. "Have you ever *seen* such a splendid bed? No more sleeping
on that dirty straw, eh? Listen, it's all like this! Your father and I—"

"Where's father?" Tim asked.

"Now, now, your soup is getting cold!"

"Where's *father?*" cried Tim.

"The woodcutter's coming soon, I promise. He has a present for you!"
She stole a glance at the Usher before the fire, then whispered to Tim. "He
doesn't understand women."

"Father?" Tim asked, confused.

She indicated the Usher with a flick of her eyebrows. "The empty one."

Her expression changed abruptly, as if someone had tugged a cord
around her neck. She flinched, then her eyes got dreamy. "John-John's re-

ally changed." She sighed, smiling a secret smile, and her cheeks seemed to burn. "I remember when nothing could have dragged him out of his woodshed. You know how he was about his projects." Tim nodded, thinking, This is new. She never talked this way to me before. "Some nights I'd fall asleep, hearing him sanding away." She swung her head to and fro as if enjoying the memory of a dance. "Sanding, sanding, sanding. Like some chorus of bugs. But now." She sighed again and held the back of her hand to one of her warm cheeks. "Goodness! He's a different man." The tiniest giggle escaped her. "I have to *kick* him out of bed." Tim smiled, glad for her apparent happiness, pleased at the prospect of his father's joy, and totally baffled at what it was they were so satisfied about.

Twinkling, said the man within, as if the child were dense.

She cupped his face in her cool hands and gave him the gift that every boy longs for from his mother. "I will never leave you again, Tim. Never. I am yours forever. As long as we're together, you'll never grow up, never grow old, never be lonely—I promise. You'll never get sick, and you'll never die. What more could any boy want?"

To say Tim received these words with unbounded joy would be true. But it would be truer to say that the words overwhelmed him. Somehow, he knew they were false. And part of him was shocked, for his mother had never lied to him before.

"Mother?" he asked. "Are you alright?"

"Alright?" she answered, as if the question were absurd. She crossed her arms over her chest. "Tim! I have you! I have everything I need!" She leaned in close and confided, "You wouldn't believe the pantry! Or the games. There's even a bath with water that never goes cold! How would you like a pet dog?"

"Two dogs!" said the Usher, then coughed loudly.

"Three dogs!" said his mother clasping her hands together. "Three dogs you can call your very own!"

Just then, the woodcutter poked his head through the metal-plated door. It was a wonder Tim recognized him, for it looked as though all his hair had been singed off, he had no eyebrows, and his face was charred and black and blistered. But Tim knew him by his eyes, and in them he saw something he would never forget: a fierce joy, the look of someone defeated, in horrible pain, but someone who knew he had struck a lucky fatal blow to his opponent.

"Nobody's quick enough for three!" he said, smiling.

Marty sat up in the humming boat that skimmed down the middle of a turquoise channel. The Usher stood with his back to her, his feet braced against the angled sides of the bow.

"If you've harmed the boy, I'll see you drowned!"

The Usher raised his bad hand. "Peace. The boy is safe. Have some dinner." And he reached down and pulled up a net full of fish that twitched and slapped against the wooden bottom.

"Impossible!" Marty spat. "No one could eat this many fish."

"But you're starving," said the Usher kindly. "And you mustn't let them go to waste."

The net squirmed at her feet. Marty could not remember the last time she had eaten. "This is no common catch. None of these fish swim together."

"All the more a delicacy!" said the Usher. "Indulge yourself!"

Her mouth was watering, so she reached down and quickly ate one fish, and then another. The fish were boneless; they consisted entirely of meat—they were delicious. And, for a moment, you could say she felt no hunger. But it would be truer to say she felt nothing.

Marty heard a nagging buzz and turned. Behind her, a large insect was resting its chin on the stern of the boat; it hummed like a dittykaid in the mating and wore a quicksilver helmet like a fly dipped in liquid moonlight. Its tail churned in the water as a maple seedling spins its way to earth, trailing a frothy wake and propeling the rickety boat across the channel. Jewels shaped like glyphs and scribbler marks adorned its gleaming head. To Marty it seemed something both living and not, something born yet smithy-wrought. She was about to ask the Usher to explain when she noticed his odd stance in the bow. "Aren't your ankles getting tired?"

The Usher chuckled. "Don't you worry about me. Have some more fish."

"No, thank you."

"Ohh, I insist. Have some more."

"I'm quite full. I've already had two."

"Have three," suggested the Usher. Then Marty saw his shoulders jolting up and down as he coughed.

Suddenly, there was a splash and Marty felt her heart drop to her stomach. The Listener poked his tiny white head over the side of the boat. His pale hand touched hers quickly, and an understanding beyond words passed between them in that family way that no one on the outside could ever hope to grasp. The little one closed his eyes for a moment, as if he savored a smell. She noticed he had command of his body, and was overjoyed. He nodded his head in the direction of the Usher. "He doesn't know about you," he croaked, then giggled as if it were a wonderful joke. "Nobody's quick enough for three!"

Simon was standing in an open field. Huge clouds rolled overhead and the sun came pouring through the blue. In his hand he held a broadsword smeared with blood, and at his feet lay the body of his victim, facedown: a harmless-looking pile of flesh cloaked in black. With a flick of his toes he turned over the body and saw it was the Usher. Joy washed over him and a song rose in his heart. He had done the impossible: The shadow had passed. The enemy was slain. Perhaps, after all, his power was superior!

To say that he felt all this was true. But it would be truer to say that it felt him. An unspoken contradiction lodged inside his mind and did battle with his triumph.

A heavy hand lay on his shoulder and he whirled about.

It was Jason, just as he had seen him last. But, no—there was an enormous difference. Something he didn't know the word for. Like an image that stubbornly lingers on the margins of memory. This was Jason as he had been: solemn, fierce. Alive.

No, he reminded himself. Not alive.

"My Prince," the horse said with a slight bow and a smile. He wore a strange white smock, and his bare feet and hairy arms were all that it revealed. There was an odd thin band about his wrist and Jason's full name was printed backward on it: last name first.

"I killed you," said Simon, utterly miserable.

Jason shrugged. "It was a fair fight. You had no choice."

"Can you stay long?" Simon asked suddenly, conscious of how precious this time was, and how fragile: Visits with the dead were said to be brief affairs.

"No, I'm afraid the timer is ticking."

Timer? thought Simon.

"But, take heart, my Prince. You're going to make a great King."

As if that were any comfort.

Then Jason drew his hand from behind his back to show him three walnut halves resting in his huge palm. The big man looked down at the body of the Usher and smiled, then turned back and shared it with Simon: The smile grew wry as it passed between them, like a private joke. "Do you remember?" he asked.

For a moment Simon struggled to grasp another slippery memory. Then, as if the key had finally turned inside the lock, something shifted open inside of him, and he recalled. The trickster. The court. The festival. Jason whispering in his ear: explaining the magic.

"Your move. Your Majesty," the man said turning. Simon watched him walk away in the garment that seemed to glow whiter than a cloud: It was open in the back and tied at the neck and the waist with a type of bow. He strolled down the hill, leaving Simon with the answer to a riddle and the body of the Usher at his feet. When Jason was a throw away, Simon realized they might never see each other again and he called out, "Jason!"

The huge man turned and held up an arm to shade his eyes.

Then Simon said something he had never said to anyone before. Perhaps that made it easier to say. Perhaps he knew this was his last chance to say it and he could not bear letting it go unsaid. Or perhaps he was merely following the impulse of a dream—for dreams allow us leeway onto paths we'd waking never dare to take.

"I love you!" the King called fiercely.

Jason said nothing. But his grin appeared wide and white under the blade of shadow that hid the rest of his face. A warm, satisfied smile it was. Then he dropped his arm and turned away, and in a moment, disappeared over the green hill.

For a time Simon watched the space where his tutor had last been. Then, shaking off the feelings that swarmed inside him, he observed the field. The sky. And then his victim. He smelled the air and remembered once again the story Jason had called up from his past. And soon he understood that everything about this place was unreal: He was spellbound. Flinging his sword aside with disdain he squatted next to the body, and relief flooded through his muscles. He was perfectly still for a moment, his eyes focused on the crippled hand of the Usher. He licked his lips, chuckled, and spoke casually to the corpse.

"When I was four, a trickster came to Court. She claimed she could make a pea disappear under three walnut shells—and she could! Try as I might, I could never find the pea after she shuffled the shells. But as I watched, Jason leaned over and told me the secret. The trick, he said, was not to use three peas. One at a time and it'll work, but he assured me: 'Nobody's quick enough for three.' "

The body coughed once.

Simon smiled, looked directly at the pale head, and said the breaking spell. "Usher, nobody's quick enough for three!"

Like a flint striking light into a dark room, the madness was dispelled. Tim, Marty, and Simon stood side by side in the throne room of the Night Usher. They were glad to be back.

As he turned to face them the Usher trembled and coughed into his good hand. Obviously, he had gotten into the habit of winning: Defeat settled into his face like suffocation. He opened his mouth and a horrible scream came forth, and then he was gone.

Chapter twenty-nine

IT WAS THE BIRD'S FAULT, thought the Usher. Always the bird. He grumbled to himself as he dashed through the winding passageways, the secret doors only he and that arrogant Prefect of his knew. Where was Satch, anyway? Never there when needed. Always off somewhere pinching his students. Still, he ran a tight ship. And he had a gift for management which the Usher, preoccupied with his studies, had neither the patience nor the inclination to undertake. Let the wolf handle it.

He caught himself against a doorway and coughed. His palm held a glob of greenish sputum, and looking at it, he realized his health was perhaps less robust then he let on to his boys. But then physical exertion wasn't something he was used to.

It was the bird. Always the bird. He had no cough until the bird had shown him the apparatuses and their secret commands. Could there have been a poison emanating from the glowing jewels, passing through the air and entering his small frame? But that was illogical. As a scientist he knew that poison was not ambulatory. It required a medium, either liquid or solid, to traverse between materials. And vapor was spiritual medium and thus by nature incapable of hosting anything detrimental to body or spirit. Besides, since his Transformation, his sense of smell had developed into an instrument he could trust. He had smelled nothing.

Where was the bird? Of course, he would never call it that aloud. It was a private joke he relished when he knew the bird was off on one of its sprees: fetching boys, starting fires, or hunting game. Once it had appeared at the window of his tower with the foot of a child in its beak. He had presumed to scold the bird about the uses such a specimen could have served in his laboratory. But the beast had spit it out on a perfectly good chair, flown past his head, the wing tip flicking his ear, and had lectured him on the appetite of a symbiote. How dare the bird presume to instruct him? He who had freed it, he who had spent his entire life pursuing the arts that had made possible its release from prison.

"Not prison," the bird had corrected him. "Stasis." But it was a distinction that did slight justice to the Usher's genius.

And where was the bird now? Where was the bird when he had cast the dream spell and sent the three upstarts into their reverie realms? He hadn't needed any help doing that. He stood on a stool, drew the ring of keys from his pocket, and using his good hand, unlocked a cabinet. From the top shelf he removed a vial of dried willow leaves and shook a few into his bad palm. They looked like boats stuck in a low-tide muck. He flicked them into his mouth and chewed eagerly. The feeling would start on his tongue—a pleasant numbing that would soon spread down his throat into his spine. In a minute he would not feel the stars of pain in his lungs or the sour knot in his stomach. In a minute he would feel strong again.

He sat on the floor to let the feeling come. It was a position he would never allow himself to be seen in by any of his students. Although, from time to time, Satch had been present when he had taken his daily constitutional. After all, his dosage—he had begun to call it that when the pain had forced him to triple it—was purely medicinal. And nothing to be ashamed about. He was no drunkard. He retained command of all his reason. It was just his body that had rebelled. And the bird. Always the bird.

First it was little things. Like insisting he watch it feed. As if there were anything to be gained by observing such butchery. "Do you see?" the bird would ask him. "Do you see how the bone snaps here with just the slightest bit of pressure?" He had no inclination to observe these rituals. He was a man of learning, bent on higher thoughts. What did he care about the best way to skin a dog? What possible interest could he have mustered in the precise way a squirrel's tail, dipped in honey, could be used to coax ants from their volcanoes? Books! He'd pleaded to the bird. Bring me books. And occasionally it did. Apparatuses! he commanded. Show me your collection! And less and less frequently, it complied.

Eventually the bird had insisted on revealing the secrets of the human "organism." And not being a man of prejudice, and not wanting to show his fear, he had submitted to a series of what the bird called "inspections." Curious, what a body could endure. But, finally, he had to ask in the calmest voice possible: What are you doing? What possible benefit could be derived from this? And when he could bear it no longer he'd simply say: Please or Not again or That hurts.

It had never occurred to him that he would grow to fear the bird. Of course he could have spelled it into oblivion with a wave of his hand but something, well, everything about the bird, restrained him. Still, fear was a small price to pay for the worlds that had opened to him. The vast realms of knowledge that scrolled and stuttered before his eyes when he consulted the bird's ghost window. The dream journeys where he would weave and hover over landscapes in his ether body, as the bird sometimes hovered over the candles in his study, its claws just out of reach of the lapping flames, teasing them—somehow beyond their burning.

It had all been worth it to travel in Between. To glimpse other worlds, other times. Places past words, past knowing, past even the imaginings of his ample and analytical mind. Places where limbless yet intelligent creatures thrived happily inside the skin of others like maggots in a carcass. Albino mermen who constructed entire cities of glowing green bubbles on the ocean floor and had so perfected their diet that they only ate each other. Spiderlike parasites as big as his hand that rode on the spines of talking beasts. Brilliant venomous plants which trapped and feasted on flies. Sentient rocks. Conscious clouds.

And aeons forward. Days yet to be. He would catch himself staring openmouthed at the ghost window, unaware of time, in a place beyond thought, overwhelmed by the flashing yet soothing imagery whose messages felt encoded yet all the same approachable, almost intimate. At times he felt as if he were being asked to purchase foodstuffs and apparatuses whose purpose and appeal were at best trivial. Yet the images spoke with fierce eloquence and economy, condensing the most vivid tales into stories as the finest tapestries do, promising all manner of satisfaction: rest, peace, relief, respect, beauty, fertility, power, freedom, honor, and, often, romantic success—which struck him as singularly implausible. Is this how the future conducted itself? Was the only use of such marvels the perfection of hygiene, the excellence of inebriation, the variety of meals? At times his impression was that the ghost window had been possessed by the spirit of some mad tinker who, through the wonders of this dream machine, had unlimited access to the appetites and longings of the entire civilized world. Must every image be a transaction? the Usher wondered. Would invention be reduced to commerce? Shall Science become a mere tool of the marketplace? Where was truth? Where was insight? Where was knowledge?

Yet as he delved deeper he found hope.

There were bubble-headed shining birds of polished silver screaming through dark turbulent skies discharging projectiles of death. The blossoming magnificence of fire that armies someday would spew forth upon their enemies. The crystal lenses they wore upon their noses that mitigated their flawed vision. The clever instruments of time the futures used to dissect reality into increments and numbers. Their opulent and rampant slave apparatuses, which executed the most mundane tasks so efficiently. The precision of their surgeons. The industry and quality of their slaughterhouses. The colorful mayhem of their spectator sports.

He would have given anything to have been born then.

It had been worth it. All of it.

Besides, the bird had promised him everything he ever wanted. And he had no reason to doubt him. Still, as his studies flourished, the long sought Golden Dream he had pursued so fervently had somehow receded into a bank of fog. He found himself stopping in the middle of a lecture to watch a flock of birds outside the classroom window, to wonder, what was he doing? What exactly was the Golden Dream he had pursued? Knowledge? He had it in abundance. He knew more than any man alive— he had no doubts about that. Power? With a word he could have any of his students skinned. What then? He wondered. And for a moment, watching the birds stream by the window, conscious of the careful faces at their desks, staring and waiting for him to complete his thought, he wondered what was it all for? Why had he started? What had he gained?

He was the Usher, he reminded himself. He had his school and his responsibilities. He would set up his rule, secure his rightful authority. And having achieved all the power the bird had promised him? What then?

What then?

And in that terrible moment he knew, as all men eventually know that someday they will die, he knew: He had no clue.

He examined the scarred tissue of his right palm and saw again the barren scorched landscape. A palmist (before he had raped her) had read his hand and said she saw a fire that burned on nothing. A fire without tinder or heat. And he had taken it as an omen that all his experiments would one day yield the ultimate: Transformation.

It had happened. More than he dreamed. But still it nagged him that for all his mastery, he could find no way of healing his own hand. Nothing worked for long. It continued to ache and throb as if he still held it over the candle. It was the bird's fault. He would have to ask it. The bird would know why.

In his mind he held the brief joy of watching his adversaries succumb to his dream spell, standing like sleepwalkers in his study, the arrogant child's drool reeling down like a silver cord to his feet. How dare this peasant bastard challenge him with his purity and his presumptuous air sorcery! If he wouldn't have enjoyed his death so much, he'd have let the bird instruct him on the neural capacity of the body.

And the young King, standing like an idiot hero, his legs splayed apart, his hands hanging like a simian's, his ridiculous face cocked to the side, imagining his victory. Of course, he'd had potential. His listening aid was the pinnacle of the Usher's craft. It gave him almost as much satisfaction as the day he'd taken the brute Jason's mind and made it adore him. Yet, it was true—why not admit it?—the King had been a setback. He had expected an ally and a puppet. His plan had been to enlist him, not to engage him in combat. This was an outcome that had never occurred to him.

Like the frog. Shimmering sickly green before his fire, arms so thin and twisted they hardly deserved the name. His voice an abomination: as intelligent and viscous as the expulsions of the bird's apparatuses. His knobby back and stump rump, those bulging eyes that seemed to see you even though they looked the other way—it was all too much. He could not think of the Waterman without a shudder.

It reminded him, he could not say why, of the first birth he had ever attended with the bird. A wide-eyed thick-witted seamstress with a deep voice, whose wet cooing whimpers made his skin crawl. Who once, in the throes of labor, had tried to touch him on the head. He had opened her up and found inside the transparent sac . . . wonders: a blue and red and purple cauliflower with a tail that corkscrewed about the curd-covered human sprig, joining it at the entrance to the tiny belly, like a serpent worming into a hole.

"Nourishment is mutual," the bird had explained. "The baby feeds on the blood of the mother. The mother thrives on the youth of the child. It is the most natural thing in the world. It is symbiosis."

He also learned that by severing the twisted cord, the foetus would spasm and gulp, attempting to breathe the fluid in which it was preserved, and thus, eventually drown.

So much to learn. He sighed. So much to learn.

A dog was sniffing his feet and he realized he'd done it again: let the medicine get the better of him. Focus, he scolded his body, using one of the secret words. Focus.

"Is the courtyard ready?" he asked the dog, not remembering its name. It nodded eagerly; he gained his feet.

"Good boy," he said, scratching it behind the ear and striding forward to settle his ambush.

Chapter thirty

"AFTER HIM!" SIMON SHOUTED. As they sped down the spiral staircase, they heard the Usher yell, "Fetch my boys!" And then, the sound of boots on stone diminished as he ran away.

They could not find him.

For a short while they were lost in a maze of doors and steps. The Book House was a labyrinth of dark rooms and hallways leading nowhere. At the fountain where Marty had found her entry, they paused and listened.

A dog barked.

Following the sound, they dashed up a staircase, and finally found an archway that opened onto the courtyard.

They stepped into the middle of a blizzard. The snow stung their faces and the wind cut through their clothing mercilessly: They could barely see their hands stretched out before them.

"Be gone!" Tim shouted, and his voice was lost in the wild rush of wind and snow.

The wail receded, the whirlwind lost its power, and far across the courtyard as the swirls of snow wound down to silence, they saw their enemy.

The Night Usher stood by the main gate surrounded by his school of boys, their faces blank as snow. One of the small boys gave a low guttural bark. He was joined by several others, and soon all the boys were barking. Their horrible chorus echoed off the high stone walls.

The Usher stood in the middle of a pack of wild dogs. They clawed the ground, bared their teeth.

And then, they charged.

It was all Tim could do to keep the black man inside from bolting once he saw the magic dogs.

Simon stepped forward and cast a wall of fire before them, but they dove senselessly through it. Then the King hurled a freezing spell and the dogs faltered, as if they were running through water. Finally, one by one, they were paralyzed midstep. The Usher wailed, spelled open the front gates, and dashed through. Simon, Tim, and Marty followed, dodging the frozen dogs.

The Usher had just passed through the gates when it began to rain. But it was no ordinary rain. To the three that watched it looked like a rain of stones. Stumplike objects fell from the walls of the old Book House. One knocked the Usher to the ground and he screamed a single word. Several more fell directly upon him and he screamed no more. The rain continued: More and more of the objects fell, each landing on the one before it. There was the sound of stone falling on stone, until a high pile of oddly shaped rocks completely covered the body of the Usher of the Night.

"The Lie Catchers!" cheered Tim. "The Griffs! He *said* he would send help!"

The Griffs had scaled the ivy walls and waited for their chance. Their unique capacity to detect lies also made them deadly weapons. On contact with the Usher's body they had turned to stone and crushed him.

Simon examined the pile of Griffs sadly. To him they resembled a heap of discarded statues—so flawed the sculptor had abandoned them, unfinished. To Tim, though, their mouthless faces somehow suggested peace.

He gently touched the crown of one Griff. It shifted suddenly, and startled, he tripped backward.

Simon whispered, "I'm hoping to wake up any time now."

A tiny black bird squirmed out of the pile, chirping nervously and looking to and fro as if confused. It bounded from one Griff to another, then flew off past the row of shabby pikestaffs toward the big boulder that lay beside the road to the Book House.

Tim screamed when the little bird coasted into the open mouth of a huge black bird perched on top of the rock. The monster swallowed its meal with one gulp, then burped. There was a smile in its voice when Tomen called out to them. "He was mostly illusion, anyway. I used him up long ago."

The creature shook its head furiously and laughed a laugh that sounded like a shriek. "You can't harm me, lads! I am spirit. Pure and simple. Your magic's no good on me!"

The moment had come. Tim shook as he looked the bird straight in the eye. The more he feared, the more he hated. The more he hated, the more he wanted to harm. The more he wanted to harm, the less the Teacher's instructions made sense. And, somewhere in a dark corner of his mind, he heard a whisper.

The man inside was saying, It's a bird. Hell, *anyone* can kill a bird.

Tim begged up the strongest winds he knew. He wrapped them in a tempest and mixed in the most potent thunder call he could reckon. Instantly, the air about them stirred, and a gale tore out of the west, shredding the leaves off all the trees for miles. It dove down at the Beast and in its wake came three shafts of lightning with a deafening crackle and a burst of light that cast a bright gold glow on the snowed-in land. The impact of the explosion knocked them to the ground. When the light cleared, this is what they saw: The snow had melted in a huge circle around the rock. The rock was cracked down the middle. But Tomen stood unscathed and laughing.

The boy covered his eyes and sobbed.

"Tim, in my former life, I composed some of those spells. I named those winds before you even breathed! My name is Tomen!"

Trembling, Simon stepped up and yelled out spell after spell, charm after charm, curse after curse, until he choked with exhaustion and collapsed to his knees. His earth magic was useless; Tomen swallowed his spells like food. He had truly met his superior.

The black bird snickered and called out grimly, "King Simon! To think that I once wanted your heart! Such incompetence! Such barren spells! They were crude tricks to dazzle children in my day. I am Tomen!"

"I'm sorry, Tim," said Simon. But he could not comfort the boy, so he sat and waited for his death.

Tomen strutted back and forth, laughing, hopping over the crack in the middle of the boulder. Then it cast its eyes on Marty. "It is my custom to know the names of all my meals. Perhaps you could enlighten me, Waterman?"

Marty began to walk slowly toward the boulder.

"No!" Tim cried out.

"Surely you can tell me what you are called?" said the Beast patiently.

Marty said nothing and walked on.

"Don't!" yelled Simon.

"Your race is a rare and tasty breed. The unusual aging process enhances the flavor." Tomen laughed at the joke. Marty strode on without a word.

"Peculiar that you should be out in daylight. Isn't your kind partial to night?"

Marty approached the boulder with her eyes downcast. The Beast stared down at the frail, blue-green creature.

"I knew the first of your kind. I taught it the chants and gave it music. I observed your silly customs and stifling traditions. Come, frog, tell me your name!"

Marty paused briefly at the foot of the rock to gaze back over her shoulder at Tim and Simon. Then she looked up into the eyes of the Beast, and uttered simply, "I will tell you when you are killing me."

Tomen cackled with delight. "A final act of defiance, eh? Oh, you fine, foolish, noble frog!"

The black beast pounced viciously and dug its claws into Marty's sides, smashing her to the ground. Perched upon its victim, the bird arched back its head and gave a shout of pure triumph.

"I am Victory! I am Power! I am Tomen!"

Marty's eyes stared up weakly at the Beast, and she said her dying words:

"And I am Mother Death."

The bird froze. Time stood still, and for a long moment the earth held its breath.

Tomen had heard it whispered in the air—a rumor or a prophesy. *Someday one would come. A different one. A Guardian. A female of great power.*

So Tomen had instructed the Usher to poison the water, to spoil it especially for mothers and girls, and to recruit only boys. The bird had made the fires to kill the women and spoil the air so that any pregnant woman would grow ill. It had every reason to believe that after all these precautions it was finally safe.

Tomen shifted, but found itself strangely anchored, as if between its claws it carried the weight of the whole world. Tomen shook and twisted violently and still it could not free itself from its victim. Its wings beat frantically, but to no avail. Tim and Simon lifted their eyes and watched as Tomen's body began to shiver. It raged and contorted and was racked by cruel spasms.

"No!" Tomen screamed. "No!"

Feathers flew off the bird like water off a shaking dog. Soon it became an obese red animal—a bald body covered with sores that festered and oozed. The stench was abominable and the Beast appeared to be growing.

One wing, then the other seemed to stretch to a breaking point as if something were trying to wrench them off. The wings became human arms, awkwardly extending from the body of a plucked bird. A tortured voice tore itself out of the creature, screaming in protest.

"It cannot be! I am spirit!"

Two spindly legs shot from the belly of the Beast and kicked the ground spasmodically: grotesque arms and legs connected to a miniature torso. It swayed on the dirt and lengthened like a shadow into the body of a man with the head of a bird.

"*Awwkk!*" it screamed. "There is no such power!"

Now the creature was on its knees, wrapping its shivering body in its arms. The bird head wailed and cursed and rolled, and finally, the beak broke off with a snap. As the head swelled, its eyes bent forward and a wedge protruded to become a nose. A small mouth burst out of the face and a streak of white hair sprouted on the crown.

Seeing how the Beast was now a naked human cowering in the mud, Tim and Simon gained their feet and stepped closer.

"Don't touch!" screamed the man. "It hurts! It hurts!"

He was an ancient, sickly old man and he looked like he had died a thousand deaths before he actually did.

Under his body they found no trace of their companion but a shallow puddle.

They dug a grave and buried him. Simon spelled half the split boulder over the plot. When they returned to the Book House they found the courtyard full of boys curled up and sleeping in the snow. Soon after, a great thaw began, and in a few days, summer had returned to the Southland.

Chapter thirty-one

FOR DAYS TIM WOULD SAY nothing to Simon. He followed him silently, like a sleepwalker, as they made their journey back to his castle. Once Simon turned to find Tim standing trancelike, some fifty paces behind, as if he had forgotten how to walk. A few days of this and Simon grew irritated. "Dammit, Tim! We *won*, didn't we?"

At this Tim burst into tears and Simon could have kicked himself. Obviously, the boy was grieving for Marty. He kept forgetting that he was a child.

But days later, as they lingered by a pond of noisy ducks, he began to wonder if it wasn't something more than grief. Then he realized—like a man who wakes to find himself late—that for Tim it *wasn't* over. His battle had never really been with the Usher or Tomen, but the sickness they had spread. The great spoiling that required a great healing. And his struggle was far more terrible, for he had to destroy not an enemy but a friend: the wind. Simon recalled the torment he endured when he fought Jason. But for Tim, the wind posed no great threat, offered him love not danger, power not defeat. Even the wizards couldn't erase their greatest magic from the world. How could anyone expect this boy to surrender his incredible gift? But then again, maybe only a child was capable of doing it.

"It's the wind, isn't it, Tim?"

"Yes. I can't do it."

"Why not? You told me yourself that every wind you ride is sick. You said you could smell it."

"That's it, don't you see? That's the secret. Wind Wizardry's not like yours or any other magic. It's not a tool or a weapon. Your magic can only change. Mine can destroy." He snorted bitterly. "Such a gift."

"I don't understand," said Simon.

"The wind isn't just *awake*, Simon. It's alive!"

"Alive?"

"They have names. Venturi. Cyclone. Lyraloe. They have feelings." Tim held his hands over his ears. "They laugh. I can hear them laughing."

Oh dear, thought Simon. I never imagined. "That's why the wizards could put them to *sleep*, but they couldn't . . ."

"They loved them as I do. They were so much like each other. They put their spirits into the winds. They're the closest thing they had to children, the only thing they could create."

"Children?"

"So wild. So trusting. They'd do anything for me. Or anybody they liked enough."

Anything? thought Simon. No wonder they're so dangerous. "You'd be putting them out of their misery," he offered.

"You mean I'd be putting them to death." Tim gave him a grim smile. It was an expression he had never seen on the boy's face before. And for a frightening moment, Simon thought he was looking at a man wearing the body of a child.

It passed when Tim said, "I will never fly again, never see the other side of clouds, never feel that embrace. I will have nothing."

That was a boy speaking. He remembered how it felt. How every ending seemed to be the last.

He laid his arm around Tim's shoulders. "You'll still have me, Tim. I'm not Marty, or your parents, or the wind—no doubt I'm the poorest of the lot. But . . ." He could say no more.

Tim thought of Marty. How she had tried to warn him that eventually the wind would spoil everything it touched. It had happened and he hadn't even noticed. He had hesitated; he had not done what he was told. He could have put the wind to sleep and Tomen would have been disarmed. He could have spared Marty her death, but he loved the wind too much, and hated Tomen too much; he couldn't resist revenge. The frog's words came back to him then: "It will cost the life of my people and it will cost you all your power." Oh Marty, he thought, you knew. You knew!

Below them the ducks had grown silent on the pond.

The next morning Simon sat on a hilltop watching Tim take one long last flight. It was like watching someone dance with an invisible partner. Tim swooped and twirled and once he cried out, but it wasn't clear if it was from pleasure or pain. He disappeared into a cloud and when he emerged his clothes were wet as with dew, and when the sun caught him, Tim sparkled. Finally, he came soaring back, his purple cloak whipping in the breeze as he coasted down and landed next to Simon. The King saw his eyes were full of tears.

Tim looked up. "They don't know. They think I want to play." Then he lifted his arms to the sky and called out in a voice that cracked and soared: "Go to sleep now! Now and forever!"

Simon could have sworn he heard a long groan sear across the sky. For a moment he thought it might storm—the air was gripped with tension and a dark, dark cloud trembled overhead. But then an awesome stillness settled on the day, like the echo of a dying breath. Birds chirped and down the hill two butterflies quivered over the grass. Simon found Tim sleeping. He did not wake up until the following day.

"Whatever became of the poor boy?" the Captain asked with mock sympathy.

The Teller shrugged.

Tim never forgave himself for Marty's death, and he never recovered from losing the wind. It was as if he had lost a limb—and the memory of it, the vivid absence still clung to his spine through imaginary nerves. And though it was gone, it would never leave him. No one but Simon knew this. People would say he looked constantly distracted: There were long pauses in his speech, and walking down the corridors of Simon's castle he was often politely asked if he was lost. He grew to become, not a bitter man, but one who walked in a permanent state of diminishment—like a hero come home from war who knows that the peak of his life has passed and that he was never as noble as he seemed. And so he came to understand, finally, the white eagle's words:

"Those few who choose the Way of the Wind dread and cherish it forever."

Chapter thirty-two

THERE WERE NO MORE FIRES to plague the land—that is, no more than usual. Once again the water ran clear and cold. The wind has not been ridden since. The young sorcerers who had begun to rise to influence in various towns disappeared on the same hour of the same day, and down each of their main roads an unfamiliar stray dog was seen roaming in search of a master. The Usher's Book House stood empty for years until a wandering troupe of players came upon the worn, abandoned structure and made it their home. In the tower they found the ashen remnants of a great library. One of them, an artist, saw beauty in the stone Griffs and placed them at intervals along the battlements, where he fancied they would guard against enemies.

Nemot's grave still stands today.

The practice of magic died off and many spells were forgotten. But it was said that King Simon of the North could mend an ailing child with the wave of his hand, that he could prophesy eclipses and talk to birds. Great stories were told of his wisdom and power—some of them were true. But in the days he ruled, when asked about such things, he would scoff and make light of them. Nevertheless, he was a kind and honored man and he grew into a legend.

King Simon had a jester/fool of some renown: a moody man, whom the King treated with special favor and affection. Some say he was the son Simon never had or the one bastard child he decided to keep. Wild things were claimed about him. That he was a chronicler who found a doorway into Time. That he had learned to read the past as if it were the present, and spent his life deciphering the forgotten secrets of the wizards that had turned into legends. Some even say he learned to disappear.

The rumors grew: He came from the White Moon Mountains (where people do not dream) and he had carved a dragon's rib into a pipe. Upon it he played strange songs, the likes of which no one had ever heard before. But it was said his most marvelous gift by far was his way with stories. Rapt listeners sat cross-legged at his feet, and he could make them laugh and weep in the same breath.

One of his favorite stories (which Simon often asked him to repeat) was about an old woodcutter named Timothy who lived by a small lake deep in the North Woods.

One day in the middle of a cold, cold winter, the woodcutter was coming home over the frozen lake dragging a bundle of branches. It was his habit to watch the ice under his feet for thickness and cracks, so as to avoid an icy plunge. As he made his way along, he thought he saw his shadow move away from him. Then he thought it changed colors. Finally he saw a great fish swimming under the clear ice beneath him. He had never seen a fish do that, so he stopped and knelt down, hoping to get a better look. As he pressed his face close to the ice to see past his own reflection, he saw another face looking up at him.

He was not frightened, for in his many days he had seen many strange sights. And besides, it was such a kind face. He spoke to the creature and told it to stand away for a moment. His hand shook as he drew his axe from his belt and struck it to the ice. Soon he had made a hole large enough for the biggest fish, and to his amazement, out squirmed the creature with the kind face.

For a while, all he could do was stare.

It was small like a child, its skin was the color of a lake on a bright, warm day, and it had deep scars on both sides. The man was astounded when the creature asked him if he had a fire. They walked together to the woodcutter's cabin. It sat quietly before the fire and had many helpings of hot soup. The woodcutter was glad for the company, even though it was strange, and through the night he talked to the creature like a man who had not spoken in years. Morning came and the man fell asleep in his chair. The creature from the lake did not sleep, but watched the fire till noon, when the woodcutter awoke.

THE Gift

"Oh!" he exclaimed when he saw it again. "Then it wasn't a dream!"

He took its hand and begged it to stay, and the creature agreed, smiling. They were together a long, long time.

And they talked before many fires.

Chapter thirty-three

AFTER A TIME, THE GO-BOY, Nib, asked, "Is that all, Teller?"

"No," replied the little man who stood in the bow. "That's just an ending. Did you know that there are only three kinds of endings? Those that stop, those that pause, and those that begin."

"Which is this?" asked the boy.

"The last: an ending that begins." From his pocket the Teller pulled a tiny green shell. For a moment, he held it between his finger and thumb and turned it about, taking it in with his eyes. Then he looked over the faces of the sailors who had stayed the nightwatch at his feet, to hear his long sad tale of the last magic makers: Tim, Simon, Marty, Tomen, and the Usher. And as they watched they realized that he was looking at their Captain, the tall, hard, one-handed man who sat above them at the helm, as he always did, tugging at the yellow jewel that rested in his ear. And as he spoke, the Teller's eyes never left the Captain's face, so eventually they wondered that the Captain did not fall upon him with blows, for they well knew his temper and the slander in the Teller's words was as clear as Sotton's Bay. He didn't flinch or pause, not even when the Captain's knuckles went white on the worn rail.

There once was a man who hated women. Hated them worse than he hated the face he saw every day when he looked over the gunwale down into the water. That's right: He was a sailor. This was a convenient profession as it gave him leave to be off the poisoned land where women walked. So he would not have to look upon their faces and be troubled.

No one knows why he hated women. A woman partly made him. A woman carried him and bore him. Perhaps she died and he never forgave her that. Perhaps she orphaned him and he longed for her still. Perhaps she never left him but kept him past his growing as some mothers are known to do. Or perhaps she was simply a bad woman. But then, in his mind, all women were bad.

But there is another possibility.

Perhaps he was spurned by his first love. Every man is spurned sooner or later. But this one would not take "No." He needed her too much. And his need frightened him like a child lost in a black forest. And he despised her for making him this needy.

So he followed his love after she had spurned him and took his love from her as a stranger. He robbed her of her body's gift, and in the taking, lost everything he loved.

But this sailor found there was a pleasure in this taking.

It did not sate his hunger.

It did not fill his empty places.

In fact, it left him quite unsatisfied.

The pleasure he learned to substitute for love was power.

He found he could make women fear him. He found that when he made them fear him, he wasn't afraid of them and he didn't need them. He didn't even need to touch them. Still, he found the touching made them fear him more.

Now you will imagine this man a monster. And so he was.

A monster who grew himself under the shape of a man. A strong man. A leader of men. Does this surprise you? It takes a great deal of strength to hold a monster prisoner inside yourself and never let anyone catch a glimpse of it. But he did. He was that strong.

Now we come to the difficult part of the story. The part that no one wants to hear. Because it does not make anyone feel nobler, or wiser, or happier. It is not one of those stories. It merely tells the truth.

This man who was a monster had a family.

He was a father.

He had a daughter.

One day his daughter (who did not, by the way, know her father was a monster) came to him and said, "Father? I am with child."

And the monster who was a father was ashamed of his daughter (imagine that). And he told her that she could hide herself upon his boat as long as she agreed to sail with him to a distant port and sell the baby to the market there and return home with him and their name intact. He did this to punish her.

But as she sailed upon her father's boat and as her birthing day drew near, the daughter wept and wept and begged her father to let her keep the child. But he would have none of it. He was a monster and the last thing a monster needs is a bad name.

Her birth was hard, but no harder than relinquishing her babe.

And on the voyage home the daughter despaired. And not wanting to live without the child, and not able to bear the voyage any longer, she drowned herself. One night she leapt overboard. She did not know the nets were out and she'd be dragged up in the afternoon. She hadn't thought that far—

The sailors heard a sheath of steel behind them, and turning, saw their one-handed Captain drawn and leaping from the highrail to the deck, coming at the Teller in the bow. "Watermen! Dragons! Wizards! Monsters!" he scoffed. "Can any man say these tales are true?"

"So it is lies that have angered you?" asked the Teller as he fiddled with the small green shell in his hand.

The Captain closed in, his heavy boot heels thudding on the foredeck as the men gave him wide berth. "I'll suffer no slander on my boat! Not from a jester! Or didn'tcha think I was sharp enough to catch that, Master Tim?"

"Captain, please!" the Go-Boy, Nib, pleaded, but the man hilted his face and knocked him to the deck, saying, "I'll serve you next," then turned back to the Teller.

One sailor reached out to stop him but the Captain slashed and laid open his arm.

He stood before the Teller and looked down before he squashed him. "Jonas Johnson owes no safe passage to ugly little men with poison tongues."

"That is not your name," said the Teller calmly. "Or did you lose that as you lost your hand?"

Something moved in the Captain's eyes. Any sailor who saw it backed away. Finally, he tilted his head to one side and let his blade swing lazily before the Teller's face.

"Come," said Tim. "We are men of power. Such deceptions do not become us."

After the longest moment, the Captain smiled and asked a question none of the sailors understood. "How?"

Tim shrugged. "Even Tomen left a body. We never found yours."

"How's the King?" the Captain said with relish.

Tim looked at the deck. "He still fears you. He wanted to believe you died under the Griffs. He doesn't understand Between."

"But you do," said the Captain levelly.

"It's too easy, you know. Wearing other people as if they were clothes. You learn just enough to miss them when you have to shed them. A terrible gift, don't you think? Understanding the core of someone, yet being unable to change them."

"It seems you've given the matter a great deal of thought." The Captain nodded.

"I've had lifetimes to consider it. I have worn many bodies to find you. I have been many men. Many creatures. Once, I was an eagle. I know their stories inside out. And now they are a part of me. Do you know what I've concluded? That it's better to stay in one body. We're not meant for infinite choices. In a way it spoils it. I suppose the wizards came to the same conclusion. One body. One life."

"As, eventually, I did." The Captain nodded.

"You could have chosen another time. I might not have found you."

The Captain raised his brows. "It never occurred to me you'd be looking."

"That's a lie, isn't it?" The Teller smiled. "Why else would you cut off your hand but to avoid detection? The truth is: I never would have stopped."

"How did you find me?"

"Weren't you listening? I wore you on the day you unbound Tomen. And the day you escaped us in your Book House. I caught your scent. You've never searched for anyone you've worn before?"

"This one." The Captain smiled, tapping his chest with the stub of his right hand. "I had to choose carefully. Remarkably strong. Brighter than he looks."

"And tall," the Teller added.

The Captain stopped smiling. "May I remind you whom you are addressing? I am the Usher." His eyes flicked once to the side and he gave a soft laugh. "That was good. You goaded me into the quaint custom of exchanging names. Will we battle now?" He spread his legs and stood sideways, pointing the sword at the little man's head.

"I don't suppose I could persuade you to kill yourself?"

For a moment, the Usher was speechless with anger. "Who are you to talk to me that way?"

"I am the Teller Tim. I am the Chronicler Who Has Stepped Between Worlds. Death is too good for you, Usher. But it is all I have learned to give."

As Tim sat, he covered his face with his heavy cloak, so that for a moment, it looked like a pile of shadow had occupied the bow.

The Usher barked a laugh and was on him, shredding the cloak with wild strokes of his thin blade.

The cloak collapsed as if the little man had never been within its folds.

Puzzled, the Usher turned to find the Teller standing with the rest of the crew, watching him.

"Jodi?" Tim said. "That is the name your mother gave you."

The Usher blinked three times.

The Teller kicked his legs out from under him, and a yellow jewel popped out of his ear and bounced across the deck.

Then the Teller kicked away his sword. Then kicked him in the head. Then knelt upon his shoulders.

The Usher howled into his face until the Teller grasped his head between his hands and wrenched until he nearly turned it all the way around, until it made a crack that split the night.

The body sprawled upon the grey cloak. Then, as the little Teller stood and began to tug his butchered wrap out from underneath the dead weight, the body rolled over and over, the head lolling about like a blossom on a broken stem.

The sailors gave him wide berth as he swirled the cloak up above his head and clamped it to his body with a hand.

The Teller looked about the deck for a moment, then strode over, reached down, and retrieved the yellow jewel that had once been lodged inside the Usher's ear.

"Magic," he said with disgust, and popped the jewel into his mouth and swallowed.

"Let him join his daughter," said the Teller.

For a slight time the crew hesitated.

The Teller looked up. "Toss the salty dog."

The men rushed to it and the body cleared the rail with one heave.

"Sit," said the little man, turning to the crew.

They sat. He sat.

"Listen," said the Teller, regarding them fiercely.

And they were silent.

265

Chapter thirty—four

IT SEEMED TO THE SAILORS then, on that windless night upon their drifting boat, that all the colors and sounds of the world had somehow leaked away, leaving only the Teller's face, a mask of white that hovered above the folds of his cloak like the full moon above a dark mountain, and the Teller's voice, which, after his long telling, was hoarse and full of brambles. They had no doubt that when he finally finished, he would not be able to speak for days.

"Here is what I know about the wizards.

"They had, in all, seven secrets.

"Firstly, they were tall, and they were small. They were slight, and they were stout. They were aged; they were young. They were fair, and they were dark. Their eyes were alternately blue and hazel, brown and grey, black and cataract white. They were whiskered and they were baby-skinned. They were loud and harsh, and they were sweet and soothing. They were boys and men, husbands and fathers.

"Do you see? The first secret is, they wore many faces, but they were few.

"Here is what I know about the wizards.

"That they lived among us for ages, invisible, for outside their natural habitat they were as spirits in the night, as wind on a windless day. They were a handful of beings with virtually no limitations. Pure intelligence seeking vessels to contain their thinking."

Once again the Teller removed his silver ring. He held it up to the night sky between his finger and his thumb as if to put a ring around the moon. He brought it down and stared at the perfect hollow it contained.

"Now, imagine being denied the common joys our senses grant us every moment—joys we do not even reckon as such for they've been with us always, in some ways they *are* us. Imagine never being able to smell the hair of your lover, the smoke of burning autumn leaves, the tangy steam of spiced cider. Never tasting the juice of a berry, the warm wet mouth of your lover, the crisp bitter meat of a fried loach. Never feeling a mother's touch, a father's smile, the cool rump of your sleeping lover, the wind in your face, or the rolling frothy muscles of a horse at gallop between your legs. Never knowing the warm sun on your skin, the shock as you plunge into an icy stream, or just the relief of shutting your eyes after a long long day and turning to your lover . . ."

For a time the Teller seemed to lose his voice. His head sagged between his shoulders, and he ran his hand along his bald scalp. The Go-Boy heard a change in the echo of his words, and felt, though he could not say why, that for this passage anyway, the little man was telling, not the wizards' story, but his own.

"We feel . . . so much. We are so alive that we cannot conceive what being alive might feel like to a mind that has never relished the wealth of our senses.

"Reckon it.

"Do you see? That is the second secret. They had no bodies.

"Here is what I know about the wizards.

"They had immense power.

"Their magic imbued everything they touched. Everything. So that, it was said, if a wizard drank from a stream, the stream became, for a time, aware of itself, its currents and the banks that defined it. And if they rode a cloud, the cloud retained a trace of their power, and knew itself as that particular cloud, unlike any other. And if they ate a berry off a bush, the bush would have a language which would pass on to its next bloom of fruit, and any man eating it would have, that night, a dream of growing up and down: into the bright sky, deep into the dark nourishing earth. And any tree they napped under became awake as the wizards slept, and would be filled with words it couldn't speak, longings it could only tell another tree, who, in any case, couldn't listen. Everything they touched became awake. And if, like the winds who learned to carry them, it was visited repeatedly, it became alive.

"Do you see? That is the third secret. Their magic wakened sleeping matter.

"Here is what I know about the wizards.

"They gave us stories.

"But what does that mean?

"Imagine a world without stories. Where everything was as it always was. Where nothing new happened. Where things just were. If this is difficult it is because we have been so altered from our animal nature that we cannot imagine a world without endings, a changeless world, a world of creatures who only grew in canniness and never in apprehension. Without their stories we would have remained beasts: content with survival, oblivious to death, aloof to the possible, expecting nothing new.

"It was a beautiful and horrible gift.

"Do you see? That is the fourth secret. Their stories changed the world.

"Here is what I know about the wizards.

"That their stories were lies.

"We tell each other stories to teach a lesson, or give a laugh, or share a shudder. But, whatever form they take, there is a peculiar constant about stories. They always resolve. This is because they were designed to reassure—to contain the comforting kernel of an answer. It doesn't matter to us whether or not it is a particularly good answer. Any answer will satisfy.

"Who killed her? Why does the Maker allow evil to fall on the good?

THE Gift

What does it mean to be human? What is love? These are the questions that stories purport to answer, in different ways, over and over again.

"Yet these are not the true questions. All our stories are masks for questions we cannot answer. Questions cloaked in little answers to distract us while we swim in bigger mysteries.

"Do you see? Stories are our tonic.

"And, we hope that if we tell ourselves enough stories, perhaps someday the mystery will become tolerable, will become just another tale.

"It is a lie.

"Mystery is our essence. And it cannot be contained by beginnings, middles, and endings. It was in the wizards and it is in us. And we may only ask the eternal questions as the wizards must have asked themselves, never expecting an answer.

"How did we come to be?

"How are we to live?

"What is this thing called life?

"What happens when we die?

"When will we know?

"Why are we?

"Until the Maker condescends to tell that last lost story, we are left with the questions that haunt and form our souls.

"That is the fifth secret. All is mystery.

"Here is what I know about the wizards. They found us irresistible.

"It was all they could do to leave us alone, to keep themselves out. Because once they tasted us, they wanted in. The only thing that prevented them was a peculiar fact of our humanity: the same richness of our senses that made us so intoxicating also made us deadly. For they learned that if they stayed too long inside our bodies they were trapped; they could not get out.

"This was something new. Their prisoners had become their captors.

"They lost many of their brethren to this fate: happily locked in the body of mortals. And so they learned not to overstay their welcome, for they lingered at their peril.

"Yet, eventually, they could not resist the pull of our bodies. They surrendered their immortal spirits to our mortal frames. They became us. And becoming us, they made us something new, as when any two things merge: fire and water make smoke, man and woman make children, body and mind make . . . well. You understand. Their minds played upon the substance of our bodies and slowly altered it. Until we were as different from our former selves as the wizards were from their vaporous past.

"Do you see? That is the sixth secret. We captured each other.

"Here is what I know about the wizards: They possessed.

"They could not create; they could only absorb. They could not birth; they could only occupy. They could not make life; they could only shape it to their ends. This is the legacy the wizards left us.

"For bodies may hunger or desire; but they can be satisfied. Yet a mind's thirst is never quenched, its hunger has no bounds: Having some, it wants more, having more, it wants all; having learned, it knows how little it knows, having grasped, it reaches out again: and that is its gift and curse, it may absorb but it may not be filled.

"Minds want everything.

"Do you see?

"Do you see?

"Do you see?"

The Teller sighed deeply.

"This has been a dark tale. A tale of monsters. Wizards. Dragons. Gosis. Tomen. Griffs. But, as I asked you before, and all of you confirmed by your silence, none of you has ever seen a monster. So all these tales must then be legends, right?"

The men all nodded.

"No! No! *No!*" screamed the Teller.

270

"You have learned nothing! I tell you that the monsters and the legends and the myths and all the wizards' tales are alive! They planted their stories in us and we grow them in our lives without even knowing it. We do their bidding. That is the untold story of the wizards. And there is nothing more treacherous than a story untold.

"That is the seventh great secret of the wizards. They have taken us as their hiding places."

The Teller surveyed the faces of the men. "There are many untold stories on this boat. And each of you had a part in them.

"These, then, are the tales I did not tell.

"The story of the man who made her with child and left.

"The story of the cook who gave her food and nothing else.

"The story of the man who forced her to sex, then passed her on to his mate as if she were a pet.

"The story of the man who listened to her torment through the walls and did nothing.

"The story of the man who hit her when he thought she laughed at him.

"The story of the one who showed her kindness and no mercy.

"The story of the man who hated her because she reminded him of another woman.

"The story of the man who dismissed her because she was a child.

"The story of the righteous man who scorned her because she was with child and had no husband.

"The story of the man who feared his friends and watched.

"The story of the men who raped her and thought it sport.

"The story of the father who gave his daughter to his crew.

"The story of the boy who heard it all and did not tell."

The Go-Boy, Nib's, eyes were locked upon the deck as if he were afraid they might stray somewhere else.

"Each of you, in your own way, deserves a judgement."

All the sailors trembled as if a northern wind had blown across the deck.

"But," he continued, "I am not a judge. I am the King's bodyguard."

If it were possible the men became quieter than they were before.

"And though your crimes are the crimes of monsters, you do not deserve death. These are untold tales that happen every day. Everywhere. I cannot give them all endings."

In the long silent minutes that passed upon the deck, the sailors thought of many things. Their wives. Their lovers. Their daughters. And their mothers.

"New wind," the Teller said suddenly, looking up.

The sailors saw the ripples settling on the dawn-lit fabric of their sails like silent waves.

"Doubt we'll need it, though. See that, Nib? We've drifted back."

And for the rest of his living, Nib would recount the tale, saying that it was as if in one swift casual conjure the Teller Tim had slain a beast, convicted a crew, dissolved a mystery, called up the sun, the wind, and the shore. For there it lay: a black lip of land across the pink horizon. And he watched in wonder as the small man knelt to touch briefly the long wet strip of water that divided the deck in two. He rose then, and strolled across to lean against the gunwale and look out at the golden ball of fire rising over the great salt sea they did not know was an ocean as the new wind filled their sails.

Epilogue

THE NIGHT THE TELLER RETURNED to the castle, the gate guards mistook him for a vagabond. They were new and he had, after all, been gone three years. Finally a crusty stablemate saw the interrogation in progress, intervened, and rebuked the young men thoroughly, saying "Do you not know whom yer addressing? If I were you, lads, I'd run smartly and tell the marshall: Master Tim has returned."

"*The* Tim?" one of them said after a moment. The other guard looked with new eyes at the matrix of spiderwebbing that covered his mouth, then dashed off.

The stablemate rolled his eyes. He took the small man by the arm and led him along: He had always been one whose very fragility invited such deferences. "Come inside, Teller. Looks like it was a long journey."

"Yes," Tim said, looking about, reacquainting himself with the castle where he had lived for some fifteen years. There was an air of cheer about it which he did not recognize. A new garden rimmed one wall of the keep, an unfamiliar scent of flower filled the muddy courtyard. New banners hung from the battlements, and he could have sworn he heard music. "Where's the King?"

"In the tower, of course. They'll be most happy to receive you I'm sure."

"They?"

"He's taken himself a Queen. Did you not know?"

The Teller shook his head. The idea seemed strange to him.

The old man smiled. "There's talk of an heir. Though, they don't seem in much of a hurry. Like puppies they are." He leaned in confidentially. "It's a bit much at times."

Tim smiled thinly.

"Lovely lady," the man said, helping him up the stone steps leading to the Keep.

"A Queen," the Teller said in wonder.

The stablemate grabbed the rope ring and half the great door creaked open. "We missed your stories, Tim. And your piping. But there's new music in the castle now, eh?" The old man tilted his head and listened dreamily.

A muffled air of melody came from a distant chamber; it echoed off the stone walls, and drifted in and out of hearing. The tune was new to Tim: slow and lilting, somehow it reminded him of a certain birdsong. And for a moment he thought of the white eagle, the songs she taught him, the way she smiled.

The music ceased abruptly.

He shook his head as if to ward off a charm. "When did the King . . . ?"

"Two summers after you left. There was a ball. She's from the Northern Isles. Her father's a great ally now. Look who I got!" the old man called out proudly to the guards at the tower base, who saluted the Teller. The old man leaned closer. "Some say she is a witch, but not in my hearing. I'd cuff 'em. Sure, she's a bit strange. But strange isn't black, I say."

"Indeed," the Teller agreed, and for a brief moment they stopped walking.

"Something wrong, Master Tim? Can I get you a brew?"

He was thinking about witches. And trying to remember where or whether he had ever heard a song like that before. No. Definitely not. It was . . . different. Simple and lovely and . . . it sounded like a mixture— something both conjured and captured.

A figure was running toward them from the tower doors. He wore fine yellow bedclothes that flickered in the torchlight. Rushing up, he took the

Epilogue

Teller into his arms and swung him about like a boy. When he put him down, Simon inspected Tim as if he couldn't believe he was real. The stablemate marked the fierceness of the King's face and discreetly looked away.

"I thought I'd never see you again."

The Teller smirked. "You've grown a beard."

"You smell of fish." The King smiled.

"I need a fire," the Teller said.

"With a splendid wrap like this?" he said, holding up a corner of the Teller's shredded grey cloak. "I shouldn't wonder."

They sat in the King's private chamber before the hearth. Simon insisted that Tim be wrapped in a thick quilt and given hot wine. There was a long silence, but it was the silence of fast friends: comfortable, requiring nothing to fill it. The King had donned his purple robe over his yellow clothes; he sat cross-legged on his chair, savoring his company, sipping occasionally from his jeweled goblet.

"You've caught something."

"A chill." Tim shrugged. "It'll pass."

Simon yawned. "Boring since you left, Tim. Peace treaties. Good crops. Though there's a new songstress in court—she's been a joy."

But the Teller didn't seem to be listening. "You've changed."

"Three years. Did you suppose the world would stand still?"

"You're older."

"You, too."

"Happier."

A wide grin broke out of Simon's beard. It had been held back for a while and letting it loose seemed to relieve him. "Much happier." The King's eyes danced. "She's an island woman. Her skin's dark and windwhipped. Strong body. Strong will. The people love her."

Tim had no reaction. He looked at the maroon rug that ran to the edges of the blazing hearth. "Good for you."

Epilogue

"For all of us," the King replied.

Then Tim told him of the Usher and their battle. Not the whole story. But the ending.

"You ate his jewel?" Simon asked amazed.

The Teller shrugged. "It is a molded jell. Like those festival candies: crunchy on the outside, soft in the middle."

A sour face. "How'd it taste?"

"Awful."

The King grunted.

"You seemed . . . surprised to see me," said Tim.

Simon held back a frown and twirled his golden wedding ring about his finger. "After a few months . . . I . . . well . . . I came to believe you wouldn't return. First, I didn't want to think he lived. But I knew you. And I knew you wouldn't give up. Then I thought, even if you found him . . . I couldn't believe you'd best him. It was difficult not knowing. It was easier to believe . . ."

"I had died?"

Simon swallowed. "Yes." He sighed. "I'm sorry, Tim."

The Teller met his eye and spoke mildly. "My friend, no apologies. You keep forgetting, I know you, inside and out. It is impossible for you to disappoint me."

After a moment, Simon laughed. "When will you start treating me as your elder, much less your King?"

It was an old joke and it comforted them to share it again.

They watched the fire for a while. Then Simon asked warily, "You wore him?"

"Of course." He caught Simon's look. "Don't worry," Tim lied. "I didn't stay long enough to carry him."

Simon shook his head. "How does a creature get that twisted?"

"How do any of us?"

"No." Simon scowled. "I'll not hear that from the man who saved me."

Epilogue

A silence.

"Dammit, Tim!" He slammed his goblet down and a red cascade leaped over the lip and soaked the white cloth on the tablette. "You saved us all! Can't you even now grant yourself a little of the joy we have because of you?"

"No." Tim smiled wryly. "I thought perhaps . . . after I evened the score with the Usher, maybe, but, no. Apparently joy is not my gift."

The door opened and they heard a woman's voice. "Am I interrupting?"

"My dear!" said Simon rising. "No, never. Come in. Come in!"

He gathered the woman in the bright red dress into his arms and nuzzled her neck. She gave a surprising low laugh. Her hair was black as pitch, as were her eyes which Tim briefly glimpsed before she bowed and her fine dress ballooned on the floor about her. As she stood he saw she was a tall woman; she met Simon eye to eye. A striking foreign woman—he liked her immediately, as certain animals first sense no threat, and then commonness, and sometimes kinship.

"This is the man himself," said Simon. "I warn you, dear, he's a charmer."

Tim bowed in turn and kissed the gold ring on her hand.

"So I see." She gifted him with her smile. "Ever since I saw the throne I have wanted to meet the son of the woodcutter."

It was, perhaps, the best thing she could have said. His hand lingered over hers. "I've not had the pleasure of your name."

"Clare," she said.

"Do you know what it means?" he asked a little impishly—as a jester he was expected to surprise.

An open smile. "No."

"Clear and light." He released her hand.

Her smile broadened. "Thank you."

Simon caught Tim watching her eyes as if they were a strange constellation in the night sky. "Your beauty has stunned him, my dear." Simon

Epilogue

laughed, then stepped up next to the Teller, tilted back his head, and joined him in his admiration. "She has that effect on people."

As the stablemate said: It was a bit much.

"Madam, you'll have to forgive me," Tim said, embarrassed. "I've grown unaccustomed to the company of women."

The Queen replied warmly, "Treat me as you would any friend of Simon."

"More than a friend, I suspect."

"I hope so."

"Much more," said Simon.

Tim raised an eyebrow at the giddiness in the King, and smiled at the dark woman. "I see you have bewitched him."

The Queen clamped down upon the word she was about to speak and a wall went up behind her eyes. Both men marked it.

"It's a mutual spell," she smiled graciously.

"Madam?" Tim asked. "What have I said? I've offended you."

"You couldn't have known." She swallowed. "On our islands . . . they burn witches. Or anyone they take to be so. It is, as you might imagine, not a trifling phrase where I come from."

"I'm so sorry," said Tim.

"My dear, he meant nothing."

"I'm sure of it." She gathered herself suddenly and bowing to them both, she made for the door.

"Clare?" Tim stopped her. "I am, after all, a fool. I've much to learn."

She smiled. "Then we will teach each other." And she was gone.

For a while they watched the fire. The silence grew uneasy; like a fog it filled the room.

"What is it, Tim?"

"I *am* a fool." The silver ring on his pinky glistened as the Teller pulled the quilt up to his chin. "Simon, it is as if there was a great mystery in the world which everyone understands except me."

Epilogue

The King saw then, for the first time in years, the face Tim allowed only him to see: bewildered, haunted. This was the Tim he worried for, the Tim he loved—not the dark Teller who seemed to wear a snicker on every other word, nor the great public weaver of dazzling tales, whose startling gift for mimicry made all his characters palpable and vivid, not even the wild boy who had ridden the wind and healed the King but could not heal himself—but this. This not-quite-man who wore the lives of others like a heavy chain of many links. For years Simon had wished that someday, someday Tim would shed his ghost and come happy into the man he knew was there. It was as if he was stuck at the bottom of the well, still hiding there, still a frightened lad listening to the fire devour his world, hoping for something that would never be his again, a child who had been robbed of his childhood and had found nothing in the many years since to replace it. He's still in the well, thought Simon. And as long as he stays there, there's always the chance he'll find his home when he emerges.

He would have given anything to know the counterspell to this.

The Teller made several false starts before he managed to say: "I mean, I get along fine with women, don't I?"

The King smiled gently. "You regard them, if I may say, perhaps, too highly."

Simon had managed to surprise him: not a frequent occurrence. "What?"

"They are not such strange creatures as you make them, my friend."

"This is something you know?" Tim said with a heartrending wonder.

"Something I've learned." He smiled.

"The learning stone has given me the memories of many beds, Simon. But, I don't, it's not about twinkling. I know that."

"No. It's not," Simon agreed.

"I've never touched a woman like that."

"I know," said Simon softly.

Epilogue

Tim lost himself in the fire. "I'm an ugly thing that no woman would want to touch."

"No." A pain insisted itself into Simon's face. "No. My friend. Say rather that you would never let a woman close enough to touch you." The King sniggered at himself. "I feel foolish counseling such a learned man— will you allow me?"

"Of course."

Simon needed a long drink before he could continue. He wiped his mouth. "You will not believe yourself worthy of a woman. Therefore you shield yourself. And no woman can know you."

"Mothers have known me," Tim said darkly. "Both of them dead. I couldn't shield them."

"Women are more than mothers, Tim. That is only a small part of what they are."

A long, painful pause.

"What's it like, Simon." Tim asked suddenly. "To feel that. Trust?"

"Yes."

"Joy?"

"Yes."

"Peace?"

Simon covered his eyes. Someday, he thought. Someday. Finally he said, "You've never felt it? In all the lives you've worn?"

Tim's brows pressed together and his eyes squinted as if he was straining to see a sail on the horizon. "I think it is a thing you cannot learn from others. The stone only lets me touch the lives of those concordant with my own. We have to share something for me to get in." He shrugged. "Sometimes we're orphans. Sometimes killers." He closed his eyes, remembering, searching. "I've worn men who fear them, men who need them, men who take them." He opened his eyes. "But fear . . . is a shadow. Need is not right. And taking is not getting." He sighed. "I've never known a woman like that: from the inside . . . or the outside."

Epilogue

"Then you have not lived."

The Teller nodded sadly. "I am still a child."

The King couldn't bring himself to agree, although his silence spoke volumes.

There was a knock on the door.

At the King's beckon, a short stout woman entered and curtsied. Tim saw her face was dark and round, her eyes an icy blue. She wore a simple black robe bound by a white strand of twine, a bronze green dress peeked through the opening of her cloak. The more Tim looked, the more he seemed to see her.

"Your Majesty, my lady asked me to bring a gift to your guest." It was a high girlish voice: Her body had grown but not her voice.

The men rose and saw that in her chubby palms she held out a small golden pipe with perfect diamond holes along the spine.

"What gift would that be?" asked Simon.

"My song," said the woman, shyly. "A wind I've written for friends returning from long journeys."

"She has a marvelous way with melody, Tim—you'll see. Tim?"

The Teller had been staring at the woman's face. And he found it difficult to look elsewhere. It was a face of great openness and mystery—a face that could tell stories.

"I'm sorry," said the King, laying a hand on the Teller and indicating the small, round, chinless woman. "Tim, this is the Queen's songstress, Maggie. Maggie . . . Master Tim."

Their bows extended perhaps longer than necessary; each seemed reluctant to be the first to rise. Neither spoke when they did.

The King said. "Sit! Please. Be comfortable!"

The Teller smiled and held out a hand to guide the round, sweet-scented woman to a chair closer to the hearth.

"He plays a fine pipe himself," Simon said.

"So I'm told," Maggie said.

Epilogue

Tim shrugged.

Finally Tim ventured, "I—I heard you when I arrived."

The woman swallowed. "I may have been practicing."

"It seemed an air of birdsong."

The woman looked to the side. "I make a poor try at various calls . . . to warm up."

Simon scoffed. "Maggie's far too modest."

"Indeed," the Teller agreed. "Was it a whippoorwill?"

The woman blushed and nodded.

"You caught it splendidly. I myself find birdsong a magical thing—unrepeatable even with practice. I believe one would have to be a bird to master it."

Tim noticed it first: The woman seemed to grow a chin as she pushed her face deeper into her chest. He thought there might have been a mouse in the corner for her eyes seemed fixed upon the floor. But following her gaze he could find nothing. Then he saw Simon flick a glance at the woman from under his brows. He appeared about to say something, then thought better of it. Tim looked at the woman. Tim looked at Simon. And felt a great self-fury rise into his face. I will never learn this, he thought. Never.

"I've done it again, haven't I, Simon?" he said, splitting his sad and puzzled look between the King and the little woman.

Simon held up a hand to silence Tim. Then he addressed the songstress. "Maggie? Peace now. No one has been talking about you, I swear."

Tim was totally lost by this remark.

The small woman looked up a little. Just a little.

"This is your home now. And will be for as long as you like, do you hear?"

The woman began to sniffle.

Epilogue

"This is my closest friend. I have no secrets from him. But this is not mine to tell."

Tim saw her gathering her courage, her bottom lip forced its way upward until it made a horseshoe. "My mistress has had some training . . ."

So the rumors are true, thought Tim. But what an odd way to start a story.

"She saved my life."

"Yes?" Tim said with a half smile. What was she talking about?

"I have been a woman but three years," she said quietly, as if it were a shameful thing.

I would have put her older than that, thought Tim.

"I'm not very good at it yet." She stood abruptly. "I must go."

"Please," said the King. "Please sit."

The woman sat back and her fingers clung to the golden pipe as if it were a branch over a cliff.

"Shall I?" the King asked her gently.

She nodded and once again her lip braced itself.

"When Maggie was a child, her father used to do tricks. He'd practice spells on her. One of his favorites was to make her a bird. I'd thought transmogrification a dead art, but apparently, he found a book. One day he left her in that shape too long and she was stuck. He ended up losing her in a gamble. Maggie was passed on from hand to hand—The Amazing Talking Bird they called her—who, when prompted, could repeat any human phrase. Small wonder. Eventually, she was given as a present to my wife. She was not long in her company when Clare knew the truth. Luckily she possessed the skill to turn her back. Is that fair, Maggie?"

"Yes, your Majesty." Tears welled up in the corners of her eyes. "It's silly." She sighed. "But I keep thinking someone's going to put me back into the cage." She laughed bravely.

After a moment, the Teller said, "I understand."

Her eyes met the little man's.

Epilogue

"I have been many birds, myself," said the Teller. "An eagle, a hawk, a sparrow—too many to name."

When she realized he was not teasing her, a knowing that can only be shared by those who have worn the mystery of another passed between them.

Tim leaned forward. "Flying." He smiled gently. "To see the other side of clouds . . . That is the hardest part to let go, is it not?"

"Yes." The word spilled out of her and she looked in wonder at the only person who had ever understood the haunting memory of flight.

"It's difficult being more than one thing," Tim said.

"Yes," she said.

"I mean it's a privilege as well. But, no matter which eyes you choose to look out of, something seems not right with the world."

"Like having two homes." She nodded. "Earth . . ."

"And sky," he said.

"And never being able to rest in either."

"I understand," said Tim.

She swallowed a gratitude beyond words. "Then you are the first."

The fire crackled. And both the small woman and the small man held to the slender thread of silence, each wanting the other to fill it, each unsure of how to begin, both stunned by the sudden harmony they felt with a stranger. Simon thought he heard a speechless hum of longing and astonishment fill the space between them, a fragile thing that at any moment could be broken.

The King stood then and yawned brassily. "Excuse me, I've lost all track of time."

They looked at him as if he were spoiling everything.

"Forgive me. I must be retiring. My wife hates a cold bed."

The man and the woman stood at the same time as if their chairs had been kicked out from under them.

The woman blushed. "Oh, but your Majesty, you must stay!"

Epilogue

"No, no, no." He dismissed the suggestion with a wave which seemed to give the woman hope and seemed to leave the Teller speechless. "My guest deserves better company than me. You must entertain him, Maggie."

"Simon," said Tim awkwardly looking about. "I—I—"

"Now, I'll suffer no impudence from my jester!" He mock scowled and laid a hand on Tim's shoulder. "I'll hear all your stories in the morning. But for now, I command you to listen to this good woman's music. I myself cannot do it justice."

"Simon." the little man bit his lip.

Again the King yawned extravagantly.

"If Master Tim would indulge me." The woman bowed in the Teller's direction.

The gesture left him stuttering. "Of course. Of course." He nodded happily to her. Then turning to Simon, he shared a private look of panic. "Of course."

"Sit," the King commanded, forcing the stiff Teller down into his chair.

Simon turned to Maggie and gently passed his palm through the air. "Play."

The songstress blushed deeply. "As you wish." She bowed slightly and looked with unguarded curiosity at the Teller.

For a moment, Simon felt as if he had already left the room. "In the morning then," he said, moving to the door. There, he paused and turned.

"Teller?" said the King.

"Eh?" Tim said after a moment, reluctantly lifting his eyes from the woman with the golden pipe.

Simon regarded him sternly. "Don't do all the talking."

Gently closing the chamber door, the King couldn't help lingering a moment to listen to the muted conversation on the other side.

"Maggie?" he heard Tim say in a familiar voice. "It is a lovely name. Do you know what it means?"

Epilogue

"No, sir."

"Then I'll tell you. Black Bird Who Sings Like a Lady."

There was a high sound of wonder from the woman.

"I am glad it pleases you. Now, will you play for me?"

"I'd love to, Master Tim."

"Just Tim, if you please. I am nobody's master."

Simon smiled, thinking: Mage takes rook. Mate.

For a moment, the King turned his head to one side as if his eaves-dropping had been interrupted by another voice. But the hallway was silent.

"Yes," he said. "It *is* a thin door. Come out. Someone's liable to step on you there."

The shadows near the doorway shifted and the fledgling unsquatted into the light.

"You're Nib?"

The Go-Boy nodded guiltily.

"It's all right," the King said. "One can't help what one hears." A purple strand ran down the middle of the lad's forehead. "That's a nasty bruise."

The boy volunteered no explanation.

"Perhaps someday you'll tell me the story?"

Nib nodded.

"The Teller shouldn't have left his page out in this drafty hall. You've got a proper bed? Off to it, then."

"Thank you, Simon," the lad said bowing.

The King did not correct him, but watched until he turned the corner. Then strolling down the corridor, he allowed himself a skip or two, then caught himself and collected himself and made his way upstairs to his wife and their bed.

A song began to play.

To know that life can be truly capricious; that one is not omnipotent; that without magic as the ultimate defense, there is pain at times which hurts more than words can describe. And after the grief and the mourning, not only for the lost objects of one's fantasies, but for the fantasies and illusions themselves, to be able to live relatively without illusion . . . That the gates to that Eden of infancy are closed, barred by angels with fiery swords.
That mother is dead, forever, and ever, and ever.

—Fred Hahn,
"On Magic and Change"
Voices (10/1975): 4–13